UNCLEAN

Jeff E. Frazier

Tate Publishing, LLC

Isaiah 6:51

Then I said,

Woe is me!

for I am undone;

for I am a man

of unclean lips,

and I dwell in the

midst of a people

of unclean lips:

for mine eyes

have seen

the King,

the Lord of Hosts.

This Book is dedicated to
the loving memory of

Joseph Steven Ayres

Special Thanks:

To the following for their special effort
and assistance that made this book possible:
First and foremost, I want to thank

The Holy Spirit,

(without whose guidance,
this book would not have been written)

Others who were beneficial:
Fred Jenkins and Charles Putegnat

From the Author

I wrote this book from the perspective of the people that might have known Jesus and witnessed many of the events that pointed to the fact that Jesus of Nazareth is truly the Savior of the world.

In order to get a clearer understanding of the events that took place (as recorded in the Four Gospels of Jesus Christ) I had to combine the information from different books of the Gospels. As you read this book and if you come to a spot that does not match what you believe the Bible to say, please read all four Gospels versions of the same event. This will enable you to see how I had information from one Gospel that was not in another.

I tried very hard, and I pray that I did not stray from the true meaning of the Holy Bible.

Please enjoy . . .

UNCLEAN

CHAPTER I

Uriah intently studied the insects that crawled between the blades of grass. He wondered how a grasshopper would taste. They were probably crunchy like the cake his mother had cooked in the oil. The taste of the fried cake was still fresh in his mouth. He had eaten the last morsel of it just moments ago, but he was still hungry. Uriah trained daily in the ways of his people, but he could not remember if grasshoppers were on the list of items lawful for men to eat. Just eating one grasshopper would not hurt anything, he thought. He cautiously moved his young hand toward the green creature. He had his doubts that he could even catch it. Slowly and purposefully his fingers began to encase the insect in them.

With his thoughts so concentrated on the little insect, he did not hear the first bleat of the sheep. The second cry snapped him out of his fixed attentiveness on the insect. In his mind he could hear his father say, "Watch the sheep, Son!" He jumped up and looked around to see what had startled the flock. Uriah saw his father on the next hill and he was glad to see that he faced the opposite direction. It relieved him to know that his father had not caught him being so irresponsible. Uriah knew it took great dedication and concentration to become a good shepherd. The world was full of creatures that sought to devour the sheep. For him to allow his mind to drift away from his duties, even to the thoughts of his father, would be a violation of the responsibilities that his father had entrusted to him. Obediently, Uriah scanned the area for wolves, wild dogs, bears, or even a lion.

Uriah did not see what had disturbed the flock, but he was trained to sound the alarm even if the possibility of a threat existed. He continued to scan the vicinity as he pulled the ram's horn from the leather pouch that hung around his waist. With puckered lips and a lung full of air he brought the horn to his mouth. The sound that vibrated out of the large end of the horn sounded rather dismal compared to the loud duress blast that his father had tried to teach him.

John heard the duress call come from the hill from which Uriah tended a small segment of the flock. It was not the customary emergency signal, but he knew his son was only a novice with the instrument. He began to visually search the countryside nearest Uriah, but it was the movement on the distant hill that caught John's attention. John stood up to get a better look, and he used his hand to block out the brightness of the sun.

Uriah abandoned his position and ran over to the hill where his father stood. He knew that everything was not as it should be, something troubled his father. "What is it?" he asked and then looked in the direction of his father's gaze. "I do not see anything. Father, what is it?" he asked again.

"Uriah, have you forgotten an important lesson about how to watch out for predators?" his father asked. Uriah just shrugged his shoulders. John had not looked at his son, but he knew what his reply had been. "Look for movement," he said. "Camouflage can hide them, but movement will give them away every time," he reminded his pupil.

As always, Uriah had looked directly at his father when his father instructed him. It was a custom of his people that showed respect for the teacher. He hated some customs, others he thought he would never understand, but he really cherished this one. As Uriah began to turn his head in the same direction of his father's gaze, he reached up with his left hand and grasped the rough and callused hand of the sheep herder whom he loved dearly. Uriah struck the same pose of his father and stared toward the eastern horizon. "I see it now," he shouted with true youthful excitement, "but I still cannot tell what it is."

John knelt down next to his young son and looked directly into his eyes to make sure that Uriah's attention was on him rather than the distraction on the far hill. Uriah hoped that he would not be scolded. With urgency John said, "Run quickly into town and inform the council that a large caravan is passing to the east of us." As Uriah started to run away, John shouted, "Tell them that they bear different banners as though they are from different tribes or countries, and their numbers are great.

"Samuel!" John shouted to his eldest son who stood in the midst of the flock on a different hill. "Begin to herd the sheep for the trip home." John had not let Uriah know that he had noticed him playing. John's sons had tended the flock, but he tended to the sheep of his fold.

As Uriah ran through the dusty streets of the town that he knew as his home, the townspeople were alerted by the expression of fear on his young face. They could tell something was amiss, and began to follow after him. Several of the women called out to him, but he ignored them. Uriah would dare not disobey his father again. Many of the older men, who always sat at the place of council, did so rightfully; others just had nothing more important to do. The old men just stared at the young lad when he interrupted their conversation with one breathless word. "There," he said with his finger pointed to the direction from which he came.

Some men grumbled, but one kind man asked, "Uriah! What has you so troubled?"

Uriah quickly and breathlessly related to the council the news his father had instructed him to tell. He also advised them that his father would be there shortly with more information about what had happened outside their town. Many of the people who stood just outside the room became very frightened and burst out of the building to sound the alarm to the people in the area.

Like a fire on parched wood in the desert, word of the great caravan spread quickly through the town. The men who were not present were summoned to attend this meeting to address the issue of how to deal with the great caravan that passed to the east of their town.

Many quarrels broke out as confusion filled the room. Terror was sensed on the lips of some of the men who were usually considered brave. Some had suggested that they ignore them, and maybe they would pass through peacefully. Some of the younger men, who tended to be more aggressive, suggested taking up arms and pursuing them. That idea was quickly rejected, because it was not their custom to attack strangers. The mention of the size of the caravan compared to the number of men in the town who were able to fight caused many of the hot-tempered men to calm their loud protests.

The crowd of worried men hushed as John entered the room. John was immediately ushered to the front of the room. He explained that the caravan had established a camp, and had set up sentries on the perimeter.

"Can you tell where they are from?" someone from the center of the room shouted.

"The origins of their banners are not common to this area of the country," John stressed. I could speculate that they are from countries far to the east," John related to them.

"Countries?" someone asked.

"Even though they are traveling together, they are definitely from different countries," John said confidently. John had concluded his comments and as he sat down, the quarrels began again.

The quarreling ceased when Josephus spoke. "Brothers," he said as he slowly stood up. He cleared his throat, and with the dignity of being the chief elder said, "I believe that these men mean us no harm. There have been no reports from any sector of Israel of any evil deeds by these men. True, they may be great in number, but are they greater than Rome? This is not an invasion of our country for the purpose to carry away the spoils of the land. From the explanation by our brother John, they seem not to brandish any signs of war, except that for the purpose of self-defense. We will send an unarmed group of our most trusted men," he stated as he turned to look at the younger group of men, "Who are not prone to jump so hastily into a fight."

The accused knew of whom he spoke, and nervously shuffled their feet on the dirt floor. The tops of Jeru's sandals gathered dust that came up from under his feet as he shuffled.

"We will send these men to greet them and offer them our hospitality," Josephus said as though the discussion had been concluded and the determination was expected to be followed.

With that decree, the men were chosen and given further instructions. Among those chosen was John, for his great vision even in hours of darkness. Mashic was also selected for his ability to talk with anyone, even with those who did not speak the same language as his. All of the men chosen were well mannered, yet could still fight if the need presented itself. Of those omitted from the selection, was Jeru.

Mashic was glad that Jeru had not been chosen, for he knew that Jeru was quick to demonstrate his temper, even in a public meeting. It was well known among the whole town that Jeru's temper was as hot as his hair was red. Mashic was glad that Josephus' reason that Jeru was not chosen, was because of Jeru's wife. Jeru's wife was great with child and Jeru would need to be nearby. No one knew more than Mashic, that Jeru always let these decisions hurt his spirit too deeply. Even though they were of different families, they were closer to each other than most brothers.

As day gave way to night, the men walked away from the safety of their homes to what could be their deaths. The chosen men met at the edge of town. Many of the wives followed them in the distance. One of the women was Sara, Mashic's wife. She was young and beautiful, yet had not born a child for Mashic. Some of the townspeople had already labeled her "barren" even though they had not been wed but for a short time. The women of the town began to hide themselves in the bushes and rocks on the hill, and watched with great fear as their husbands descended the hill to the camp below.

The men were more afraid for their families than for themselves. If provoked, the people of the caravan could retaliate and send armed men into the village. The men from the small town could see the campfires of the foreigners as they burned brightly in the darkness of the night. The smells of cooked meat from the camp greeted the missionaries of the small town before even the outermost sentry could be seen. They were on a mission of peace, but would they be perceived as thieves and robbers? They stopped and allowed themselves to be seen when they neared the camp. They wanted to make sure that a sentry would not mistake them as hostile and threatening.

In one quick move, the sentry quickly vanished behind a clump of debris that had once been a mighty tree. He drew his bow and arrow, and warned the occupants of the camp of the approaching men. Mashic motioned for the men that had joined him to remain where they stood. Mashic approached the sentry with outstretched arms, and showed the sentry that his hands were empty. As he walked toward the sentry, he slowly turned himself around to let the foreigner know he was unarmed.

By the time Mashic had finished his demonstration of peaceful intentions, another man from the camp had augmented the other sentry's position. Mashic related in his native tongue and with gestures that he was from a nearby village and had come to seek council with the members of the caravan. "That's if they would be so kind as to speak to sheep herders, fishermen, and carpenters?" Mashic asked. The man seemed to have understood Mashic's intentions, and vanished into the night back toward the camp.

Mashic had only seen one man other than the sentry, but he knew that there were other men out in the darkness. He knew they were outnumbered, and unprepared for battle. He prayed that these men were on a peaceful mission. Several of Mashic's companions had called out to him and inquired as to what had happened. Mashic reassured them that all was as it should be, and to fear not. After a few more moments of silence the man from the camp returned, and motioned for Mashic and his kinsman to follow him into the camp.

All of the men of the village were awed by the wealth of the men in this caravan. The foreigners did not flash their wealth as to be extravagant, but it was hard to camouflage their well-woven fabrics and polished metals. Their guide would look back at them from time to time and would motion for them to move more quickly. The local countrymen now felt as though they were the visitors. They were not in a foreign land, but now felt as though they were the ones who had trespassed on another man's land. The guide stopped at a large tent that appeared to be reserved for meetings. The man opened the flap of the tent and gestured for them to enter. One by one the representatives from the small town entered into an abode of men of unknown origins.

Greetings and salutations were exchanged. The sheep herders, fishermen and carpenters were received as openly as noblemen and princes. Each man was given a plush pillow on which to make themselves comfortable.

Fortunately for all, an interpreter journeyed with the kings. Mashic was quite surprised to see a twelve-year-old boy as an interpreter. Some of the men from the village had wisely perceived that the interpreter was probably a slave, because of the ring in the boy's ear.

The lords of the camp were peaceful by intent but remained rather evasive about the true nature of their expedition even though the question had been asked several times. Small talk about their families, countries, and customs were discussed many times by each person in the tent.

Mashic did not want to insult the visitors, but knew the fear that his fellow countrymen felt. Mashic decided to ask yet of his hosts, one more time, the purpose of their journey. With the question asked, the mood of the room changed. Everyone could feel the atmosphere in the tent transform from one of joyousness to that of the utmost seriousness.

One of the hosts arose from his chair, and walked over to the door of the tent. With his left hand he pulled open the fabric of the door, and with his right hand he pointed to the star that shone brightly in the sky. Through the interpreter, the king explained what the learned men and astrologers from his country had told him what the appearance of this special star meant. The Hebrews heard, but only one understood the full meaning of what was proclaimed. The king returned to his seat and requested food and drink for all who were in the tent.

Time had moved more swiftly than any of the men dared imagine. It was not until one of the hosts began to fall asleep that it became evident to all that they should depart with friendly farewells. One of the hosts suggested to their guests that their family members in the town might be worried about them.

When they were reminded of their loved ones, they knew the meeting was over. Even though it distressed them to leave the camp, they prepared to leave. Hugs and brotherly kisses were exchanged and the men exited the tent. All of the men were in the same condition as when they had entered, save one. By physical and health standards he was still the same man, but he was a changed man. They began to walk back to the town of Nazareth.

From the distance, no one could tell what events had unfolded within the camp of the mysterious band of men from the East. It had been many hours, and all the women had become restless. Sara knew her God would protect the man who possessed her undying love. It was very quiet, Sara thought to herself, but at least no screams of disaster had come from the camp.

Sara shouted with excitement when she saw her husband, who climbed up the hill on which she and many other women were hidden among the rocks and bushes. "They have returned!" she shouted to the other women who could not see the men. Sara took the time to count the group of men and shouted, "All of them, all of them have returned!" At once the women sprang from the places that they hid and ran to greet their husbands.

Sara was not the first woman to jump from her refuge in the rocks, but she was the first to greet her husband. Sara grasped Mashic tightly around the chest and cried out loudly, "Praise the Lord; Praise the Lord God of our fathers for your safe return." Even though Mashic had remained silent and she had not looked upon his face, she knew something must have happened to him at the camp of the men from the East. She began to grow fearful to look into the dark warm eyes of her beloved husband. She was afraid to see what change had occurred within the heart of her Mashic.

"Sara," he whispered.

She now knew that she must look into his soul and see the change in him. She wanted to hold him tighter than she did now, but when he whispered her name again, she submitted to his voice. The fear she once had, vanished from her as her eyes looked into the windows of the heart of Mashic. When Mashic was assured that his wife could sense his internal peace, he turned to look at the caravan that camped at the base of the hill.

"They are on their way to Jerusalem. The star that is before them, will lead them where the King of the Jews has been born," he said.

"King of the Jews?" she asked him.

"They have traveled for almost two years to reach Israel, and their journey is almost complete," he said, as though he were a part of their quest. "Sara, the Messiah has been born," he said with excitement.

He was no longer the boy she had grown up with, nor was he the man she had married last year, Sara thought. Mashic was always a kind and gentle man, and he loved the God of Israel. Mashic was also a very devout and religious man, but something happened a short time ago that had altered his joyous presence. Mashic had never told her what was wrong, but she knew something was amiss. With this newest revelation, the spark of life had returned. It was as though the news that Mashic brought back to Nazareth was personal, private, and something just for him. This was his answer to prayer. "When would this Messiah present himself to the people of Israel?" she asked herself. What other changes would be brought into the heart of her husband?

Mashic looked back at the caravan and said, "The caravan will be leaving in the morning and John has requested to travel with them. He was granted approval to follow from a distance behind them. I also requested to join them, but I was denied." He sighed heavily and stated, "I wish I had been granted this most honorable request. What wonders does our God want to bring upon his people?" he asked and did not really expect a response from his wife.

"Come Mashic, let us return to our home," she suggested. She looked around and noticed that they were alone on the side of the hill. As they walked toward their home, the lamps of the caravan faded in the night.

†

A month had passed since the caravan from the East went by the quiet town of Nazareth. As time passed, so did the memory of the great caravan, except in the heart of one man. No one spoke of it except for Mashic, who was always in constant thought over these matters.

Even though Mashic had not been chosen to continue on in this wondrous journey, his desire to see the new king of Israel traveled with the men from the East. "Sara!" he said. "I think it is time to check on Jeru, Martha, and Salem."

"Do you wish for me to go with you?" she asked.

"No! I have some very serious matters to discuss with Jeru," he said, as he walked out the front door of their small home.

The friendship that Mashic and Jeru held for each other went deeper and greater than many brothers. It was spoken of in jest by many of the townspeople that Jeru and Mashic were Esau and Jacob reborn. These two men resembled the life of these early patriarchs of their nation. Jeru with his red hair, rough demeanor, and very muscular body, and Mashic who was smaller in frame, level headed, and his spirit favored the things of God. No one ever spoke of this comparison in the presence of Jeru, for all the people knew of the fate of Esau and Jacob. "Jacob hath I loved, and Esau hath I hated," the Lord God Jehovah had spoken to his prophets.

They were so much alike, yet they differed greatly in so many areas. When Mashic thought of the news that a child had been born to rule over the seat of David, he thought of the word, Messiah. Jeru would only think of a king, someone to cast the Romans out of Israel. Jeru had stressed many times to many people of his hatred for the Romans that held his nation in bondage. The two men had many conversations centered on the fate of their people.

When the subject of the Romans came up, Jeru sounded as though he was always ready to reach for a sword. Mashic's words sounded as though he held onto the promise of God. This was the reason Mashic decided to make this recent visit. One more conversation about this matter will not hurt, Mashic thought to himself as he walked down the street to his friend's shop.

The diversity of people who walked down the street this morning was evident to all. People from many different lands would pass through Nazareth on their way to Jerusalem. Of the people that intermingled in the town were Samaritans, Syrians, Greeks, and Romans.

Mashic had set his mind and eyes in direction of Jeru's shop and did not hear the Roman soldier yell, "Hey, Jew!"

There were many Hebrew people on the street that day, and Mashic did not know that the comment was directed toward him. He suddenly became aware that the Roman had spoken to him, when the large strong hands of the Roman grasped his shoulder.

"Hey! Hebrew! Did you hear me call you?" the soldier shouted.

Sheepishly Mashic answered, "No."

The fire in the Roman's eyes had already begun to lessen when he said, "Here! Carry my bundle!" As the law had been written, Mashic carried the Roman's bundle for a mile, and his obligation was no more. The Roman quickly found another poor victim to cast his burden upon.

The sharp edge of the carpenter's cutting tool glided effortlessly through the cedar log that Jeru had recently imported from Lebanon. Jeru's thoughts wandered from his present task to things that had not yet come to pass and he almost made a critical error in the cut in the precious timber.

With the sleeve of his garment, Jeru wiped the perspiration from his brow. Until the moment of the barely prevented error, this new laborious task had had him so absorbed that he did not realize that the sun was now at midday. Joyously he flung open the covering from the window and savored the moment. He deeply inhaled the fresh air, as if it were an expensive gift. He pulled a stool up to the window to rest his exhausted body, and let his mind drift into the same thoughts that had almost cost him a month's wages.

Jeru envisioned a day that he, his family, and his country could live in peace and freedom. He prayed that one day he could look out onto the streets of Nazareth and not have soldiers from a foreign land rule over them and his nation.

Jeru looked out over the green hills that his God had given to his fathers. He gazed at the distant mountains from where the stories passed down from generation to generation had come. Jeru could not see the small stream just outside of the town, but he knew his wife was there. In his mind, he remembered a conversation that he had accidentally overheard between his wife and some of the other women of the town. He relived the moment and he could see the face of his Martha, as she complained to the other women at the stream about him.

"I have asked him many times to use the scraps from the old clothes instead of the sleeve of his garment," she would tell the other women.

"At least he is not a fisherman," another one would say. They would laugh joyously and continue to talk about other matters.

He also let his thoughts wonder to his firstborn son, who would be asleep in the basket on the shore. These thoughts made him feel good and they warmed his heart, but what he saw down the street enraged him and cast out all of his pleasant thoughts.

The more he remembered the injustices that his country was forced to endure, the madder Jeru became. Freedom from a foreign leader was a word only known of by forefathers who had written the words that were inspired by the Spirit of God. He believed in the God of Israel, but where was the Messiah? When would the children of the Almighty be delivered from these barbarians known as Romans?

Mashic breached the entrance of the door, but halted when he noticed that Jeru was not alert to his unexpected entrance. "Jeru," he called. "Jeru," he called again. Mashic noticed a piece of wood that leaned against the wall next to the door, and gently kicked it with his foot. When the plank slammed to the floor, Jeru jumped from his seat with his fist clinched. Mashic felt sorry that he had disturbed Jeru's quiet solitude.

"Forgive me, my friend," Mashic said honestly. "I did not come here to intrude on your privacy."

"You are not intruding," Jeru replied as he let his hand relax, "Come in." Mashic greeted Jeru with a strong brotherly embrace. Neither man was ashamed of this display of affection, for it was the custom of their people, and they truly regarded each other as brothers. Jeru released himself from Mashic's grip, and offered him a place to rest.

Mashic had barely sat down when Jeru inquired of him why he made this unannounced, but welcomed visit.

"I just wanted to see how the new parents were doing," Mashic replied.

"My son is doing nicely, Praise be to the God of our fathers," Jeru responded.

"It is not the young babe that concerns me," Mashic replied.

"Have my actions been so drastic, that someone other than my wife should take notice?" Jeru asked.

"It is very noticeable, my friend. Something must be troubling you very deeply. I have not seen you in that much thought since the time of Salem's circumcision last month," commented Mashic as he began to massage his right shoulder.

"These are troublesome times for the people of Israel," Jeru said mournfully, and continued to explain to Mashic of his desire to be rid of the Roman conquerors. "Just before you entered, I saw a Roman soldier make one of our fellow countrymen carry his bundle." It was then that Jeru noticed that Mashic massaged his shoulder. "What is wrong with your shoulder?" Jeru asked.

"It is nothing," Mashic lied.

"That Roman made you carry his bundle for a mile before he could throw his superiority on someone else. That is what I have talked about all these years. My son will never know freedom," Jeru complained openly.

"Our God has brought many Gentile nations to Israel to rein over her because of her sins," Mashic explained.

"If only things could be different," Jeru stated and then realized what he had said, and he knew it was too late. He saw the expression in Mashic's eyes and Jeru knew that he was in for a lecture.

"Why fret yourself with things that you cannot change? Our God will bring to pass whatsoever he chooses. You let your tongue run wild like the wild horses in Samaria." Mashic walked around the shop and pointed at some of the valuable wood products made for sale or commission that Jeru had produced. "My eyes have gazed upon many works of art within these walls. You choose to complain about the ungodly men that rule over us, yet it was this same political structure that enacted the decree that moved your competition away. Was it not the decree to return to the family of each man's lineage for the purpose of taxation that caused Joseph to depart our town two years ago? Is it not that since his departure that requests for your carpentry work have increased? If Joseph were still here, would your career be so productive?"

Jeru sighed heavily and commented to Mashic, "Mashic, your friendship warms my heart, but your words are sharper than most of my cutting tools. They have pricked my heart. Having great faith has always been a stumbling block for me. It has been about four hundred years since the word of the Lord was given through the prophets. Has our God forsaken Israel forever?"

Mashic passionately interrupted Jeru's oration, "Maybe it is Israel who has forsaken her God? The children of Israel were in captivity for almost four hundred years in Egypt before God raised up Moses to deliver his people." Mashic went on to say, "The first occasion of deliverance was to bring the people out from among the oppressor. The next event will be to liberate the people by removing the oppressor from within the nation."

With a question on his lips Jeru stated, "You speak as though Moses has returned to free his people yet again."

Mashic walked over to the window and stared out at the hills as Jeru had done so intently just moments earlier. Mashic placed one hand on each side of the window opening, and lowered his head. After he let out a loud, long, and painful sigh, Mashic expounded, "One greater than Moses will come to deliver God's people."

"Are you a prophet? Are you one who receives word from Jehovah?" Jeru asked.

"No. No. No," Mashic moaned. He turned around to face Jeru and said, "Yet I know within my heart, and bear witness of the fact that men of great wisdom have gone forth to Jerusalem in search of the male child, born to be king over all of Israel."

Jeru snarled back at Mashic with the comment, "If these kings were so wise, then tell me why these men went to Jerusalem instead of Bethlehem? Every learned man in Israel knows that the Messiah is to be born in Bethlehem, the City of David.

Mashic responded, "I cannot answer that rebuke, but I know our God has a reason that he led them to Jerusalem first. There are many prophecies that must be fulfilled to signify the coming of the Messiah.

Just perhaps their going to Jerusalem first would bring to pass one such prophecy."

"If the Messiah is among us, you will be able to see him because you look for His coming," Jeru said with doubtful words.

"And am I led to believe that you look not for Him?" Mashic asked with his head slightly cocked to one side.

The noon air in the workshop was thick from the heat of the sun and made it uncomfortable, but the tension between the two friends made it unbearable. Jeru had suggested that they venture outside to get some fresh air, and then both men felt ashamed at their actions. Neither could be swayed, yet neither really expected the other to break. Jeru placed his hand on Mashic's shoulder and they walked toward the door. As they walked together, Mashic promised within his heart not to bring this subject up again with Jeru.

Mashic momentarily halted in mid-stride when Jeru said, "Mashic, my friend, let's cease these type of conversations between you and me. I fear that they will only lead to future troubles."

Mashic was startled by the revelation that he and Jeru thought the same thoughts at the same time. As they emerged from the confines of the carpenter's shop, Mashic turned to Jeru and said, "This thing you suggest is a wise thing for us to do. I must leave now. Sara expects me to be home for the noon meal."

As Jeru raised his hand to Mashic, a gesture of acknowledgment of his departure, a large commotion was heard at the other end of the street. "What is going on?" Jeru asked. Both men began to run toward the disturbance.

As they neared the area of the confusion, some of the men had already run into their homes and retrieved whatever weapons of war that they could find. The women had run away in many different directions as they screamed for their children. The children began to cry even though they did not know what had happened. Without missing a step, the women scooped up their young ones and dashed for their own homes.

When Jeru and Mashic arrived at the center of the turmoil, the man who had started this mass confusion was ushered into the chambers of the council. Mashic remembered the confusion that had filled this same hall just a month ago. The noise of all the people as they tried to shout over one another was unbearable, and it only added to the madness in the room. The man that had been escorted into the building had been hidden from Mashic's and Jeru's view by the throng of people. "What is happening?" Mashic asked the man who had just been able to press his way out from the middle of the room.

"John has returned," the man replied.

"Why is there such madness among our people?" Mashic asked.

"I do not know," he replied. "Maybe Josephus can calm things down when he arrives," he went on to say and then exited.

The volume of the conversations in the room lessened as Josephus walked to the front of the room and sat down in the chair of honor. "I understand that John has returned to Nazareth after he followed the kings from the East. We will set this time aside to let John relate his news to us all. Some of this news is very troubling and will bring distress to many in this room. In order for all here and the ones who wait in their homes to get the complete details, please everyone remain quiet until John has completed his oration." Josephus held out his hand toward John, and motioned for John to come forward.

John's wife screamed when John collapsed to the floor before he could reach the spot where Josephus sat. Someone quickly brought a damp cloth and put it on John's face. Another helped John to his feet after he recovered from the strain of whatever had tormented his soul. It was very visible to everyone in the room that John had begun to cry. John just stood motionless in the crowded room.

Everyone knew that John was not a public speaker, and many presumed that was the reason for his hesitance to speak. No one knew that it was the knowledge of the horror that had pressed his tongue to silence. All who were in the building jumped when John shouted, "Murderers."

Josephus motioned for a chair to be brought forward for John to sit in. When John sat down, it was evident to all those who attended this emergency town meeting that he was fully prepared to begin his recollection of the events over the past weeks. "It all started with the great caravan that had passed to the east of our town," John said. Many of the heads nodded in agreement and whispers of "I remember them," were heard throughout the room.

"The air was filled with excitement after we departed Nazareth, for Jerusalem. Everyone was thrilled to know we were on the last part of a journey in which a common man such as I could envision the king that had been born. Not just any king, but the king foretold by our fathers, and his birth displayed in the heavens. They camped outside Jerusalem, and only the kings and their closest advisers went into the city to give tribute to Herod. Some of the details and events that took place inside the palace are not fully known to me. I heard that someone told the wise men to seek for this king of the Jews in Bethlehem."

Jeru looked at Mashic and expected a smirk, but was not even noticed by the one he looked at.

"I also heard that Herod wanted to know where this child is, so he could worship him also," John continued. "They made camp outside Bethlehem, and again only the Kings and the closest advisers entered the town. I met some other shepherds who watched their flocks by night. The shepherds became very excited when they learned of the purpose of the Kings from the East. It reminded them of a special event that had happened about two years earlier. They watched their sheep this night as they were doing the night, when an angel clothed in light appeared before them," John explained.

"The angel said, 'Fear not! For this night in the City of David, born in a manger, is the Christ child wrapped in swaddling clothes.' The shepherds told me that they went into the town and saw with their own eyes what the angel had described to them. They had gone back many times to look for them after the time of the census was completed but were unable to find the child or his parents. We decided to walk into the town to see for ourselves, this Christ child. We could see the house where the child lived, but we were unable to advance any closer than a block from the house because of the amount of people thronged around it. It was my assumption that the majority of the people that had crowded around this small home did not fully understand the importance of what was happening right before their own eyes. They saw kings and pageantries unlike anything that they have seen before, but they missed the true king, the King of the Jews.

"The other shepherds decided to try and see this child the next morning, when the crowd would be smaller, but I felt a need to see him right then. I began to push my way through the crowd. As I advanced through the crowd, I realized that my first conclusions were correct. These people, my countrymen, the people known as the children of

Abraham, Isaac and Jacob, were only there to see the visitors. They had no comprehension of what unfolded before their eyes. When I got to the front of the crowd, one of the kings brought the child to the front door. He was an ordinary looking child, until he looked directly at me. The child looked inside me. He knew me. The child possessed such peace. It is too hard for a common shepherd to understand, much less try to explain. The king turned and went back inside. I knew I had to see this child again. The other shepherds and I decided to go to the city again the next day just after the sun rose, and before the streets became crowded. I felt I must meet the parents of this blessed child." John paused.

The suspense had gripped everyone in the room, and no one dared to breathe too loudly. Each word that John had spoken meant life for their nation. If what he said was true, the Messiah had indeed been born. His words told of favorable things, but his present state of mind told them that a horrible fate awaited their nation.

"I awoke the following morning, and I was horrified when I noticed that the caravan had departed during the night. I asked some people where the caravan had gone and they pointed in the opposite direction from which we came," John told them. "I ran through the streets of Bethlehem in hopes that I would find out what had happened. Panic had gripped me, and I could not think clearly. All at once my mind recalled the house at which the promised child had lived. As quickly as I could, I ran to the house. Again horror greeted me, as a hungry wolf would greet a young lamb. In this house, I hoped to find answers, but the house was as empty as my questions that had gone unanswered.

"It was not completely empty as though they had moved, but vacant as though they abandoned it in a hurry with no plans to return. I began this short trek to Bethlehem, and believed that there was a King born among us. I saw Him, yet I knew him not."

"Surely that alone would not give any man reason to display such theatrics as you did earlier," someone from within the masses shouted. Mumbling broke out throughout the building.

John jumped to his feet and pointed in the direction of the scornful man and scowled, "It discouraged me that I missed an opportunity to meet the Messiah, but what happened next was too monstrous for any man to witness."

The room once again became deathly silent. John still stood before the people of his town, and breathed heavily before he said, "The sound of the horses' hooves as they raced down the small stone streets silenced all other noises. I asked myself, where did they come from? Why were they here? When the screaming began, the sound of the horses' hooves became only a faint sound, like rain on the roof, rather than the thunder it had been just moments ago," John said through his tears.

The men in the congregation began to get restless, while the women began to cry as John continued to tell of the horrors that he saw. "House by house, life by life, death by death those murderers advanced through the city in search of their prey. The soldiers would easily break down the flimsy barriers intended to hinder their entrance into the homes. The soldiers would emerge from the den of death that they had just created with satisfaction on their face, and blood on their swords. Wails of despair, like none I have ever heard, came from every Hebrew family's house. It was at this time that I would call the barren and childless blessed."

"What did they do?" someone asked.

"They killed every male child under the age of two years," John answered painfully.

Horror-driven panic erupted furiously throughout the room. A majority of the men ran from the building to protect their families. Jeru was numbered among those that fled. John continued to disclose the horrors that took place in Bethlehem, yet no one had noticed that his speech had transformed to babble. "Rachel, Rachel crying for her children, because they were not," John screamed.

Mashic's own words returned to him, "Just perhaps their going to Jerusalem first will bring to pass one such prophecy," as John continued to mention Rachel crying for her children.

Josephus stood and tried to calm the people, "Fear not! Do not panic." His words were as though he had not even spoken. He yelled against the noise, "If this army with its thousands of horses had wanted to spread this destruction to our town as well, surely they would have arrived here long before John." They heeded not to his words and dashed back and forth as they tried to get out of the building. One of the panic-stricken men collided with Josephus, which caused him to tumble to the floor. Mashic quickly rushed to Josephus' side and helped him to his feet. "Thank you," he said. "This will cause unrest in many homes for many weeks to come," Josephus said sadly. Mashic nodded his head in agreement, and escorted the chief elder out of the now nearly cleared room.

Jeru burst through the door of his home and found his wife, who nursed their young male child. "Martha? Are you okay?" Jeru shouted uncontrollably.

Martha wanted to scold Jeru because he almost woke the infant up. However, when she saw the terror in his face she instantly and wisely decided that it was best to let her husband speak. Jeru frantically searched for his sword or any weapon he could find, while he described in as much detail as he could what he had heard John tell the crowd. Martha was not afraid for her own life, but she wept bitterly for the mothers who had lost their baby sons.

CHAPTER II

Two Years Later

Jeru, Martha, and Salem played joyfully on the hillside. The grass glistened brightly in the sun from the greenness of the season, and was soft to the touch of the bottoms of their feet. Joyfulness had returned to Nazareth. Many familiar activities had returned to the nation. They watched their young son struggle to his feet, and waddle across the new grass. Jeru mentioned to his wife how relieved he felt about the change of events.

The death of Herod had caused the fear to fade from the hearts of the Jewish people. All of Israel knew Herod was responsible for the massacre in Bethlehem. Everyone rejoiced when they heard of Herod's death. Jeru was one among many who had brought praise unto God for the death of this murderer.

He thought within his mind, "Now with the constant fear of death for my son diminished, I can return to a normal life. As normal as possible, with a foreign power in charge of the land of my fathers," he corrected himself.

Because of the extra activity, warm sun, and the cool breeze, Salem fell into a peaceful midday sleep on the soft grass. Jeru quickly seized the opportunity of the moment and drew Martha to his side. "I love you," he whispered.

"Jeru, I have always known you to be crazy!" she said as she laughed. Jeru tried to give her a passionate kiss. She only half tried to resist. "You have a shop to attend to!" she attempted to say in a scolding manner, but it came out in laughter.

"Let the shop be! I have neglected my family enough this season. I have done well. The name of Jeru is spread throughout the area for my craftsmanship, and many wait for my service. Let them wait one more day!" he said.

"God does not bless a prideful spirit," Martha said.

His mood changed immediately and he stood up. This rebuke caused an attitude change in Jeru and now he was ready to return to the town.

Martha tried to apologize for her rebuke, and explained her love for him. "I would rather see you die at the hand of the enemy than by the rebuke of our God," she said as she tried to explain her motives. She knew he had heard, but she knew his understanding was weak.

The children of Abraham, as they were called, had been taught and knew the stories of people who had died because of their sin. To die at the enemy of your people during battle was honorable, but to die at the hand of a just and holy God was eternally disgraceful.

Jeru lowered his hand as to offer his wife assistance to get up off the ground. Before she could take his hand, Jeru withdrew his out-stretched hand. He used his hand to shield out the rays of the sun to get a better look at the movement in the distance. When Martha saw that Jeru's attention was on something else, she asked, "What do you see, Jeru?"

"It looks like a man, a woman, and a child. The child appears to be just a couple of years older than our Salem. They appear to be very poor, for they do not carry very many possessions," Jeru explained to her.

"Can you tell who it is?" she asked.

"Not from this distance," he responded.

"I will find out at the well!" she said confidently.

"I bet you will," Jeru said as a joke.

Quickly and unexpectedly for Jeru, Martha pulled at his feet with both of her hands, which caused Jeru to fall to the ground. She pounced on him as precisely and purposely as a mother lion on a defenseless animal of prey.

"Okay! Okay! I'm sorry!" he said as he laughed. They both burst into tears of laughter and joy. So joyous was their commotion that Salem awoke from his slumber.

They walked down the streets of the town they called home. Some of the older men who sat under the eaves of their shops smiled in their hearts as they watched the family walk by. The people who accidentally saw the glimpses exchanged between Jeru and Martha smiled openly at the young devoted love. It was good to once again see joy in the streets of Nazareth.

Martha and Salem continued on to their home, and Jeru promised that he would not be long at the shop. She did not believe him and gave him a glance that anyone would know meant she did not believe his comments, but smiled when he said "I promise!"

When Jeru opened the door of his shop, he stepped back as the released heat from the closed room hit him. He quickly opened the cover of the window to allow for a cross breeze in the shop. He could see Mashic walking up the street, and Jeru called out for him to come inside.

Jeru noticed that Mashic's face was flushed and his eyes were red. "Mashic, have you been crying?" Jeru asked out of true compassion. These two men had their differences, but still regarded each other as brothers. Jeru hoped it would always remain this way.

Through his tears, Mashic replied, "John has gone on to be with his fathers!"

"I still do not understand how he lasted this long. I would not have endured as long as he did," Jeru commented.

"Life is such a mystery to me. How could it be so strong, but so fragile at the same time," Mashic said.

"His mind had been extinguished like a small fire at the end of a long night when he witnessed the massacre, and now his spirit has departed as well," Jeru said mournfully.

"His family will suffer from this loss. At least he had sons who can take care of his wife," Mashic said regrettably.

Jeru knew Mashic has suffered privately from not having any children to call his own. Yet he knew Mashic loved Sara too deeply to put her aside in shame. Mashic was a true patriarch, and if Abraham and Sarah could live childless all those years, so could Mashic, Jeru thought. "Mashic," Jeru said as he placed his hand on his friend's shoulder, "Should anything ever happen to me, would you please take care of Martha, and my Salem?" Jeru asked passionately.

Mashic wept even deeper. They both sat in the still of the shop and dared not break the silence. The solitude was interrupted when Martha entered the room. "I just heard about John," she said. They all cried together. "At least his sons can care for their mother," Martha commented mournfully.

"John never recovered from the illness that struck his mind after he ventured to Bethlehem with the caravan," Jeru reflected.

"We must go mourn the loss of our brother with his family," suggested Mashic. It was not until he had spoken of mourning the death of his friend, that he realized maybe they would be mourning him, if he made that journey with the kings instead of John. The hand of providence of their God was truly wonderful and strange, Mashic thought.

He was a more sensitive man than what John had been; maybe he would not have survived as long. Inwardly he praised God for his wisdom, but outwardly he mourned the passing of his friend, fellow countryman, and Hebrew.

"Mashic, I left Salem with Sara. He went back to sleep, but should be awake soon. I will leave you two alone and go take care of him," Martha commented. She departed the shop, and the silence returned instantly.

Neither man wanted to face the mournful family, but neither wanted to seem as if they did not care. They cared deeply for the family. Though Mashic was a great speaker, even he could not speak to a mournful wife and her children. Mashic could only try to offer hope and comfort to them. Jeru was a person who cared, but was completely inept to share his thoughts or show sympathy. The two men left the shop in sadness.

John was buried as directed by the customs of his people. Mashic noticed that someone whom he had not seen for many years had attended the burial of John. The man looked very familiar. Finally he remembered that it was Joseph. Since Joseph was of the lineage of David, Joseph had departed for Bethlehem just after Caesar Augustus' decree for the census.

Mashic decided that he would go see Joseph and his wife Mary and see if they needed anything. Mashic remembered that Mary had left many months before Joseph. Mary had gone to be with her cousin Elisabeth. It had been told that Elisabeth, the wife of Zachariah the priest, also expected a child. Mashic had heard that Elisabeth was great in years, and this was their first child. It made him be hopeful. But the talk in the town caused his own fears that Sara was indeed barren to weigh heavily on him.

The death of John and the extra time that he had spent with his family had caused Jeru's work to falter, so he worked feverishly to catch up on the back orders. Large sweat drops rolled off his face onto the dirt floor. Jeru had worked so hard and long, he had not had time to clean up as he worked.

Mashic made a comment about the cleanliness of the shop when he entered, and then offered, "Can I help you?"

The offer of assistance was denied, and Jeru replied, "It would hurt Martha's spirit if a man did her job!"

"I understand. I know you have been very busy lately, and I wondered if you had heard about Joseph," Mashic asked.

"The only thing I heard was that he had returned to Nazareth!" Jeru replied.

Despite Jeru's comment, Mashic picked up the scrap pieces of wood that had been cut away from Jeru's craftsmanship. "Do you know where he has returned from?" Mashic asked smugly.

"If it is not Bethlehem, then I do not know," Jeru answered as though he was more concerned with his work.

Mashic said, "He just returned from," he paused to let the suspense build, "Egypt!" He did not have to wait long for Jeru's reply.

"Egypt?" Jeru asked as he ceased his laborious task.

"The whole story told about them, was that Joseph and Mary left for Bethlehem to partake in the census. She gave birth to their son, Jesus, soon after they arrived. They stayed there for several years before they went to Egypt. Only recently had Joseph decided to come back to Nazareth," and Mashic concluded his oration of events.

"Bethlehem, I can understand, but why would any man from Israel want to go live in Egypt?" Jeru asked?

"Maybe you should drop by his home and ask him," Mashic replied. "He has a son that is about two years older than Salem," Mashic remarked.

"That must have been the family I saw entering the town the day John died," Jeru stated.

"You did not realize who they were?" Mashic asked.

"No, they were too far away! We could see them as they entered the city, but we could not tell who they were," Jeru answered. "I wonder how this child will be called." Jeru asked.

"I do not understand what you mean!" Mashic answered.

"How will their son be called? A babe born in Bethlehem perhaps, or the one that came out of Egypt, or Jesus of Nazareth?" Jeru asked.

"I do not have an answer for you," Mashic replied. "Have you made plans to speak with him?" Mashic asked.

"Why are you so interested in Joseph's and my relationship?" Jeru asked sharply.

"I did not want Joseph to think of you as unkind," Mashic reiterated. He paused as though he were in a deep thought and then asked, "Are you afraid of the competition? Do I sense jealousy or contempt for Joseph?"

"If you came to hinder my progress, you have been very effective," Jeru said sharply to his friend.

"I did not mean to hinder nor offend you, my friend. Joseph was my friend and your friend for many years. Just because he left our town for several years does not give you the right to show him disrespect. Friendships lost in the chasm of time can be restored," Mashic reminded Jeru.

"I am sorry, Mashic, for my unjustified attack on you," Jeru lamented.

Mashic accepted his apology and both men remained silent until their wives entered. After Martha entered with Salem, Sara entered with bread and cooked fish. The women were very joyful, and both noticed immediately the tension that was in the room. "Have we interrupted something?" Sara asked. Both men shook their heads. The conversation then became light and casual, much to the relief of both families.

The gold, red, and blue colors were poetically displayed in the sky as the sun set quietly this day and as it had done many other days since the God of Israel had created it. Mashic and Sara knew it was time to return to the humble house they called home. They looked like silhouettes as they walked down the dusty street in Nazareth. Jeru and Martha watched their friends turn at the corner and vanish from sight.

Martha reached down and lifted up Salem, who slumbered. Jeru offered to carry his son, and Martha accepted his offer gladly. Even though Salem was still a young child, he was getting heavy, especially when he was asleep. As Jeru walked out the door of the shop, Martha began to clean up the shop. Jeru looked back and saw what had detained his wife. He just shook his head and continued to walk. Jeru knew that if he told her to leave this mess until tomorrow, it would only fall on deaf ears.

CHAPTER III

Eight Years Later

Jeru stopped at the entrance of his prosperous establishment to watch his wife, who was cleaning up his shop. As a joke, he said to her, "Things will never change. You will always be cleaning!"

Without a moment's hesitation, Martha replied, "As long as you make these messes, my dear husband, I will have to clean them up!"

When Jeru began to assist his wife to clean up his shop, she asked, "Where is Salem?"

"After his studies were complete, he headed out to play on the hillside," Jeru answered. "He is safe," he told her before she had time to ask, "Mashic said that he would watch over him and the other boys. Mashic deserves to have children. He is such a caring man," Jeru said reflectively. "He is a true friend. A man of honor," Jeru added to his statement.

"But he does not have to work as hard as you my dear," she said, complimenting Jeru because he was such a great provider for his family.

"I wonder sometimes if it is a choice of his not to work so hard, or if it is a justification since he does not have any heirs?" Jeru asked even though he knew that he should not have asked it openly before his wife.

"Neither way really matters! He is your friend," Martha explained as she put the broom away. "Now, your shop is ready for you to mess up all over again," she said with her hands on her still trim hips.

Martha left the shop after she received a very passionate and loving kiss from the proprietor of the establishment. He watched her walk out of the shop, and down the street toward their home. Jeru knew he was blessed with a happy and healthy family. He prayed daily to the God of his fathers to bless his family.

A short time later, Mashic knocked loudly on the seal of the door and then entered the shop. Jeru did not have to look up because he knew who it was. "What can I do for you this time, my friend?" Jeru asked.

"You must not think badly of me that I would come here only in a time of need," Mashic replied. "Even though you have tried to test me, I will respond only in kindness. I will only accomplish the task that I was instructed to come here to do. Sara wanted to know if there is anything that we can do to assist you and your family as you prepare for the trip to Jerusalem tomorrow," Mashic asked with true friendly intentions.

"Your offer is counted as a worthy deed, but all preparations for the journey to Jerusalem are complete," Jeru said pride fully. It was then that he realized that he talked with the man that he had left his son with and asked, "Where is Salem? Is he with Sara?"

"No. He had a question to ask of his mother, so, as I was on my way to take him home, we saw Martha and Salem went with her," Mashic replied.

Jeru noticed that Mashic had been looking around his shop ever since he walked in and Jeru stated, "The expression on your face tells me that you have another question or two to ask of me!"

"You have read me well. I do have another question. I do not see an animal in which you can take to the sacrifice. Have you obtained your sacrifice?" Mashic asked.

"No, I have not purchased a sacrifice yet. I will acquire a lamb when I get to the Temple!" Jeru said boastfully. "Besides, I would have to leave the creature at my home instead of here at the shop. They are too much trouble to have to take all the way to Jerusalem."

Most people would get their offering prior to their arrival in Jerusalem. The price at the Temple was always greatly increased. Only the wealthy, those who could not attain one earlier, or the foolish, would buy their sacrifice there.

Of all the things Jeru could have said to hurt his lifelong friend, this was the one thing that hurt. Everyone in town knew Jeru had been very successful, but to boast made it almost sinful. It was not as much what he said, but the attitude that prompted Jeru to let the words spew from his mouth. To a trusted friend, those types of words were worse than if he had vomited in his presence. Jeru could afford to pay a higher price in the Temple than bring one with him.

Mashic made his ends meet, but he was content, and that was the reason Mashic had already purchased turtle doves. Other people, like Joseph, still struggled, especially with Mary and all those children. Joseph was considered blessed by the arrows in his quill, but still his family had to be provided for.

"Lambs purchased in Jerusalem to be offered for sacrifice will cost almost twice as much there as they would if purchased prior to your departure!" Mashic said with concern for Jeru's livelihood.

"I cannot take the time for these matters now. Since I will have to take time off anyway for the feast, I might as well use that time to obtain an offering," Jeru replied very sternly to Mashic.

"Then I will disturb you no longer," Mashic said as he exited.

Jeru was not quite sure if Mashic had left with an injured heart or not. "I will talk with him later to make sure he is not troubled," he said to himself, but the occasion never presented itself, and the seed of dissention had been planted.

Salem entered the shop almost immediately after Mashic departed. "Father," he announced to let his father know that he was there.

"Yes, Son, what do you want?" Jeru asked.

"Mother said if it is okay with you, that I could go play in the fields north of town with the other boys. They wanted me to come back and finish the game we started earlier," he said almost desperately. "I'll be home before the evening meal," he stated as though he knew what the next question was.

"Do not go into the forest!" Jeru stated.

"I promise!" Salem said.

Jeru gave a nod and Salem's feet were already in motion when Jeru said, "Do not," and he was out the door when his father finished the familiar sentence, "Be late, and be careful."

Jeru ran over to the door and watched his ten-year-old son run playfully along the street with the other boys his age. Jeru smiled openly and inwardly and then returned to his work.

Salem and the other boys began to imitate the soldier stories that were part of their heritage. One boy pretended to pick up stones and then started to swing the sling over his head and shouted, "I'm David.

Which one of you dog gentiles wants to be Goliath?" he dared the other children.

"That's not fair. You were David last time. David always won!" another boy protested.

"Except with Bathsheba," one of the older boys said.

"Oh yes he did," the oldest boy commented.

Salem, who was the youngest, said, "I do not understand." The group of boys immediately began to laugh and jeer him. "I really do not understand," he honestly proclaimed.

The oldest boy then said, "Let's go into the forest."

"Yeah!" was the response from the small band of boys, save one.

The oldest noticed that Salem had not responded and then asked him, "What about you, Salem?"

"My father said . . ." Salem began to quote his father's demand.

"Your father said? Is your father here now? How will he know?" the group began to bombard him all at once.

"Okay, okay," he said reluctantly.

"This will be fun," the oldest boy said.

The brave pretend warriors of the nation of Israel began their imaginary campaign into the forest of their dreaded enemy. "Some of us may not come back alive," the oldest boy proclaimed suspiciously.

Salem was very nervous as they disappeared into the forest and away from view of the town. He was not sure what scared him most–that he had disobeyed his father or to actually be in this forbidden forest.

"Come look at this!" one of the boys shouted. "Be quiet, or you'll scare him," he also said. The boys gathered together around the excited boy.

"What is it?" Salem whispered quietly.

Before any of the boys could answer his question, a man inside the bushes jumped out and yelled, "Get away from me!"

The crowd of boys leaped and scattered like a covey of doves surprised by an intruder. The man yelled, "Unclean! Unclean! Unclean!" as the boys raced away.

The oldest boy stopped, and almost immediately the others stopped as well, except for Salem. "Salem!" he shouted. "He will not hurt you. Come back," he yelled. Salem very reluctantly returned to the group. "Have you ever stoned a leper before?" he asked. None of the boys had ever stoned anyone before, much less a leper, but Salem was the only one who admitted to never having done it. The oldest boy picks up a stone and yelled, "Come on, let's get him!" The once frightened, now angry mob quickly picked up their evil tools of justice and pursued the man.

Usually children could not run faster than adults, but this man was very slow in his steps, even though he was aware of his pursuers. The oldest boy drew his arm back, and let the stone fly through the air. The stone collided heavily on the man's shoulder and he fell to the ground. The man was dressed in very thin and filthy rags, and tried desperately to use them as armor against the assault. Each boy let the missile go from their hand, aimed at the defenseless target.

Salem threw his stone at the man, but prayed that it would miss him. One of the other boys punched Salem on the arm when the other boy realized that the rock missed its target. Salem acted like the assault to the arm did not hurt, but it was his heart that was in real agony. After the band of young boys had a victorious campaign in the forest, they started to walk back toward Nazareth. Salem, at the end of the line as always, looked back at the leper. The leper looked directly at him, and Salem could see the tears run down the man's face. Salem began to weep, but quickly wiped his eyes. Even though the temperature was rather high that day, Salem shivered as he walked from the forest. He knew he could never share this event with his father.

Salem returned to the village in distress. As he walked past Mashic's home, he glanced over to make sure he had passed unnoticed, but frowned when Sara called out for Salem to come over.

"Mashic, come out front. Salem has come to visit us," Sara called out. "Why the long face, Salem? Is something wrong?" she asked.

"Nothing is wrong!" Salem lied.

Mashic appeared in the door just as Salem had lied to Sara. Mashic knew that the words from the young boy's mouth were false, but this was not the time to scold. "It is so good to see you, young man!" Mashic said as Sara went inside the house. Mashic talked to Salem about many subjects that were of no importance.

The wise older man used a technique that the fishermen used to get the information out of Salem that he wanted. He kept throwing the net out again and again, and sooner or later the fisherman would catch the right fish. As always, Mashic maintained his reputation as a great conversationalist with the young boy that sat next to him. It was not his ability to speak that had given Mashic his notoriety, but it was the way he listened that really distinguished him from most men.

Mashic's ears perked up when Salem said the word, "Forest."

The restrictions that Jeru had set for Salem not to go into the forest were well known by Mashic and he very carefully asked, trying not to sound judgmental, "Have you been in the forest?"

Salem wept bitterly, and confessed the whole story to Mashic. It comforted Salem to know that Mashic would listen and understand him. Mashic knew what he must tell Salem, even before Salem began his confession. As Salem concluded his story, Mashic put his arm around Salem and said, "Even though the law requires us to do things that might not seem right for us, each of us must do what is right. The reason we obey the law is just as important as obeying it."

After Salem gained his composure, he asked, "Where do lepers live? When I saw that man asleep in the forest, it really scared me. Where was his home?"

"Unless the leper is very wealthy, he will have no home, no family, nothing!" Mashic answered. "I have heard of a place in the land of Samaria, where lepers can live in somewhat relative safety," Mashic told the young boy. It was like he had cut his bowels open with a knife to tell his young friend of such matters. No matter how much the truth hurt, it was still the truth. Mashic put one hand on each of Salem's small shoulders and turned his body so he could look directly into the boy's eyes. "You know you must tell your father about this incident?" Mashic asked sternly, but patiently. Salem nodded his head, and then Mashic hugged him tightly. "Do you want me to talk to your father first?" Mashic asked with great concern.

"No, thank you. I think my father would be insulted if he knew I talked to someone else first!" Salem admitted honestly.

"Wise decision, young man," Mashic said as he stood up and he saluted him with the salute the Roman's used. They both laughed. Mashic knelt down and said, "I love you like a son. Be strong and do what is right before our God!"

Salem began to walk away, but stopped after just a few steps. He turned to Mashic and asked, "Mashic, why do you always say things

Jeff Frazier

like my God, or our God, and my father always says the God of our fathers?"

"I do not have the answer to that question," Mashic answered ashamedly. After Salem walked away Mashic whispered to himself, "But I wish I did." Tears rolled down his face as he watched the young boy walk toward his home. "Son, I wish I knew."

Salem openly confessed his sins to his father, and was prepared to accept any punishment that his father had deemed appropriate. Jeru was inwardly very pleased that his son was unharmed, but his emotions had begun to slide to the side of unreasonable anger for Salem's disobedience.

Jeru instructed Salem on what his punishment would be, and then said, "I am glad to see that you are unharmed. Your punishment is not too severe and it will soon pass, and the trip to Jerusalem will soften the impact some." Salem nodded to signify that he understood and left the room. Salem decided not to ask his father the question Mashic did not know the answer to, and he could hear the voice of the uncle figure in his life say, "Wise decision, young man."

†

The people from Nazareth that made the trek to Jerusalem were those who were required to go, and those who wholly enjoyed the feast times of their faith. Jeru was among them, but his thoughts were on his shop. They traveled in large groups for protection from bandits. All of the townspeople praised the Lord that the trip to Jerusalem went without any unpleasant events.

The feasts were conducted in the order of their traditions, but Mashic had his doubts if the true spirit of the festival had been preserved. The majority of the people in Jerusalem ate, drank, and consumed in merriment. Had the reason for the feast been forgotten? Mashic should have been joyous, but his heart was heavily burdened.

Jeru and his family had separated from the mass that had made the journey to Jerusalem soon after their arrival. Mashic had kept a close watch on the mobs of people for several days, but he had not seen Jeru, or his family.

At the end of the third day of the celebration, they practically ran over each other at the corner of the Temple. "I am sorry, Jeru. I did not mean to run into you in my haste," Mashic said.

"It is I who should watch more closely!" Jeru stated.

Mashic looked in the cart that Jeru pulled, and smiled when he noticed that Salem was asleep. "Is he too big to be pulled around by his parents?" Mashic asked.

Jeru smiled and replied, "A young boy of ten should be able to keep up, and stay awake." Then Jeru leaned close to Mashic's ear and pretended to whisper, but spoke loud enough for the two women to hear, "His mother has spoiled him terribly."

Mashic came to Martha's defense and replied, "We all know that it is Sara and I who should accept the blame for Salem's spoiled state." Salem awoke from his sleep, looked at Mashic, smiled and fell asleep again. They laughed at the young boy.

"Yes, you two have contributed to the condition of Salem!" Jeru replied.

"Have you made plans to return to Nazareth?" Sara asked.

"We are on our way back to Nazareth. Our religious obligations are fulfilled, and there are many matters at home that I must attend to," Jeru said as though he needed an excuse for why he left early.

"You will always do what you think is right!" Mashic commented. In order not to sound as if he had just insulted his fellow countryman, he said, "I will pray that your trip home is a safe one." Friendly hugs and kisses were exchanged, and they were soon out of sight within the massive crowd.

According to the laws of Moses, the feast days were complete, so the people had begun to return home. The return trip was not as organized as the trip to Jerusalem. The people from Nazareth had departed to Jerusalem as a group, but returned to Nazareth as stragglers and wanderers. Many of the older children were expected to find a relative and stay with them until they got home, and some people decided to stay for a couple of extra days.

Mashic and Sara had discussed a possible visit to her sister in Jericho, but they had not yet made up their mind. "A decision must be made before we get too far out of Jerusalem," he told her gently. Mashic opened his mouth to tell Sara that he had decided to take her to see her sister but was interrupted when Joseph and Mary ran up to them. They appeared to be deeply distressed.

"Have you seen Jesus?" Joseph asked.

"Have you seen my son?" Mary asked before Mashic could answer Joseph's question.

"No, I have not seen him, but Sara and I will be glad to help you look for him," Mashic respectfully offered their assistance. They discussed all the possibilities of where Jesus could be.

"Could he be farther ahead? Maybe he is with another family member?" Mashic asked.

"Maybe he got lost and went in the wrong direction!" Mary stated fearfully. When Sara asked, "Could he still be in Jerusalem?" even without further discussion they knew that Sara was correct, and that Jesus must still be in Jerusalem.

Joseph and Mary had left their other children with some other friends from Nazareth, and promised that they would be back to get them after they found Jesus. Joseph, Mary, Mashic, and Sara quickly returned to Jerusalem. Neither Mary nor Joseph could think of any place where Jesus could be.

They searched for three days and still could not find him, so they decided to concentrate on the major sites of the city. Mary finally remembered where Jesus always seemed to be drawn, and shouted with excitement, "The Temple!"

Joseph and Mary entered the Temple before Mashic and Sara. Mashic could see the young boy Jesus, who was now twelve years old, sitting in the seat of the teacher. "This is strange," Mashic said softly.

Mashic was close enough to hear Mary when she asked Jesus in what sounded like a rebuke, "Where have you been? You should have known that we would be worried about you?" The question that was asked was a proper one for a worried and concerned mother to ask, but the answer from the young Jesus shook Mashic's belief on who this son of a carpenter was.

The trip back to Nazareth was quiet and pleasant, but Mashic was troubled, or at least appeared to be. Sara had only asked him one time at the start of their travel home with, "Is there something wrong?" When he only responded with a slight movement of his head, she knew better than to ask him again.

†

Mashic had rested for several days after he returned from Jerusalem. Then he decided to visit his friend, Jeru. As Mashic approached the carpenter's shop door, he could see that Jeru still labored tirelessly even as the hours of darkness approached. Mashic was really distressed with his relationship with Jeru. Jeru had become very obsessed with success. He stood at the door of the shop and waited a few moments before he let Jeru know he was there. The shadow caused by the oil lamp on the other side of the room made Jeru look like a very large, muscular man. Jeru's distinct features were not visible because of the shadows caused by the light. "Jeru, are you in?" Mashic asked.

"Yes, can I help you?" Jeru asked and then noticed that it was Mashic. "Come in, Come in!" Jeru said.

"I am sorry that I have not had a chance to see you lately, but the trip to Jerusalem was a little more eventful than I had expected," Mashic said. Mashic unfolded the events of the days after Jeru left Jerusalem. While Mashic spoke, he got the impression that Jeru did not really listen to what he told him. Mashic, an expert listener, knew if someone listened to him or not. The impression Jeru gave Mashic was that Jeru wanted to finish his work unhindered. Mashic continued his version of the occurrence despite Jeru's reluctance to hear the details.

When he got to the part about Jesus that sat in the seat of the teacher, Jeru interrupted Mashic's story and asked, "What is wrong with that child? Have his parents ever trained him not to sit in chairs that were intended for someone else?"

Mashic explained to Jeru, "Jesus was the teacher. Jesus had confounded all the teachers with his wisdom and his knowledge of the scriptures. All the people present were aware of his abilities." Mashic struggled to continue the rest of his story.

A smile erupted on Jeru's face when Mashic told him how Mary publicly rebuked Jesus. "She said, 'Where have you been? Do you not know that we were worried about you?' The answer he gave to his mother shocked me!" Mashic continued. "Jesus said, 'Did you not know that I should be at my father's house? I should be doing my father's business!'" Mashic quoted the young boy from Nazareth.

"That boy does not know what business his father is in!" Jeru responded.

The Sabbath was near, and he had to start making preparations soon, so Mashic used this as excuse to terminate this conversation. "I must leave now," Mashic said as he walked toward the exit.

Jeru laughed and said, "Father's business!"

Dccp sorrow came over Mashic after he related the story to Jeru. Mashic walked home saddened by the hardness of his fellow countryman's heart. The sorrow he felt could not quench the elation that had come over him since he had witnessed the events in Jerusalem. There was something within his soul that wanted to tell everyone of what he had seen.

CHAPTER IV

Eighteen Years Later

Mashic approached the entrance of the establishment that he had walked to so many times before. No one was happier than Mashic that the quarrels between himself and Jeru had diminished over the last eighteen years. The fact that the subject of Jesus had very seldom come into their conversations helped control the number of verbal confrontations. Mashic had not forgotten his zeal for the man called Jesus, but he did not display it publicly.

He walked in the shop and did knock first. He saw the figure of a man that stood in the corner. Nighttime quickly approached, but the man was still engulfed in the task that sat before him. "How many days have I witnessed this sight," Mashic said quietly to himself. "Jeru, are you in?" Mashic called out as though he was not sure who worked in the shadows.

The man ceased his labor and turned to face the man at the door. The man said "No! I am not Jeru. It is I, Salem," he said as he turned so the light could reflect off of him, so that Mashic to see him clearly.

Mashic smiled with embarrassment and said, "Salem, my young friend. My! My! I thought you were Jeru, when he was your age. Your work ethics compare greatly to his as well."

"I normally do not work this late, but I have a special assignment. A wealthy man in Cana has consigned me to make him this wedding bench. His eldest daughter is to be wed soon, and I must finish it tonight," Salem said.

"You need not explain your actions to me!" Mashic replied. "You are a grown man. Your stature and desires are already molded by the man who trained you all these years, yet I hope that they are not set in mortar. Besides, no man has ever burned the oil in his lamps like Jeru has!" Mashic emphasized.

"That is a very truthful statement," agreed Salem.

"It is late, so I will bother you no longer," Mashic said honestly. Mashic started to walk toward the door, stopped, looked at Salem's work and said, "Magnificent craftsmanship, Salem."

"Thank you!" Salem answered and watched the friend of his father exit the shop that bore both his father's and his name. Salem labored heavily and purposefully into the hours of darkness. With the job completed, he laid his head down on the bench that had required many hours away from his wife.

†

Salem awoke from his slumber with his head on a pile of clean rags. He sprang to his feet when he noticed the morning light that came through the window, and the sound of children's laughter echoed radiantly down the streets of Nazareth. He ran home and entered the house of his family. It pleased Salem that his parents were not home because it was not good for a man to be rebuked by his wife in front of others. He had prepared himself for the onslaught of accusations, and threats from his wife of ten years, but the silence he received was unbearable. Without any questions asked, Salem explained, "I fell asleep in the shop," to the woman who ignored his justifications. "I had to finish the wedding bench. A generous bonus is in store for us, if I deliver the bench before tomorrow!" he emphasized.

"I knew where you were!" she finally responded. "Who do you think put your thick head on the soft pile of rags during the night?" she asked. Salem did not answer her because he just then realized that the way he fell asleep was different from the way he woke up. "I love you so much, and I hate to see you destroy your health this way!" she lovingly scolded him. "You are all I have. The Lord has chosen to bind up my womb, and you are the only person I truly love," she lamented.

Salem walked over to her and held her close to him. "I will never give you a reason to worry about me again. My heart ached because I had not told you of my whereabouts, and let you worry needlessly!" Salem proclaimed to her. He became consumed with her kiss, and he knew at this moment how the friend of his father had felt all these years, without a son to call his own. There was something missing, but they continued through life as if they had all they needed.

He had been instructed for many years by Mashic on the concerns of spiritual matters, and Salem knew there had to be a reason that the God of Israel had chosen to seal the womb of his wife. At times Salem thought he had two fathers. Jeru was the man who raised and trained him in the ways of business. His other father was Mashic, who trained him in the ways of life. Both worlds seemed to collide within his spirit. Salem had been trained for business, but his heart wanted the things of the God of his fathers.

"Life is good, but your business must never falter," Jeru had told him.

"Business is good, but never let it consume you," the friend of his father and who was now his friend had said.

Salem shook his head several times to clear the confusion of different teaching from his mind. With his thoughts again on Cana and to please his wife, Salem asked Elizabeth, "I want to ask you if you would like to go with me to Cana to deliver this wedding bench?" He prayed silently that his voice had not betrayed him. He hoped he sounded as though he had asked her from a true heart rather than the thought that had just come to him. The latter was more to the truth.

"Well then, ask!" she replied.

"Will you honor me and make this journey with me to Cana?" he asked.

"It would be my delight!" she sweetly answered her husband.

Salem had learned one of his most important lessons of life from Mashic while he grew up. Mashic never said a word about the subject, but the way Mashic demonstrated his style of life spoke louder than any oration given by a Pharisee. Salem had learned to love his wife, regardless of the conditions that their God had chosen for their lives. Elizabeth, like Sara, was barren. He had known men that would abuse their wives if the man believed them to be barren. He even heard of some men that went as far as giving their wife a bill of divorcement. Salem's father had always treated his mother well, but at least she bore him one son. Salem wondered how his father would have treated his mother had he never been born.

From past experiences, Salem knew that to let Elizabeth join him on this delivery would slow him down. He could not complain or change his mind because he had already asked her to go with him. Salem remembered what Solomon had once said, "It is better for a man to live on top of the house than with a contemptuous wife."

Their departure had already been delayed by one hour, while Elizabeth gathered materials for their joint venture. Salem maintained his patience with her, even though she requested to stop frequently. With each interruption of the delivery, Salem would calculate the amount of the bonus he lost. He loved his wife, and to spend this time with her was more precious than any gold. Salem chided himself while he calculated his losses, and his desire to be with Elizabeth at the same time. No matter how hard he tried not to recount the amounts, he would do it anyway.

Jeru did not make this trip, but Salem could still hear the words of his father, "You must tend to your father's business," in his mind. Salem had never heard anyone use that phrase before, and wondered why his father always emphasized it when Jesus could hear what he said. Jesus would never respond even though it was apparent that the remark was aimed at him.

Salem thanked the God of his fathers silently when they reached the city of Cana. They found the house without any difficulty, and presented the wedding bench to the father of the bride. The man was pleased with the craftsmanship and of the detail carved into the grain of the wood. Salem received his payment gracefully, and did not insult the man and count the money in his presence. Salem could tell by the weight of the bag that his payment was in full, and the bonus was there as well. Salem felt all the more sorrowful that he had counted his losses on the way to Cana. Another voice of the past came into his head, "Do what is right and holy and the Lord God will bless you!"

"Thank you, Mashic," Salem whispered to himself.

"What did you say?" Elizabeth asked.

"I just thanked a friend for his help," Salem said. He knew from the expression on her face that she did not understand what he talked about.

The father of the bride insisted that Salem and his wife stay for the festivities. They refused at first, but were convinced to stay when the host had prodded them all the more. They were even given a nice room to sleep in. The father of the bride had promised that the feast would be very eventful, and there was no way that anyone could have known what was about to take place.

Elizabeth noticed that Mary, Jesus' mother, had already arrived for the wedding. It was Salem who had noticed that Jesus was not there. Word had gotten around that Jesus had gone to visit his cousin John. John, the son of a priest, was an unusual character, born when his parents were very old. It was the custom of his people to add a name to a person to help distinguish one John from another John. For the son of Zacharias, the name, "The Baptist," was added. John had been known to eat wild locusts and honey.

"What would Jesus, or anyone, have to do with such a man?" one of the other guests at the wedding had told Salem. The same man said, "John has preached, 'Repent, for the kingdom of heaven is at hand.' How strange of a message is that?"

The feast began on time, and Salem noticed that Jesus had arrived sometime later. Several other men followed Jesus. They appeared to be his pupils. "What could he teach them?" Salem thought to himself. "Jesus is only a carpenter, is he not? Maybe he will teach them how to a build a temple."

Salem knew the wine was almost gone, and he planned to leave when the wine was gone. His attention was drawn to the other side of the room where Jesus and Mary, his mother, both stood. He could tell that Mary told Jesus something, but he could not hear what was said.

It seemed to Salem that Jesus had answered his mother, and that Jesus was not too overly concerned with whatever problem she had brought to him. Then Mary motioned for the servants. She said something to them and the servants turned to Jesus. Jesus gave the servants what appeared to be instructions, and the servants left immediately to obey.

Salem watched attentively the actions of his fellow townsman. Salem concentrated so intently on Jesus that he did not hear Elizabeth ask, "Why do you watch Jesus in the manner that you do?" Since Salem did not respond to her question, she slowly sank back into her chair and tried desperately to find out what had captivated her husband.

The servants picked up the jugs that were used to cleanse the hands of the Jewish people before they ate and dipped the water out of the jugs. Jesus motioned for the governor of the feast to be served. Salem sat close enough to the governor to overhear him say, "Most hosts will serve the good wine first, and when every man is full of wine, then will serve the lesser wine." The governor of the feast turned to the father of the bride and said, "This is the best wine."

Salem was shocked by what the man had said and waited patiently to be served. He questioned whether the governor was sober enough to tell the difference between good wine and dirty water. The cup was set before him. The color of the wine and fragrance were excellent, yet he chose not to drink.

Another man at the feast challenged Salem, "Go ahead! Drink it! It is very good wine." Salem pushed the cup aside, for he believed it to be only water from the jugs. Jeru had taught Salem well.

Salem remained quiet on the return trip home. Elizabeth tried several times unsuccessfully to occupy his mind with other thoughts. Upon their return to Nazareth, Salem dove intensely into his work.

The time of the Passover was near and Salem knew Jesus would go to Jerusalem after he left Cana. Joseph had always taken his family to Jerusalem every year for the Passover while they grew up. Salem, who had been trained by Jeru, returned to Nazareth and resumed his work alongside of the man he called father.

Salem told Jeru all the details of the trip, save the incident of Jesus and the water and wine. Salem knew Jesus, the son of Joseph, and he was also keenly aware that his father hated Jesus, and it was best not to talk about Jesus at all. Salem had noticed that Mashic had always shown interest in the man called Jesus of Nazareth, and wondered if one day this would strain or even obliterate a friendship that had lasted for more than forty years.

CHAPTER V

As always, Mashic attended the feast of the Passover each year. Mashic did not just attend; he thrust himself into the purpose, into the spirit of the event. Many of his countrymen had forgotten the importance of the feast. Each year Mashic's excitement grew as each feast approached. Just as his enthusiasm grew, so did his distaste for some of the manmade customs that were tagged onto the festivities, and never seemed to let go. This year would be no different.

Every year Mashic was more enthusiastic as plans were made to attend the feast, and each year Jeru and Salem would spend more time in the shop. Each year Mashic would set money aside to make the trip, and each year he would have to haggle with the vendors at the Temple over the prices of the animals to be used as a sacrifice. The prices always seemed to be higher than the year before. He recalled one year when they even tried to sell him a blemished offering. Many years before, Mashic would bring his offering with him, but now it was not possible. Offerings not bought at the Temple would have to be inspected and approved before they could be presented.

The symbolism of what the Passover meant was cherished deeply by the Jewish people. This was a people that had once been in bondage under Egypt, but had been delivered by the hand of their God. This feast was a remembrance of the hard times they suffered in Egypt, and the wondrous things God did for them. They remembered the perfect lamb that had been sacrificed. They remembered the spotless lamb whose blood covered the homes of the people who believed and obeyed the commandment of God. Death would Passover them that night. He lived in the land that this same God had given to his fathers before him and brought them back to after their bondage in Egypt.

Mashic endured great agony to witness the shame that these vendors had perpetrated in the Temple of their one and only God. While Mashic haggled with a man that perceived Mashic to be a prospective customer, a loud disturbance caught everyone's attention. Mashic walked

Jeff Frazier

away from the seller of turtle doves and sheep to get a better view of the disturbance. Many people scampered away from the commotion. The fear on the people's faces that fled told Mashic that there was a madman in the Temple. He was astounded when he saw that the center of the disturbance was a man from his own hometown that he recognized.

The man overturned tables, and shouted at the money changers. The man accused these men of vile things. The gold and silver coins sang a metallic song when they collided with the polished stone floor of the Temple. All of the animals began to sound alarms of their own, and this all added to the eruption of chaos. Birds escaped their confines and flew to freedom. The jackasses bayed and kicked wildly. People ran in all directions to escape the onslaught of this confusion.

Never in all of his life had Mashic witnessed such a scene. Mashic dodged people, animals, and debris that flew by as he stood there. He witnessed what he wished he could do and probably should have done himself. His respect for the man called Jesus of Nazareth just increased. Mashic could not wait to get to Nazareth and tell everyone what he had seen.

†

The father and son carpenters in Nazareth both smiled when they saw Mashic walk down the dusty street that passed in front of their shop. They knew that upon Mashic's return from Jerusalem, he would stop at their shop to relate all the events that occurred on his most recent trip. Mashic was a source of laughter for these two carpenters. Mashic's joyous attitude and love of life brightened their day, even though they did not always want to hear his newest story. They both respected Mashic's privacy, and would not ask him about his journeys. They knew all too well that Mashic would share with them everything he had done or learned, even if they did not want to hear it.

Neither Salem nor Jeru was surprised when Mashic told them every detail of the Temple incident. Mashic took on the responsibility to tell his friends what had happened because they just never seemed to be able to make it to Jerusalem anymore. No matter what the religious requirements were, they always had some issue that prevented the journey that was their obligation.

Jeru responded with a belligerent barrage of insults toward Jesus when he heard that Jesus had cast out the money changers from the

Temple. Salem was shocked by this newest verbalization of venom from his father. Mashic, however, was not surprised by this angry example of hatred.

When Mashic tried to defend the fellow carpenter from Nazareth, he was strongly rebuked by Jeru. "What did you say? He screamed at the money changers? Oh yes, 'Why have you turned my father's house into a den of thieves?' Did I quote that correctly? This Jesus must have an obsession with the Temple; he called it the house of his father," Jeru said. Both Salem and Mashic knew that Jeru had dredged up an old incident that happened many years earlier. They knew Jeru spoke of the time when Jesus was twelve years old and taught in the Temple. This was the second time Jesus had called the Temple "My Father's house."

Mashic responded angrily, "Those men have stolen from their own people for years! It was about time someone did something to those thieves!"

Salem tried to be a mediator and said, "You both have made valid points. You both have had different points of view before, why let this latest incident cause a hindrance in your friendship?" The argument ceased, but Salem was not convinced that the men were satisfied.

Mashic walked toward the door, stopped, turned toward Jeru and stated, "Jesus has traveled from synagogue to synagogue throughout all of Israel. One day he will return to this town, the town where he grew up."

"And of what importance will that be to me?" Jeru asked.

"Many people follow after him, and are amazed at what he has taught," Mashic responded. "We will need to hear him, and decide what we will do with this carpenter from Nazareth," he said, then departed the shop.

Salem shivered when Jeru said, "Yes, we will have to decide what we will do with this man, Jesus."

Jeru said, "That must have been the reason that Mashic made so many extra trips from Nazareth to other sections of Israel." Jeru just shook his head in disgust. Not another word was spoken in the shop that day by either man.

†

The Sabbath was just three days away when Jesus returned to Nazareth. Word had spread that Jesus was to speak in the synagogue, and a lot of people planned to be there. No one was really sure what he would say, but it really did not matter. They did not want to miss the action.

Mashic made his usual visit to the carpenter's shop, and reminded the proprietors of the establishment that Jesus was to speak in the synagogue on the next Sabbath. Jeru seemed uninterested, as expected. Salem promised that he would be there.

Later that evening Salem and some of his childhood friends relaxed by a fire. They discussed current events, and exaggerated about things they had done recently. They occasionally mentioned the things they did as young boys, but no one brought up the story of the leper. The topics were usually light in nature, but as the discussion continued, it took on a more serious tone. Uriah, the son of John, asked, "Have you heard that Jesus is back in town?" Everyone acknowledged Uriah's comment.

"Has not it been almost a year since Jesus first left to travel throughout all of Israel, to partake in this venture of his?" someone else asked.

Salem was deep in thought about other matters until someone asked Salem specifically if he had heard that Jesus had gone through Samaria.

"Samaria? Why would any good Jew go through that forbidden section of land?" Uriah asked. Uriah went on to tell of the rumor that he had heard about when Jesus talked with a harlot at Jacob's well. Very tactfully, Uriah told of how Jesus and his disciples traveled through Samaria. He stressed the important detail that Jesus had stopped in the middle of the day and asked a Samaritan woman to get him some water. Every good Jew knew that if a woman went to draw water when the sun was at mid day, it meant that the woman was a harlot. "Everyone in the town of Sychar heard about it," Uriah continued. Very purposely, like any good religious person would do, Uriah left out the part about how the harlot had turned from her sinful ways, and left a half-truth in the mind of the other men. It had not been long since Jesus went through Samaria, but rumors traveled faster than the winds across the sea in Galilee.

"It's like he is on a campaign or something!" one of the fireside critics said. Everyone there laughed heartily.

"Maybe he wants to be king?" Salem suggested. Immediately the cheers ceased at the seriousness of Salem's comment. They pretended as though the comment had not been made, but the damage had already been done. Salem realized his mistake, and in a vain attempt to discard the remark got up to stir the coals on the fire. As Salem stirred the embers with a small branch, a fragment of the red hot coals leapt from the fire and landed on his hand. All of the men saw it, and were astonished to see that Salem did not react to the ember that continued to burn his flesh.

"Salem! There is a hot coal on your hand!" Uriah shouted.

Salem quickly brushed the coal from his hand, and tried to dismiss the incident. When Salem returned to his seat, he pretended not to notice that his friend's had moved away from him. The smell of his burnt flesh made him ill, but he knew that it was not the smell that caused his friends to move away. Just a short time later, one by one, the men made excuses to leave. Soon Salem was alone in the darkness on a starless night, except for the faint glow of the fire that was about out.

Elizabeth knew the location of her husband and his friends' campfire and decided to see what had detained him. When she approached what was left of the fire, she could see Salem rubbing his hand. He tried to hide it when she called out to him.

"What are you doing here?" he asked.

"I was worried about you," she answered. "It is time to come home," she stated.

"I will be home shortly, go on without me!" he commanded, and she obeyed.

†

Elizabeth grew nervous when she woke up alone. The sun was up and her husband was nowhere to be seen. "He must be at the shop!" she said to herself quietly, but agonized whether to go see him or not.

Salem did not go home that night. He went to the shop instead, and was busy in his work when Jeru arrived early that morning. Jeru commented on how early Salem was, and how proud he was of his son, and how well they worked together. Jeru noticed the bandage on Salem's hand, but decided not to ask him anything about it. Jeru knew that his only son would tell him when he was ready. Jeru was keenly aware that every time he would come close to Salem, Salem would move away. That too would be discussed when his son was ready to talk. Jeru began to talk about matters of weather, family, and their future jobs.

When Elizabeth entered the shop, she noticed that both men had stopped from their talk. She could tell that she had arrived at an inconvenient moment and it made her uncomfortable that they were uncomfortable. After a few moments, she excused herself. When she got to the door, she turned to the Jeru and said "Father, I wish to speak to you later if it would be no trouble." She turned to her husband. "That is if it is okay with you, my husband?" Salem nodded.

Jeru replied, "Later in the day!" and then waved his right hand to let her know to leave the shop.

Later that day, when Salem had left the shop to make a delivery, Elizabeth seized the opportunity to talk with Jeru. Elizabeth meekly asked, "Father? May I speak to you?"

Jeru paused from his labor and beckoned her over to where he stood. He could tell that she was very worried. He tried to calm her with details of how wonderful a provider her husband was, but it was a vain attempt to pull her from her sadness. He could not stand to feel her pain any longer and forced himself to ask, "Why have you sought an audience with me, my daughter?"

She began to weep bitterly and moaned the name of his son. Jeru promised to speak to him, if he had been unkind to her. She assured him that his son was very kind to her, but it was his health that concerned her. She told him of the incident at the campfire, as told to her by one of the witnesses. She continued to share her concerns with Jeru for well over an hour. She reminded Jeru of how it was with them, until just recently. Her face glowed when she spoke of their love for each other. The greatest concern of all, was that Salem had denied her. Salem had begun to shun her. He would not touch her, and he would not let her touch him. "I have been faithful in all things. Do you know of anything that I have done to dishonor him?"

"No, he has spoken of no such matters to me." Jeru's heart became heavy, but he pretended, for the sake of his family, that the incident was of little or no concern for worry. "Salem has earned a good name for himself!" he said as he tried to reassure her, but Jeru was very worried. Truly Jeru was worried about his son, his life, his future. There were always things to worry about, Jeru thought.

†

The Sabbath day came this week as it always had during his life, yet today was very different. Something made Mashic very tense. He prayed that the hearts of the people might be right. Mashic smiled when he saw Jeru enter at the last moment. They exchanged friendly acknowledgments and each sat in their own designated place.

The minister delivered the book of the prophet Esaias to Jesus. Jesus stood up to read, and when he opened the book, he found the place where it was written: "The Spirit of the Lord is upon me, because he hath anointed me to preach the Gospel to the poor; he hath sent me to heal the brokenhearted, to preach deliverance to the captives, and recovering of sight to the blind, to set at liberty them that are bruised, to preach the acceptable year of the Lord." Jesus closed the book and gave it again to the minister, and sat down. And the eyes of everyone that were in the synagogue were fastened on Jesus. And Jesus said unto them, "This day is this scripture fulfilled in your ears."

And all bare him witness, and wondered at the gracious words which proceeded out of his mouth. And they said, "Is this not Joseph's son?" It was very hard for these men to accept the son of a carpenter to be anything but a carpenter. The man they looked at was not of any noble blood. To look at him caused no emotions of the heart. He was just the son of one of their own, nothing more.

And Jesus said unto them, "You will surely say unto me this proverb, 'Physician, heal thyself: whatsoever we have heard done in Capernaum, do also in thy country.' Verily I say unto you, No prophet is accepted in his own country. But I tell you of a truth, many widows were in Israel in the days of Elias; when the heaven was shut three years and six months, when great famine was throughout all the land; but unto none of them was Elias sent, save unto Sarepta, a city of Sidon unto a woman that was a widow. And many lepers were in Israel in the time of Eliseus the prophet; and none of them was cleansed, saving Naaman the Syrian."

All that were in the synagogue, when they heard these things, were filled with wrath. Quickly, talk swarmed the room to throw this man out of the city. Jeru looked around the room for Mashic, but Mashic had left the building. The mob had grown angrier and to just remove this blasphemer from the city was not enough.

"Let us throw him headlong off the brow of the hill that this city was built," someone shouted.

The unruly mob grasped Jesus and removed him from the building, and then the city. As they were on their way to kill this man, Jesus passed through them and went his own way. Jesus had just walked away from the group of men that wanted to kill him. With the opportunity lost, to do their duty, each man returned to their own home, save one. Mashic rejoiced silently for the victory that he witnessed from a distance.

On the first day of the week, Jeru returned to his shop and attempted to work, but was hindered by the thoughts of the things he had witnessed the day before. Salem had not arrived yet, and Jeru took this opportunity to agonize in secret. "Where had Mashic gone?" he thought to himself. As Mashic entered the shop, Jeru asked Mashic, "Where were you yesterday, after that blasphemer finished his speech of heresy?"

"I thought it best that I should leave!" Mashic responded.

"This blasphemer should have been put to death!" Jeru said.

"Then why did you not put him to death, as the law requires?" Mashic asked.

"He walked away from us!" Jeru had to admit.

"You want me to believe that one man just walked away unhindered, while he was carried away by forty or more men?" Mashic asked derogatorily.

"He must have used witchcraft on us!" Jeru said defiantly.

"Maybe sometimes to obey the law is not always right?" Mashic said.

"What kind of heresy is this?" Jeru snarled back at Mashic.

"If we obey the law only when it is convenient to our personal beliefs, at that moment, maybe it is sin rather than righteousness!" Mashic proclaimed.

"Your comments are as foreign words to my ears! They mean nothing to me. Cease your heresy or you will force me to seek persecution against you, by the law of Moses!" Jeru threatened his lifelong friend. There was a moment of silence that seemed to span an eternity, but it was only very brief.

"What I have tried to tell you, my friend, is that we, as mere people, cannot usurp our wills over the Lord God almighty," Mashic commented. "If it was God's will for you to throw Jesus off the cliff, then so be it," he added, "But if not, then there is a greater power that operates here"

"Are you a follower of Jesus?" Jeru finally asked.

"Yes!" Mashic proclaimed.

Very angrily Jeru turned toward the man in his shop and said, "Then you are no friend of mine! You should have no place of authority in the town council!"

"I am aware of that, and I am prepared. All of my possessions are packed and ready for my soon departure from this now cursed town. Like your fathers before you, you have rejected a prophet, a man sent from God, or even greater than a prophet, the Messiah!" Mashic stated. "When the crowd got angry in the synagogue yesterday, I knew that I must prepare to leave this town, for it is written: No prophet is accepted in his own country! One of the prophecies that pertain to the coming of the Messiah is that he would be rejected by his own. The town of Nazareth has set forth the standard to reject the chosen one of God, and for that reason I must leave this town. It is I who has chosen what is right, but you foolishly accept what is wrong!" Mashic stated.

"The words that spew from your mouth are as vile and vomit. I do not want to hear anymore of your refuse!" Jeru thundered loudly.

"All these years I hoped you would see what I have seen. All the signs are before you, yet you choose to remain sightless. Jesus is the Messiah." Mashic could see Jeru's body tense as he held even tighter to the cutting tool. Mashic knew this was his last opportunity to express what he understood from his lifelong search for the King of Israel. "It all started, as you well remember, with the Kings of the East that passed by Nazareth. When one of them pointed to the star that shown brightly in the heavens, I knew the Messiah was born. Jesus was the one the star shone for. Then John returned with the story of the shepherds who watched their flocks by night. Jesus was that baby in the manger. Then John told the dreadful news of the massacre in Bethlehem. Jesus was born in Bethlehem, and his family lived in Bethlehem up to the moment of the massacre, yet he escaped. Then there was Joseph, Mary, and Jesus, who all returned from Egypt just after Herod died. Jesus taught the teachers in the Temple when he was only twelve years old, and those men were truly amazed at his wisdom. Everything about Jesus points to him to be the Messiah!" Mashic said, as he ended his statement.

"Jesus can not be a king. What army will he rise up? Those men that follow after him can not even lead themselves. He's got fishermen and tax collectors as his disciples. How degenerate must a king be before he can become a ruler of the people? If you must be a worthless man to be king, then let Jesus reign," Jeru said venomously.

"All the years that I have known you, you have always wanted a king to come and cast these barbaric Romans out of our land. Maybe the Messiah has come to save us from our sins, rather than from the Romans!" Mashic said then exited the building and walked away from the shop. He did not turn back to get a last look. Sara waited for him at the door of their home. She had cried up to the moment she saw him turn the corner just four doors from their home. Mashic related the story to his wife what had happened at the carpenter's shop. She wept even stronger now. Mashic could not comfort her as he should have, because his own tears flowed as though his best friend had just died.

Jeru knew this day was inevitable. He knew that Mashic believed in that fool Jesus, and it was only a matter of time before Mashic would expose his inner weaknesses. Jeru never wept for anyone. Nor could he weep now, but it did hinder his ability to indulge in his work. He decided to return home. Martha would be glad to see that he finally planned to slow down. Jeru dreaded to tell Martha of the incident at the shop with Mashic, but she probably already knew anyway. He stopped just as he closed the door to the shop. "Should I wait until Salem returns?" he asked himself. "No, business has been slow lately!" Jeru reminded himself.

As he walked home, a thought struck him as hard as if he had been hit by lightning. Jeru cycled the thoughts in his memory about how Elizabeth had come to him, and was very concerned about Salem's health. And how he had been burned, and could not feel the pain! The business had been slow since the night Salem was at the campfire. Did everyone in the town know something about his son that he did not even know about? These thoughts infuriated him. Jeru had determined that that day he would get the truth from Salem about the secret he had kept from his family.

When Jeru entered the room, Martha knew immediately that something was terribly wrong. The last time Jeru had come home early was so long ago that the memory of that event was covered with layers of dust. She waited for the most opportune moment to question him. The rough tone in Jeru's voice was because of his present unnerved condition. Martha wept bitterly as Jeru unveiled the details of Mashic's betrayal to the faith of their fathers. There were not enough bottles to capture all the tears in. Martha's loving wife side of her personality was in full charge as Jeru spoke of Mashic. She quickly changed to her godly endowed mother instincts when Jeru began to speak about their son.

The old, but still very muscular carpenter showed deep signs that he was about to lose all of the strength that he still had. She acknowledged that she had noticed the bandage on her son's hand. It had been painful for him to reveal the sordid details of Mashic's conversion, but it felt like suicide to tell his beloved of his dreadful suspicions about their son. Jeru embraced her before he said the one word that could break the tender heart of the mother of their only son. The heads of the neighbors and many of the passersby turned when Martha's screams echoed off the sides of the houses and down the street. The cries were so dreadful and painful that many of the people who had heard it began to pray silently.

"Someone must have died!" a man said.

The woman who walked with him replied "No! A mother has lost a son."

CHAPTER VI

The sharp edge of the carpenter's cutting tool glided effortlessly through the cedar log that Salem and Jeru had recently imported from Lebanon. Salem's thoughts wandered from his present task to things that he knew he could not change and he almost made a critical error in the cut in the precious timber. Salem rested a few minutes and began to work again. The mark was clearly visible on the wood and to proceed past it would cost them a month's pay. His concentration was at its peak, yet the tool slipped and marred the precious cedar, and the expensive cutting tool landed on the floor.

Salem cursed himself because he had made such a crucial error. More wood would have to be purchased, and he would have to spend a good part of the remainder of the day once again sharpening the tool. Salem bent over to retrieve the cutting instrument from the floor. While his body was still bowed down, a pair of feet came into view. Salem knew that his father had entered the shop, and that he would inspect his work.

When Salem stood up, he could see Jeru as he looked at the gash in the wood. It amazed Salem that Jeru said nothing about the useless log on the work bench. His father had ceased to correct him since the day that he and Elizabeth were wed, but for him to completely ignore this monumental error was unlike him.

The mouth of Jeru opened as to say something, but the silence that came from it shocked Salem. Jeru closed his mouth, but when he tried to speak again, there was a commotion at the door that made both men cast their attention in that direction. Martha and Elizabeth both entered the shop. It was not that they walked heavily as to bring attention to themselves when they entered a room, but it was the presence of doom in their cries that no one could ignore.

Immediately, Jeru turned back to Salem. Salem's face showed alarm, but then reflected that of a person who had been caught in the midst of crime. "I know why you are here, and why the worried look on your faces!" Salem stated. Salem removed the bandage on his hand. The three spectators dared not to breathe as the mystery unfolded. When the last wrap of the bandage came from around his hand, it began to gently drift toward the floor in a poetic type of dance. Every eye followed its journey downward, as it spiraled, twisted, and then coiled up in a diseased heap on the floor.

Salem rolled back the sleeve of his garment to expose his arm. "I thought it was from too much sun. Then I thought it was from too much work. The tools were harder and harder to hold. My strength diminished more each day. Forgive me, my dear Elizabeth. I know that you must have condemned yourself for me when I did not come to you, and rejected your attempts of affection. I was not sure of my condition, and did not want to infect anyone else," Salem said.

"You know what the law requirements are," Jeru started to say. He did not finish his rebuke because he saw the eyes of Martha that spoke very loudly and clearly, the "Be sympathetic, you can quote the law later," look.

"What will you do?" Martha asked through her tears.

"A good friend of mine once told me of a place where I can go and remain there the rest of my days," Salem stated in a monotone voice. He did not divulge his intentions, because he did not want anyone to follow him to his destination. "I will leave as soon as I can gather up my essentials," Salem said with a crackled voice.

"Go show yourself to the priest first. There might be a chance we are wrong!" Martha pleaded.

"I will go show myself before the priest for your benefit, but I know that I am accursed with this affliction," Salem responded sorrowfully.

Elizabeth stepped toward her husband. Martha grabbed Elizabeth and prevented her to touch Salem. Martha knew that Elizabeth's intention to touch her husband was honorable and instinctive, but foolish all the same. To touch someone who had this unclean disease would condemn her as well. It was a simple act, but once it was done, it could not be undone. "One death in the family was too much," Martha whispered in Elizabeth's ear. "Do not condemn yourself and your child!"

Salem's bowels ached from the torture that he had placed his family in. He motioned with his whitened hand for his family to step aside so he could pass. He did not want to infect any of the people that he loved with his touch. Faintness grasped tightly to the wife of the diseased man after he had exited the shop and was no longer in sight. She fell into the weak arms of her mother-in-law, but was quickly supported by Jeru.

"It must be too much for her to bear," Jeru said.

"It is not her heart!" Martha stated. "It is her womb. She is with child." She knew what question was in her husband's mind, but answered it before he asked it. "She conceived this child the last time she knew him. Almost a month ago," she stated.

"Does Salem know?" Jeru asked.

"No. It was her wish that he did not know. She was so concerned about Salem's health that she was leery of burdening him with it."

"If that is her wish, then I will honor it!" he said as he lifted her up and carried her home. Many of their fellow citizens stared at them as Jeru carried the young woman down the street. Martha quickly went to the earthen vessel to dampen a cloth to administer to Elizabeth's face. "Salem. Salem, my dear Salem," Elizabeth moaned. Her body went limp again, and then she went into a deep sleep.

The news of the soon birth of his first and now only grandchild was diminished terribly by the declared death of the child's father. Jeru knew that Salem was not actually dead yet. Was it a law, or was it custom, that when a person was infected with this disease, that person would be considered dead? That person, now dead, would not have any inheritance rights, no social rights, nothing. The only thing Jeru knew was that his son was dead.

Quietly Martha approached Jeru and asked, "Should we let Mashic know?"

"No! He is dead as well," Jeru said with venom in his mouth.

Martha turned away and ran from the house. She did not like the words of her husband. "My son is not dead! My son is not dead!" she repeated to herself over and over as she ran down the streets.

The words of Jeru echoed like thunder in her ears as she ran "No! He is dead as well!" When Jeru said He is dead, he spoke of Mashic, but the words "as well" meant her son.

"My son is not dead! My son is not dead!" she said with even more intensity. "Why must I run? Where can I run to?" she asked herself. When she saw the house that belonged to Mashic and Sara, she instinctively went to the door and knocked. "What did I do that for? They are gone from my life as well." Martha jumped back when the door opened.

"Martha? What are you doing here?" Sara asked.

Martha did not answer.

"Would you like to come inside?" Sara asked and moved to the side to allow passage for the unexpected, but welcomed guest.

They were glad to see each other, but the joy soon drowned by the sorrowful news of what had happened. It took Martha over an hour to tell Sara all the details. Martha would cry for awhile, and then she would continue just before she would start to cry anew.

After Martha had completed her story, she said, as she placed her hand on the top of her lifelong friend's hand, "I am so glad you were here for me! My greatest fear was that you and Mashic had already left town."

Now it was Sara's turn to cry. This was the first time in her life that she had ever told anyone about her Mashic. She began with the story of the caravan that came from the East so many years ago and ended with the recent event at the synagogue this past Sabbath.

Martha knew that the version she had just heard was very different than that told to her by her husband. This version put thoughts into her head she knew that she could never discuss this with Jeru. When the tears subsided, Martha asked, "I thought you had left with Mashic. Why did you stay behind?"

"I had convinced him that it would be best that I stay behind for a couple of days and then I would meet with him in Capernaum after the next Sabbath," she stated.

"Capernaum?" Martha questioned.

"Mashic heard that Jesus was to teach in the synagogue there!" Sara related.

Martha panicked when she noticed that the sun was about to set. "What will I tell Jeru?" she asked, and did not expect an answer.

Immediately after Martha left, Sara began to prepare for the journey to Capernaum. She could not wait; she had to tell Mashic what had happened.

†

Jeff Frazier

Like a thief in the night, Salem crept into the house, and tried to avoid a collision with any objects that would make the occupants of the house aware of his presence. Slowly, he lifted his foot high into the air and brought it down to the floor. He knew it would be better to step on something than to kick it. This maneuver proved to be ineffective by this untrained, would-be intruder. Salem was accomplished at many things, one was that he was a master carpenter, but to walk silently through the dark of night was not his forte. The right side of his foot caught the left side of the cooker's stool which, tumbled over and caused a thunderous sound when it hit the wooden floor.

The whole family awoke in a highly frightened state. The man of the house quickly grabbed what appeared to be a weapon used for defense. In the middle of the confusion of screams, challenges, and threats, the wick of the lamp was adjusted by one of the women of the house, and the room quickly became illuminated. In the place where the stool had been was a figure coiled up on the floor like a rejected pile of rags.

"Who are you and what do you want from us?" Jeru shouted angrily.

"I did not mean to frighten you!" the voice from the heap spoke.

"Salem?" Elizabeth asked then repeated his name with a shout. "Salem! I thought you had left for good," she continued.

"I have returned to get some belongings to help me make it through the rest of my days with this sentence of death," Salem said and did not show his face. Martha returned quickly with a bed roll and some fresh bread. Jeru retrieved some coins from the secret place and gave a large portion to this person who was no longer his son.

Jeru and Martha backed away as Salem started to move toward the door, but Elizabeth had to be restrained by Martha. They watched as the diseased man walked away, covered by his rags of despair.

Under the cover of darkness, Salem, who belonged to no family, no town or country, covered up even more of his body as he walked down the dusty street of his former home town. He carried his life with him, and his death carried him.

The roads between the cities of Israel were usually vacant in the night hours, and that was what Salem wanted. It was what he needed. Salem seized this opportunity to travel as fast as he could. Normally he would like to meet strangers on the road, but now he had to avoid them. It was the law.

As the sun began to rise, Salem ventured deep into the forest to seek shelter and concealment. He had not rested all night, and he needed to find a dark place to sleep. The sun had already begun to warm up the air when he finally located the most strategic place, or at least that was what he thought. Sleep was desperately sought after, yet it evaded him. The saddened and sickened face of his dear Elizabeth that he saw in the light of the lamp could not be shaken from his mind.

The sound of voices, boys' voices, aroused him. Even though he could not see them, he knew that they played some type of game. Salem cowered in the brush and prayed, "Please do not let them find me!" over and over again.

"Look!" shouted the oldest boy. The rest of the boys crowded around the boy that Salem had perceived to be the leader of the band of boys. "Look! Here in the bushes!" the oldest boy shouted again.

He growled like a bear, and leapt from his secluded place. "Unclean! Unclean! Unclean," Salem yelled. The boys scattered like a flock of doves disturbed by an attacking animal. Each boy screamed as though his life were about to be terminated.

Through tears of the most grievous sobs that he had ever wept in his life, Salem shouted again, "Unclean! Unclean! Unclean! I am a leper!" That was the first time he had ever uttered that word, the word that best described his condition. He whispered to himself between the tears, "I am a leper. I am a leper. I am a leper!" His tears quickly turned to fear when he heard the sound of the young boys return. He looked in their direction and was horrified to see what they carried in their hands. Salem quickly lifted up part of his garment to use as a shield against the onslaught of stones that he knew was on its way. The first thud hit the outstretched robe and bounced off harmlessly, but the second one collided solidly and caused Salem to lose his balance.

He looked up at the group of vigilantes through his robe. He could see that the youngest boy appeared reluctant to throw his stone. After the boy was prompted by his elders, he finally cast the instrument of destruction toward the person who deserved death. After all, anyone who was a leper was judged by God, and was worthy of death. The stone missed Salem completely and the other boys scolded the youngest boy for his poor aim. Salem made his escape from any further judgment while the youngest child received his chastisement. The vision of himself at the age of ten throwing a stone at a leper flashed vividly through his mind. This remembrance caused him to weep all the more. After he had successfully evaded the group of boys, Salem found solitude in a cave and went to sleep.

CHAPTER VII

The crowd was quite large outside the house of the man named Simon, and Sara wondered if she could find her husband in amongst the throngs of people. She had only arrived in Capernaum that morning, and had already heard of all the wonderful things that had happened in this town.

"The mother of Simon's wife had a fever," one woman told her. "The fever left her after the teacher rebuked it," she continued. "Rapidly, the word spread throughout the town and people with all forms of sickness began to converge on the house that belonged to Simon," the woman said to her.

"Many devils were cast out. Many people were healed of their diseases," another person had told her as she stood outside the house of Simon.

The crowd was so large no one could move. Everyone moved from one foot to the other foot as they tried to look inside, and all hoped to get inside. She could not see who was in the house, but she knew who it was. The man in the house was the Messiah. Suddenly the crowd began to part and pushed her up against a wall.

The noise of the crowd hindered Sara from hearing what was said by the people that departed the house. She got the impression that the person for whom this crowd gathered was prepared to leave but the masses of people wanted the man to stay. They all fell silent when Jesus said, "I must preach the kingdom of God to other cities also: for therefore am I sent." The people mourned silently even as they marveled as the man of God walked away from their town, and his disciples and many others followed.

Just a glimpse was all Sara got of her husband, and she shouted his name loud enough for him to hear her call over the crowd. He scanned the area quickly as though he was not sure if someone called his name or he had just heard things. His countenance brightened when he saw the beautiful face of his wife. They had to let the crowd dissipate some more before they could reach each other.

Their separation had been short, but the reunion was joyful. Mashic expressed to his wife all the things that he had heard, learned, and witnessed of Jesus. Sara did not want to quench Mashic's enthusiasm, but the sorrow in her heart was very evident. When Mashic noticed the pain on her face, he said, "There must be something very wrong! Your eyes have expressed the sorrow of your soul!"

It took her several moments of silence before she could respond. "Your observations are correct, my love. Tragedy has struck the house of your friend Jeru."

"Has someone died?" he asked.

"This tragedy is worse than death. Salem has been stricken with leprosy," she said through the tears that flowed down her face.

"This is not possible!" Mashic shouted.

"It is true, my love," she said as she moved close to her husband.

"Why has the Lord brought this deadly judgment upon an innocent man? It is I that should have received this condemnation."

Sara did not understand her husband's statement, and dared not ask what he meant. "And the news is even yet more tragic. Elizabeth is with child," she continued.

"Has Salem knowledge of this?" Mashic asked.

"No! And I am sure Elizabeth wants it to remain that way!" Sara said. "She knew that it would be more painful for him to know that he had a child that he could never see, hold, or love," Sara stated further. Mashic turned away from Sara so she could not see the pain in his soul. "What are you going to do?" she asked.

"I wish I had an answer for you, but I do not know what I can do."

"Maybe you can bring him to see Jesus?"

"Jesus of Nazareth has done many wonderful things, but I have not seen him cleanse a leper yet. Maybe there are limits, even for this man of God!" he stated as though it were a question. He looked into the eyes of his wife and asked, "Do you want to return home or journey on with me?"

"My desire is to be with you always, but I know that you seek something that I cannot find for you, so I will return home."

He nodded his head to show that he understood, and gave her a passionate kiss and yelled, "Wait!" just after she started to leave. He ran over to her and after he took her hand said, "I have friends here in Capernaum that I am staying with. I am sure that they will allow you to stay for several days, or even weeks, if the need arises," and then he led her away.

The following day Mashic knew he must continue with his quest. "I will be back in a couple of days," he told Sara and walked in the direction the crowd had departed the day before.

To follow the trail of the crowd was easy to do, even though it was almost a day old. To find Jesus had always been easy; Mashic would just look for the crowds. This time was no different. Mashic walked in the midst of the people that sat on the hillside. Many stared at him with great annoyance, because he had walked in front of them.

Jesus taught them from the shore at the lake of Gennesaret, and many were pressed in on him to teach them more of the Word of God. Mashic saw Jesus enter into one of the two boats in the lake. The boat was cast out a short distance from the bank, and Jesus taught the people from the boat.

After the lessons had ended, Jesus instructed Simon, the owner of the boat, to cast his nets out into the water. Mashic could not hear what the other man said, but the man appeared to have replied that he had fished all night, and had caught nothing. They consented to what Jesus had said and did as they were instructed. The draught of fish was so heavy it required the help of the other boat and fishermen to help retrieve the nets. The numbers of fish were so great that the nets began to break. Both boats were filled to capacity, and began to sink.

The crowd and Mashic had all moved to the shore when the latest spectacle started. Simon bowed at Jesus' knees and said, "Depart from me; for I am a sinful man, O Lord."

And Jesus said unto Simon, "Fear not, from hence forth, I shall make you fishers of men." Mashic did not know who the other men with Simon and Jesus were, but they all forsook their boats and followed after Jesus.

As Jesus came to a certain city, a man with leprosy fell on his face before Jesus. It was not hard for anyone to notice the present state of this diseased man. The signs of his affliction were as evident as a city built on a hill. There were large, scale-like areas on his body. The scale areas were ash white in color. The fingers on his hands that were not twisted were gone. The appearance of the way this man tried to cover every part of his body alerted everyone that this man was a leper.

Compassion filled Mashic's heart, for he thought of Salem and the torture that he must have been living with.

The leper besought Jesus and said, "Lord, if you will, you can make me clean."

As Jesus' hand moved toward the leper, Mashic's breath halted, his heart beat faster, and his eyes grew bigger. Do not touch him! He is a leper! Mashic wanted to shout. Mashic's mind wanted to shout but the authority that he saw on Jesus' face stopped his intentions.

Jesus put forth his hand and touched him and said, "I will: be thou clean." And immediately the leprosy departed from the man. Mashic did not hear what Jesus told the man, for he was already on his way back to Capernaum to tell Sara and his other friends what he had seen.

All the occupants of the house where Mashic and Sara stayed at in Capernaum jumped when Mashic burst through the door as he shouted, "I must go find Salem! I must go find Salem!"

"What has happened, my love?" Sara questioned him.

He started his oration with the boats and the great draught of fish. He could tell by the expression on her face that she did not understand what the fish had to do with Salem. "Please be patient," he reassured her. Their host and the rest of the family had gathered around to hear the wonders that Mashic spoke of. Several of the children cowered behind their mother when Mashic mentioned the word leprosy. Disapproval was cast on the faces of all the adults when they heard that Jesus actually touched the leper. Everyone was relieved and very excited when Mashic reassured them that the man went away completely clean.

Mashic and Sara went outside to discuss Mashic's desire to help Salem. "Do you know where he is? He did not tell anyone where he went!" Sara stated.

"I am not sure exactly where he has gone. He could have gone anywhere, but I have a strong suspicion that he has gone to Samaria."

"How can you be sure that he went there?"

"I cannot be sure. I remember one day many years ago I told a ten-year-old boy about leper camp in Samaria. Remember when Salem was a young boy and he had gone into the forest, against his father's wishes, and encountered a leper?"

"I remember that story now!"

"I had told Salem that some lepers went to a leper camp in Samaria! And that is where I hope to find him."

"What will you tell him?"

"That there is hope," he said to his wife with a very deep conviction and faith. He looked directly into her dark brown eyes and replied triumphantly, "With Jesus there is real hope!"

The following morning Mashic departed for Samaria and Sara returned to Nazareth.

CHAPTER VIII

The stench of the place alerted Salem that he was close to his objective. It had taken him a lot longer to get to his destination than he thought it would. He was not really that jubilant that he had arrived, either. He had only heard of the general location of this valley. He would have missed it entirely had he not purposely targeted it. Salem surely knew that he could not have stopped and asked for directions. He watched from the distance and he knew he was at the right location. Several people had approached the edge, but dared not venture in, cast something into the pit, and then departed very hastily. Another person, probably a leper, entered but did not leave.

Salem quietly moved to the rim of the death-ridden valley and peered over the edge. People moved about, some crawled, some hobbled. It almost looked like a regular community, except for the lifelessness of their steps. It occurred to him that this must be what a prison was like. Here bodies moved, but not alive. They were dead, but not buried. Salem thought that he had shed his last tear after he was attacked by the boys, but he shed one more when he set his foot in the valley of the lepers.

Many people moved away from his approach, but recovered to their original position when they realized that he was one of them. All of the faces looked the same to him, no matter who was behind the mask. The eyes of these outcasts were usually the only thing anyone saw. They all permeated fear, loss of hope, and death.

Salem knew that leprosy ate away the body of the unfortunate host, and as he walked he saw children without hands or feet. Visions of women that had lost their motherhood frightened him. Adult men crawled like infants across the filth-laced soil of this condemned place. Just when he thought he had seen the worst thing that any man could ever see, he looked into the face of a small child that had lost both of his eyes. Flies collected on the sockets of the boy's face. Salem had not eaten for two days, but his stomach unsuccessfully tried to empty its contents.

"Food? Got food? Give?" the diseased boy whimpered with a voice that wavered heavily in almost unrecognizable words.

Compassion took over his being, where disgust had just been. Salem thrust his hand deep into his pouch and found a small piece of bread. He clasped the morsel of life tightly in the palm of his hand, and retrieved it from the bag. Without any reservation he knelt down and placed the crumb in the boy's hand. "Here. Eat this," Salem said compassionately.

"Praise the Lord, Our God," the child said. He tried to raise the morsel to his parched lips, but was too weak to accomplish this simple, but life-sustaining task. The weak muscles of his arm failed him and dropped lifelessly to his side, and the bread fell from his contorted and disfigured fingers.

Salem retrieved it from the dust, blew off as much dirt as he could, and tried to assist the boy and placed it in the child's mouth. The child was so weak that he could not even chew the bread. It fell out of his mouth and on the ground again and broke into several pieces. Salem gathered the bread, and pondered about if he should eat or not, but he could not bring himself to eat after a leper. He cast the bread into the bushes to be eaten up by the insects.

Immediately the ravenous people sprang from their perches and converged on the discarded food. The stampede startled Salem, and he distanced himself from the onslaught. Within an instant the commotion had ended. Through the dust Salem could see that the boy did not move. He knew the boy was dead, and the Law of Moses prevented him to touch any dead thing, especially a deceased leper. A woman pushed Salem aside and then picked up the body of the child and mourned silently as she walked away.

"Even though I am no longer a man, I will never become an animal!" Salem shouted. He knew that the hours of darkness would be upon him soon, and he must find a place to rest. He wandered around the encampment and tried not to stare at the atrocities that his eyes had seen and his mind had sealed in his memory. He finally located a place that looked somewhat comfortable, and would be secure from the elements of the night. The bedroll had been spread out on the ground in what Salem thought would have been a comfortable place, but as soon as he lay down he realized that he had made an error.

Salem squirmed in the bedroll in a vain attempt to get comfortable. Three sets of eyes watched him, the new man, as he wiggled in his bedroll. It was not hard to spot the new man. The clothes he wore, the bed roll he carried might be old and worn to the owner, but to these men it was considered kingly attire. When the opportunity presented itself, the vultures leapt upon the unsuspecting victim. Salem was fortunate that he still had a majority of his physical strength to oppose this attack, but surprise and numbers were on the side of the attackers. One adversary grasped the bedroll and was about to relieve Salem of his ownership.

"Help me! Someone help me!" Salem shouted, but he was doubtful that anyone would heed his cries of distress.

The shout from the bushes startled the entire group, including Salem. So horrible was this scream, that the attackers fled with only part of the spoils that they had intended to take. Salem was still shaken, and unsure of what had happened, when a man stepped out of the bushes.

"I am Bedar, from Samaria. The town of Sychar, to be more exact," the man said as he offered what remained of his right hand in a gesture of friendship.

Salem accepted the man's offer and was helped to his feet. "Thank you for your assistance."

"I saw what you tried to do for that young boy earlier, and it moved me. Your exclamation of rejection of this place of which you are now a resident may not have been received by some, but I have heard those words before. May I ask who you are?" Bedar asked.

"I was a carpenter from Nazareth," Salem said almost silently.

Bedar's face showed that he had just become very confused. "Please remove the cloth from your face!" the man requested.

The request was granted, and Bedar grasped Salem's chin, turned his face toward the light and then offered a sigh of relief. "Praise the Lord God of Israel," Bedar said.

It was Salem's turn to show his confusion, and Bedar laughed heartily when he realized that Salem did not even have the slightest idea what he had done.

"I apologize for my rudeness, my new neighbor. I was afraid that you might have been Jesus, the carpenter from Nazareth."

"Why were you afraid of him?" Salem asked.

"I am not afraid of Jesus. I was afraid that you might have been him. Jesus is not like any other man. To see Jesus of Nazareth as a leper would be the greatest disaster for me."

"Why should he be honored by you or anyone else?" Salem asked.

Bedar motioned for him to sit, "As you should be aware of, Nazareth is not far from the border of Samaria. We know that our people here in Samaria are not considered worthy in the eyes of most Hebrews."

Salem did not acknowledge this leper's statement, but he had to look away. Salem could not look into the eyes of the man who had spoken the truth against his people.

"Soon after Jesus came through my home town, Sychar, he went to Nazareth. Did he not?" the Samaritan asked. Salem only nodded his head. "We Samaritans know of the hatred that many of Jews have for the man called Jesus, from Nazareth." Bedar was a very wise man. He knew that when he talked with a Hebrew, he had to state facts, so they would know that he knew what he was talking about. "The reports we heard were that the people from the town of Nazareth tried to kill him, but were not successful in their attempt," Bedar continued. Again, Salem only nodded, "Let me tell you what Jesus did for our people."

Bedar explained the events of that day, the day Jesus came to Sychar, the best that he could. "Now let's see. This is the version that the woman told the people of my town." He made himself comfortable because he knew that he would talk for a long time. Salem made himself comfortable also as Bedar started his story:

"She said that she had gone out to Jacob's well to draw water and it was about the sixth hour. Jesus was at the well when she arrived. Jesus said to her, 'Give me a drink.'

"Then the woman said to him, 'How is it that you, being a Jew, ask for a drink from me, a woman of Samaria?' For the Jews do not deal with the Samaritans.

"'If you knew the gift of God, and who it is that said to you, Give me a drink; you would have asked of him, and he would have given you living water.'

"The woman then said to him, 'Sir, you have nothing to draw water with, and the well is deep: where do you get this living water? Are you greater than our father Jacob, who gave us the well, and drank from it himself, and his children, and his cattle?'

"Jesus answered, 'Whoever drinks of this water shall thirst again: but whoever drinks of the water that I shall give him shall never thirst again; but the water that I shall give him shall be in him a well of water springing up into everlasting life.'

"The woman said to him, 'Sir, give me this water, so that I will not thirst neither would I have to come here to draw water.'

"Jesus said to her, 'Go, call your husband and come back here.'

"The woman said to him, 'I have no husband.'

"Then Jesus said to her, 'What you have said is true. You do not have a husband. For you have had five husbands, and the man you live with now is not your husband.'

"The woman said to Jesus, 'Sir, I perceive that you are a prophet. Our fathers worshipped in this mountain; and you say that men ought to worship in Jerusalem.'

"Jesus said to her, 'Woman, believe me, the hour will come when you shall neither in this mountain, nor at Jerusalem, worship the Father. You worship what you do not know; we worship what we do know, for salvation is from the Jews. But the hour will come, and is now; true worshippers shall worship the Father in spirit and in truth: for they are the kind of worshippers the Father seeks. God is a spirit, and they that worship him must worship him in spirit and in truth.'

"The woman said to him, 'I know that the Messiah, which is called Christ, shall come. When he comes, he will explain everything to us.'

"Jesus said to her, 'I, who speak to you, am he.'

"She returned to the city at the time his disciples got back after they had bought food in the town. She said to the men of the town, and I was one of them, 'Come; see a man, who has told me of all the things that I ever did. Is not this the Christ?' And we went out of the city to see Jesus.

"He taught us many things about God. And many of the Samaritans of that city believed on him for what that woman had testified to us, 'He told me of all the things that I ever did.'

"Many more people believed because of Jesus' own words and said to the woman, 'Now we believe not because of what you said, for we have heard him ourselves and know that this is indeed the Christ, the savior of the world.' I am numbered among the many of that city. Jesus departed two days later."

Bedar saw the bewildered look on Salem's face and acted as though he had just been insulted. "You doubt what I have related to you?"

"Your words of testimony are not doubted by me, but the version of that same story was different from what I had originally heard," Salem commented.

"Was this the version that filtered its way to Nazareth? Believe not rumors, and conversations spoken at campfires. I am a witness of the truth," Bedar said in rebuttal.

"Please forgive me if I have insulted you, and please do not be taken aback by the next question. My intentions will not be to hurt you or insult you." Bedar nodded his head to indicate that he understood and would try his best not to be offended. "If this Jesus is so powerful and is the Messiah as you claim, then what are you doing here?" Salem asked.

"Your question has not insulted me, and I will answer as truthfully as I can. You should fear not if you insult me or not. You should fear that you should invoke the judgment of the Lord our God. This curse came upon me after the Messiah passed through Samaria, but I know that I will not always remain here."

"It has not been reported that any leper has been cleansed of this dreadful affliction, save Naaman the Syrian by the prophet Elisha many hundreds of years ago," Salem said rather indignantly.

"The man from Nazareth who changed the hearts of many in Samaria is greater than the prophet Elisha, and greater than the river Jordan. The Lord has sent him to us. I know he can make me clean again," Bedar commented. He was not offended that Salem refused his testimony; he was not the first person to reject it. He felt sorry for the man, or any man who could not or would not believe. Bedar excused himself from their conversation and apologized to his new friend for having to leave. "Even lepers need their rest," Bedar added

Sleep avoided Salem the first few nights in the valley. The lack of rest, sleep and food had transformed him. He failed to wash himself when he had the opportunity on the day it rained. Many joyfully rollicked in the cool shower from above, yet Salem secluded himself from the rest of the community and away from the showers that blessed.

One valley inhabitant had asked Bedar, "Why has Salem denied himself so?"

"He has not adjusted to the realization of his fate. He is either in denial, or he has condemned himself for his present condition. He might wish that he could die, or even take his own life. For some it is better to die than to live in this misery," Bedar related to the man. After the man walked away, he said in a low voice, "But the Lord God of Israel has plans for you, Salem, my friend from Nazareth."

Each morning when Salem awoke, he would inventory his personal belongings, and then inventory his body to see what his condition was today. During one such inspection, Bedar scolded Salem, "It does not happen that fast. It is a slow, methodical deterioration of the flesh, but it is your soul that you must inventory." Salem again rejected the words of the man from the country he now was doomed to die in.

Several eating establishments that had scraps of food left over from their customers would donate their meager offerings to the people of the valley. For many this was the only way they stayed alive. He, like the others, knew the sound of the wagon that carried the vital sustenance to the edge of their jail. It had a distinct sound: clunk, clunk, thud, mixed in with a constant squeak. One of the wheels was broken and crooked. Bedar had related to Salem that the owners could easily discard the old cart should it be besieged by the lepers, and make it unclean.

Salem had recovered from his self-persecution and was now on the attack. When the sound of the wagon approached the valley, he would claw his way through the older and sicker residents so he could get the choicest morsels of food. This did not go on unnoticed by anyone, except the ones that beat Salem to the head of the line. Bedar had become very troubled with this transformation in Salem. Bedar asked a question in a low voice, "Is this what a man will become, he who rejects the Lord?"

It was the first day of the week and many were very eager for the scrap wagon to arrive, for they never delivered on the Sabbath. The remains of the discarded meals were as usual cast from as far away from the edge as possible. The stronger ones would climb up and get what ever they could, but the weaker ones would have to accept and exist on what rolled to the floor of the valley. Salem had recovered quite a bounty of food this day and was very pleased at his accomplishments.

He stuffed a majority of his spoil into his garment and quickly devoured the rest. Salem almost choked on the piece of bread that had just started down his throat when he heard someone call his name, "Salem?"

The voice was very familiar to him; it was too familiar. Again the voice called his name, "Salem." This time Salem was positive of who called his name, and he quickly covered his face and lowered his body to the ground as though he wanted to crawl away like a serpent. "Salem, do not be afraid. It is I, Mashic!" The friendly voice said.

"Go away. Depart from me. The man you seek is dead," Salem shouted from the dust pocket that he had laid in.

"The man I seek is very much alive. There is hope for you!" Mashic proclaimed.

"Go away. Depart from me. The man you seek is dead," Salem repeated his demand.

"Salem!" Mashic said as he approached the filthy diseased person he once knew as the son of his friend.

"Do not touch me. I am unclean! Do not touch me," Salem demanded.

Mashic heeded the words of the man who cowered in the dust. "I have come to give you good news."

"Good news?" Salem asked with laughter in his voice.

"There is hope for you, Salem."

"Good news of hope? That is hard to receive when your face is in the dust!"

"I did not put your face to the ground, nor did I ask you to do so."

After Salem realized that he had a true friend, a friend that accepted him, he got up off the ground, stood up, and looked directly at Mashic. "You accept me, as I am?"

"Yes!"

"What is this good news?"

After Mashic began to tell the story of the events that caused him to come to the valley of the lepers, Salem smiled, for it brought back all the memories of how Mashic loved to talk, and tell and retell stories. Salem had not spoken a word for hours, for he let Mashic expound on all the details of what he had witnessed. Finally, when Mashic paused, Salem asked, "Did Jesus actually touch that leper?"

By the way the question was asked, Mashic thought it was not a question of doubt, but of hope. He hoped Salem would follow that question like a typical Jew, with a question. He had hoped Salem would ask, "Can Jesus touch me too?" but Salem's thoughts were not as Mashic's.

"Is he clean?" Salem asked.

"Yes, the man departed completely clean!"

The mouth of Salem was closed, but his mind whirled like the chaff that was carried away by the wind from the wheat floor after it had been thrashed. It was the confusion in his mind that caused him to say, "I cannot accept it."

Mashic knew that many years of teaching could not be broken down because he retold the facts of just one event. "I understand what your thoughts are, and I know it is hard for you accept. It might have been easier for you to not have known Jesus prior to the day that he revealed himself to be the Messiah. You have only known him as the son of Joseph. I learned a long time ago, but I just recently accepted the truth of who his real Father is. I must leave now, but I will come again and I will bring you proper food and clothing."

"I cannot repay you!"

"I asked not for any payment from you," Mashic said, and then he was silent for a moment as though he was in thought. With his thoughts in order, Mashic said, "I know how you can repay me. Allow me to share with you the things I hear, and see what I have learned about Jesus. I will give you food for your body, and for your soul." When Salem did not answer, Mashic began to walk away.

"Wait!"

Mashic stopped and turned toward Salem, "Is there anything else?"

"Yes, tell me of my family! How are they doing?"

"I have not seen them, but I have heard that they still mourn for you."

Salem had to clear his throat and was still barely able to ask, "And Elizabeth?"

"The same," Mashic lied.

"Should you see them, please do not tell them where I am."

Mashic nodded his head.

"How did you find me?"

"I remembered the conversation that I had with a ten-year-old boy many years ago," Mashic said as he smiled.

"Just one more thing before you leave. I have made a friend here. His name is Bedar, from the town of Sychar. He would probably like to listen to the things you have to say about Jesus."

"Please bring him with you."

"Mashic, my friend, thank you!"

"I love you as if you were my son. I will let you know when Jesus will pass through this area, so you can go ask him to heal you!"

"I do not know if I can do that."

"Do you remember what Naaman's servant told him, when he refused to obey the man of God? The prophet Elisha had instructed Naaman to dip in the river Jordan seven times. Naaman thought that command was foolish. Naaman's servant told him, 'If he had asked any great deed of you, would you not have obeyed?' Just ask him, Salem. Seek the man of God." Mashic departed with the promise to return.

The words of his friend echoed through his mind. The events rolled over and over in his thoughts. "You accept me? Just ask him! If he had asked any great deed of you . . ." He repeated it over and over. "Yes!" thundered the answer. Salem did not know that a war for his soul waged within him, yet he was weary from battle.

Sleep, like so many nights before, evaded him. The few small segments of sleep each night, compounded by his present condition, made him a very disagreeable person. Salem tried to avoid everyone. He and Bedar had not talked for several days and the tension seemed to grow between them. Bedar concluded that Salem had begun to reflect on his sins again. "What can I do for you, my friend?" Bedar finally got the courage to ask.

"If you had a cure for sleeplessness, I would be indebted to you for the remainder of my life," Salem said.

"For a Jew, you do not know your own scriptures, do you?"

"What do you mean?"

"A man who has trouble with his sleep is a man whose heart is not right before the Lord."

"I obeyed the law. I kept the commandments as it was required of me, until I was exiled here in this horrible place."

"Being here–being a leper–does not separate us from God. It is

Jeff Frazier

what is in our heart that condemns us. The prophet Jeremiah wrote as he was instructed by God to tell the people that they had set idols in their hearts. What idol do you have in your heart?"

A vision of the carpenter's shop flashed in his mind. Salem began to weep. The shop that he had been raised in was an idol to him, and to his father. He had waited all his life for the answer to the question that he had asked his old friend. Salem heard his own voice when he was of the young age of ten ask, "Mashic, why do you always say things like, my God, or our God, and my father always says the God of our fathers?" Salem now understood that his father, Jeru, only knew the God of Israel as a title, as "Our God," while Mashic knew him as "My God." His heart was convicted, yet his mind refused to allow him to make the decision that would affect his life forever.

Bedar was not offended when Salem walked away silently, for he knew that a man's soul weighed in the balance. The only other person who was aware of Salem's torment was Bedar. The battle that raged within Salem went on for several days. Tradition would claim victory, then a still small voice would whisper, "Faith, trust, believe." Bedar was wise enough to know to let a person be while that person labored over spiritual matters. Neither Salem nor Bedar was sure of whom the victor would be. Leprosy was trivial to Salem now, compared to the war that ensued within. Bedar was concerned that Salem would make an unwise decision.

Bedar decided to walk out of the valley, even though it was a risky to do so, but he felt drawn by an unseen force that led him to the forest just outside of the valley. As he lumbered along, he took his time in the cool morning air. He heard a man approach and fell to the ground and cried with a loud voice, "Unclean! Unclean! Unclean!"

The man continued his approach as though he had not heard the cry of warning. Again Bedar shouted his warning with a loud voice. It became apparent to him that the man had heard him but had chosen to ignore the warnings. "I heard you the first time," the man replied. "Do not be afraid! I will not approach any closer. I am looking for a man whose name is Salem from Nazareth. Have you seen him?"

"Yes, I know the man you seek!"

"Good. Could you please go get him for me? My name is Mashic and I have some more good news for him!"

Bedar looked up at Mashic and replied, "You are a good man, Mashic. Salem has spoken well of you."

"And you are?"

"Bedar, I am a merchant." Then he corrected himself, "Ex-merchant from the city of Sychar!"

"Salem has spoken of you also, and I understand that you want to learn more about Jesus?"

"Oh yes, my life has not been the same since Jesus taught our people at Jacob's well, for I have seen the Messiah!"

"Go get Salem, for I have some more good news!"

Quickly, Bedar rose from the ground and returned to the valley. When Salem and Bedar returned, Mashic had a small feast spread out for the two men. Relief flooded over Salem's face and the turmoil within him subsided when he looked upon the weathered face of Mashic. They filled their bellies on food that they had not tasted in many a day. "Slow down," Mashic repeated several times, "you might hurt yourself."

They lounged in the shade of a fig tree, as Mashic began to tell them of the things that he had witnessed. Mashic acted out and fully dramatized the scene as he had seen it happen. "The house was full to capacity, and many people stood outside. So great was the multitude that many could not get in. Some men brought a man on his bed, sick with palsy. They could not get in, so they lowered him down from the roof through the tiles. And when Jesus saw their faith, he said 'Man, your sins are forgiven.' The Pharisees must have reasoned to themselves that Jesus had committed some form of blasphemy, because he told them, 'Why do you reason in your hearts? Which is easier to say, your sins are forgiven, or rise up and walk? But that you may know the Son of man has power upon earth to forgive sins.' Jesus then turned to the man with palsy and said, 'I say to you, arise and take up your bed, and go to your own house.' And the man immediately got up and walked away, and he glorified God. Everyone was amazed, and we all glorified God."

Mashic continued with his story of how Jesus, when he saw the man named Levi, told him, "Follow me." And the man followed him, and they all went to Levi's home. There were a lot of people there, and many were publicans. The Pharisees questioned Jesus as to why he ate and drank with publicans and sinners. Jesus responded, "They who are whole do not need a physician, but they who are sick. I came not to call the righteous, but the sinners to repentance."

This visit ended like the last visit. Much needed to be said. So much more to do, yet their separation had to occur. Salem's life lacked many things now, and the one thing he yearned for most at this moment was the kiss of a friend. Salem desperately wanted to embrace his friend, but he loved him too dearly to place a curse on Mashic's life. Mashic departed with the promise that he would return, and with the same desires in his heart as that of Salem. He too wanted to express his love to Salem, but he was still fearful.

As quickly as the war had abated with Mashic's presence, his departure caused the battle within Salem to escalate with even greater fury. The words that he had heard worked within him to destroy the things that he had been taught. "Follow me," and "Your sins are for-given," were as arrows shot from the weapon and they pierced his heart. The agony only grew more intense as he fought off the onslaught from what he thought was the enemy.

On the second night after Mashic's last visit, Salem won the battle within his soul when he surrendered to his God. The battle cry was sounded and the victory trumpets blasted their song of joy. Salem cried with a loud voice, "Jesus is the Son of God." As lightning from the sky would strike a tree in the meadow, so did the revelation to Salem of who Jesus really was. Joseph had been chosen to raise Jesus in the honorable profession of carpentry, but God was the true father of the man he had known as Jesus. The realization that he had battled the same God that he had been told that he worshipped caused his surrender to be his victory.

Bedar became alarmed when Salem slept for two days without an interruption, but as long as Salem had a breath, Bedar decided to let him rest. When he finally awoke, he was not the man he was before. It was as though Salem died, and someone else had taken his place. Bedar was one of the first to notice the change. The conflict was over, and the results were evident. No more was he the man who could not sleep, and who prevented many other already weary persons from rest. The man who pushed aside the weaker, so he could consume a scrap of discarded food before anyone else, could not be seen in Salem.

With a face that emitted a divine glow, Salem finally spoke the words that Bedar had already realized, "I believe!"

"I know, and I am pleased for you!"

They talked for hours about the things of the Messiah. Salem shared how he had known Jesus as they grew up. Bedar told of what Jesus had taught him and his people. The excitement grew when one person would learn something new that the person had shared. Salem was shocked to know that Bedar had never heard the story of the great caravan that passed by Nazareth on its way to Jerusalem, with its final stop in Bethlehem.

"It happened just before I was delivered into this world," Salem announced proudly.

Their talk had been interrupted by the sound of the delivery wagon that approached. Like trained performance animals, the hordes of people collected together at the place where the food would be dumped out for them. The best scraps were quickly scooped up and carted away by none other than Salem. The face of Bedar showed his displeasure in Salem, until he saw him take the food to the weaker ones. Bedar felt ashamed because he had falsely judged his friend.

In the midst of the scraps that Salem had gathered, he discovered a morsel of uncooked corn. The kernels on the ear of corn were almost completely dried. Salem was not a farmer by trade, but he knew that this corn was ready to be planted. "Bedar," Salem shouted with a great deal of excitement. "Bedar, come quickly!

There was no excitement on Bedar's face when Salem presented the meager portion of uncooked corn to him, as though it were an offering of the first fruits to the priest at the Temple. "So?" Bedar questioned the gift that Salem held in his hand.

"Do you not see what I have here?"

"My sight sees a small piece of corn."

"No, no. It is food."

"This small morsel of corn may be enough for just one meal."

"This is not for us to eat. We will plant it. We can grow our own food and no longer be dependent on these scraps from the town!"

Bedar's eyes were opened and he could see the garden of fresh, clean food that these kernels would bring forth. Bedar grasped both of Salem's shoulders and said, "Just a few moments ago, I saw only with mine eyes. Now I see with my heart and soul." Both men began to venture out to every member of the community, and expressed their excitement. Some of the greedy could not see beyond the meal that they now consumed. With patience and forbearance, they were able to gather enough raw seeds, kernels, and bulbs to begin a meager garden.

"It is just a start!" Salem said as he looked at the small pile of discarded food scraps. "Why must we live as animals? I am a highly-trained and skilled carpenter, and I still can build many things."

"Where will this talk lead us?"

"I am a carpenter, you are a merchant. Are there any brick makers living here?" Bedar nodded his head. "Farmers?" Again Bedar nodded. "Weavers?" Bedar smiled a radiant grin when he realized what Salem meant. "We can build our own city," Salem announced triumphantly.

CHAPTER IX

Many of the people in Nazareth had heard of the calamity that had been brought upon the house of Jeru. The ones that had heard of Salem's leprosy avoided any contact with any member of Jeru's family. Jeru and Martha had taken stringent steps to ensure that their home and the carpentry shop had been ceremonially and effectually cleansed, yet it meant nothing to the fearful. The stigma that Elizabeth carried the child of a leper caused even the strongest of their faith to avoid the house of Jeru. Leprosy was not only a disease of the flesh to the unfortunate host, but it also ate away at the family. Elizabeth knew that her baby was clean, and no one would be allowed to touch the child of Salem.

Martha assumed many of the duties that had once been Elizabeth's. The wife of her now deceased son was now her daughter. She protected her from the people who stared with evil glares. Jeru forbade Elizabeth to walk the streets alone, since Martha had heard one evil hearted woman say, "Someone should stone her, before she brings that creature into this world!"

It was Jeru that saw to the business concerns of the shop, or rather it was the lack thereof that really concerned him. "We should move to another town," Jeru mumbled mournfully. At first Martha had resisted and would not yield their lives to people who could not understand. As the tension grew, so did her desire to leave. Three months ago they could have taken the loss of a major disruption like this at a leisurely pace. The pressure that was built up in their community was about to force them to make a hasty decision.

The current task that Jeru had undertaken was fruitless, but he had to work to keep his mind and hands busy because the idleness tortured him severely. The lunch that Martha had brought him did not satisfy Jeru. Her desires to please him were still very admirable, but Jeru could not be placated.

"It will kill all of us if we continue on like this!" Martha said.

"I feel as if I am already dead!"

"We have a life to live, even as years are great in number."

"The child of our only son is worth the effort to begin our lives again. I am afraid that Elizabeth will not live through this child being delivered. She is so weak, and it frightens me. We could lose them both," Martha proclaimed.

Jeru took the woman he loved dearly into his arms and whispered, "For the sake of our family, we must move. It is not a choice for us now. The question that I have asked myself is, where? Where can we go?"

"The Lord God will lead us," she said prophetically.

The words had no more passed over her lips when the sun that shone brightly through the door was suddenly blocked. They could not see the face of the silhouetted figure that entered the shop, but the voice from the large dark figure thundered the question, "Salem? Are you Salem?"

"No!" Jeru answered very timidly. "He was my son, but he is dead."

"Then you will have to take his place, old man. That is, if you are a carpenter as well," the man demanded.

"I am."

"What is your name?"

"I am Jeru! And for what reason do you seek help of carpenters?"

"There is a need for carpenters in Jerusalem."

"Everyone in this town knows that my son is dead and they would have told you so. So please tell me why did you come to a carpentry shop in Nazareth in search of workers?"

"A man in Cana showed me some of the craftsmanship that he had hired a man named Salem to do. He told me that Salem lived and worked here." The soldier was through with conversations that were pointless, and he would not discuss subjects with a Jewish carpenter. "Just gather whatever possessions that you can carry and report to the governor in Jerusalem. He is the one that has requested workers. Your name will be added to this list and you will be expected to report to him within fourteen days."

"What about the other carpenters? Have you inquired of them?" Jeru asked.

At first the soldier appeared shaken by the question but he answered, "Yes, that is my responsibility, to hire workers."

"Is another carpenter from Nazareth on this list?"

The soldier appeared to be agitated by the questions from this Jew. He remembered what he was told about these people before he was assigned to work in Israel, that these Israelites loved questions. They really loved to answer questions with questions. This custom of these weak people really disgusted him and that is what prompted him to reply, "That is not for you to ask!" With a quick, regimented, military turn, the Roman exited the shop without another word spoken.

"The Lord has answered our prayers, and rather quickly did he not?" Jeru asked as though he wanted it to sound like a joke, but the tension in his voice revealed his true emotions.

"I knew this day had to come. It is late. Come, let us close up the shop and prepare to begin the move to Jerusalem. There is no reason why we should delay what must be done," Martha stated.

"Go, I will be home shortly!"

Alone in the shop, Jeru wept. After he dried his eyes, Jeru looked around the room. He rubbed his fingers on the ruts in floor that he had created as he would walk back and forth while he created his masterpieces of craftsmanship. Every tool showed their age, but each was packed away as though it were a fragile ornament. Just before he closed the door to his shop, his and Salem's shop, Jeru went over to the window and looked out at the mountains and inhaled a deep breath.

Packing up their belongings would normally have taken a long time to accomplish, but they decided to only take what was really required of them. Jeru had no trouble selecting what was important. If he could not eat it, wear it, or use it to make money, it would not be loaded onto the wagon. To cull the other household items proved to be much more difficult for Martha. Each article meant something to her, and she could not separate them from her life.

"How long will we be in Jerusalem?" Elizabeth asked.

"Not very long at all," Jeru lied. He really felt that he had not lied to her, because he really was not sure how long they would be gone. Jeru handed her an article to be loaded and asked her to put it on the wagon.

When Elizabeth was outside Jeru commented to Martha of his concerns. "With the passing of each day, her mental condition grows more serious. If she continues to decline, by the time her child is born she will be a total imbecile, and unable to care for her child. Many of the items that I have asked her to either load or to put aside should have made her respond in one way or the other, but she failed to acknowledge the importance of any item presented to her."

After the cart was loaded, and the jackass secured to the yoke, the family that had only known this town as their home began their journey to another city. What adventures would they experience? What dangers would pursue them? How many more tragedies could this family bear? The torment on Jeru and Martha was horrendous, but they were thankful for Elizabeth's sake that she was not mentally aware of what had happened. In many aspects, Elizabeth was better off than Jeru and Martha.

When they reached a certain point that Jeru knew would be his last opportunity to look back and catch a glimpse of the town of Nazareth, he let Martha and Elizabeth pass him so he could stop undetected. After he stopped and just before he turned around, he remembered what he had been told of what happened to Lot's wife who had looked back. He shivered at the possibility that God would turn him into a pillar of salt as well. Jeru reasoned with himself that what happened to Lot's wife had never happened to anyone again. He also had not specifically been instructed, "Do not look back," as Lot and his family had been.

Jeru cast a quick glance over his shoulder, and what he saw made him turn all the way around. Smoke, a lot of dark, thick smoke could be seen as it rose from the town. "There must be a home on fire in the town!" Jeru said to himself. Then the realization of what he witnessed caused him to grow ill. He looked to see if Martha and Elizabeth had stopped as well or had continued on. When he saw that they were already at the bottom of the hill, and that they could not see the evil that his eyes saw, he was glad. Jeru knew he could never tell his wife and daughter of what he had seen. He now knew he would never leave Jerusalem. "They could have waited until we were gone at least a day's journey away before they carried out their act of judgment!" Jeru said sadly.

They were all thankful that they had arrived in Jerusalem safely. Jeru was glad that the trip had not taken the whole fourteen days. As they neared the gates that granted them access to the city of Jerusalem, Elizabeth innocently stated, "God must have moved us here for a reason. Maybe he has some great purpose for us."

Thinking back to the time when Mashic had stated almost the same thing to him, Jeru said, "Maybe that old fool knew something," as they passed through the East Gate into the city of Jerusalem.

†

Jeru was thankful that they had arrived before the Sabbath, especially since this was the Passover feast. A thought came to Jeru that he might have the slightest chance that he could accidentally run into Mashic. Travel on the Sabbath for Jeru had always been a struggle. Jeru was the type of person that when he started a project, it would be finished. Not only did he know, but everyone else in Israel knew that God had established certain laws that governed what you could and could not do on the Sabbath. One such law was how far you could travel. So every Sabbath, as much as he could, Jeru would not even move. He was not a lazy man, but he would rather not start something that he could not finish.

They used the remainder of that day to look for a place to stay and to store their possessions. Fortunately they found a temporary place to lodge. It had not been easy for Jeru. The shock of how much more things cost in Jerusalem than in Nazareth made Jeru adjust his spending habits. It made it more difficult for Jeru to part with his money.

On the morning of the Sabbath, the three new residents of the big walled city began their journey to the Temple. The crowd of crippled and sick people that gathered at the side of a pool caught Elizabeth's attention and she asked, "What is that place, and what are those sick people doing there?"

Jeru answered her as though she were a young child, "It is called the Pool of Bethesda. There is a legend that at a certain time of the year an angel comes down and troubles the waters. It is said that if anyone who has an infirmity is first into the troubled waters, they will be healed of whatever affliction they have."

Elizabeth shocked them both when she said, "It would be a good thing if Salem could enter those waters." They both agreed with her, but doubted in their hearts that it would ever be possible. In a moment of inattentiveness on Jeru and Martha's part, Elizabeth wandered off. She wandered off because she sought a possible solution for Salem's affliction. Since Salem's banishment, she had lived with scales over her mind, but something drew her to the pool.

The sight of all those people with infirmities and diseases did not affect her. She concentrated on the water that healed. The people that stood around the pool did not try to stop her, nor did the vast masses hinder her from her intended destination. Many voices called out to her for her to stop and render to their aid. No voices could cause her to stop until she heard the voice of a man she recognized. The way the man spoke with authority in his voice and the fact that she knew this man caused her to stop. She took notice of the man who was at the pool. This man she knew talked to another man, who was crippled.

"Do you want to be made whole?" Jesus asked the crippled man.

A man in the crowd behind Elizabeth said, "That man has had that infirmity for thirty-eight years. There is no hope for him."

The crippled man answered Jesus, "Sir, when the water is troubled I have no man to put me into the pool. While I attempt to make my way to the pool, another enters therein, and is healed."

Jesus said to the man, "Rise, take up your bed, and walk."

Immediately the man was made whole, and he picked up his bed and walked away. Many Jews became angry at the man who carried his bed on the Sabbath, and inquired of him why he carried his bed on the Sabbath. The man replied, "The man that made me whole said, 'Take up your bed and walk.' I do not know who this man was," as he looked around to see the man that had healed him. "He must have departed."

Elizabeth could not understand why these men were so angry that someone had been healed on the Sabbath. They should have rejoiced that the man had been made whole. She became very distraught when she overheard them talk of their desire to kill Jesus. She could tell that the conversation between these men had not yet been ended, but she knew she had to leave this place. She knew she had to find her family, and then she remembered that Jeru and Martha were on their way to the Temple.

Elizabeth found Jeru and Martha not too far from where she had wandered off from them. Jeru wanted to scold Elizabeth because she had wandered off. The look he got from Martha told him he better not make that mistake. Jeru took the silent advice of his wife, and simply stated to Elizabeth his concerns for her safety, and the safety of the child that was in her womb. He still treated her as though she was ill, but Elizabeth knew she had been fully restored to her right mind. There was something in her life now that had been missing prior to the miracle at the pool. The seed of hope and faith had been planted in her soul and heart, and had taken root.

When they got to the Temple, Elizabeth could not believe her eyes when she saw Jesus was there as well. Her astonishment increased when she also saw the man that had just been healed at the pool Bethesda also entered the Temple. What happened next really compounded her confusion.

Jesus went to the man that he had healed at the pool Bethesda and said, "Behold you are whole. Sin no more, or a worse thing will come upon you!" The once afflicted man departed the Temple. Elizabeth was not certain of the man's destination, but she had her suspicions that he went back to report to the ones who had questioned him earlier, to tell them that it was Jesus of Nazareth that had healed him.

The morning of the first day of the week brought new life to the city of Jerusalem. The amount of people that moved about, conducted business, and socialized seemed to have doubled. Jeru and his family were amazed at the number of people that crowded the streets. It had been a long time since Jeru had been in Jerusalem at the Passover feast, but he would not admit it openly to anyone. With the Passover feast behind them, maybe they could find a better place to stay that would not set the family finances back so much. Jeru was glad that the confronting of Mashic in Jerusalem had not happened.

Jeru knew that at least on this day he could report to the Office of the Governor and receive a position that would provide the means of support for his family. Jeru walked into the Jewish built building that had been seized by the Romans to conduct government business. Many people conducted money transactions with the Romans. Some pleaded for help with disputes, others even pleaded for their lives.

The first thing Jeru noticed about the man behind the desk was the man's right ear. The man's ear had a rather strange scar on it. He studied the ear for a few moments, and then he knew what had caused the scar. The man must have been a slave at one time, and the only way he could remove the ring was to pull the ring through the earlobe. It even crossed Jeru's mind that the man could have been a run-a-way slave, but why would a run-a-way slave work in a Roman Office?

Jeru explained to the man behind the desk the events that resulted in his presence in Jerusalem. The official did not seem to be moved by Jeru's explanation. To Jeru's horror and dismay the official replied, "I have not heard of any request from the governor, nor have I heard of you. Be gone!"

"But I–"

The official interrupted Jeru's rebuttal with the wave of his hand, and a rather large man that wore the battle array of the military walked up behind Jeru and gave him a quick and forceful shove. That action caught Jeru unaware and caused him to fall to the floor. Jeru got to his feet, brushed himself off and exited the building that had once been an honorable place for his people, but now was desecrated. The fall to the floor did not cause any injuries to his body, but it hurt his spirit. He had not even been given the opportunity to explain the fire that he had seen after he left Nazareth.

He did not want his wife to worry needlessly, so Jeru walked the streets of this almost foreign city to look for employment. He did not know anyone here, and no one knew him. He scanned the crowds as he walked down the streets. Out of desperation Jeru decided to ask if anyone needed the services of a carpenter. The looks and stares that he got made him feel older than he really was.

As Elizabeth sat at the window so she could watch the action of the streets below, she asked, "Do you think Jeru will find a better place for us?"

"I hope so, my dear child." Martha was afraid that Elizabeth planned to take of her own life and suggested in a sympathetic tone, "Please move away from that window. You cannot be sure of the stability of these old structures."

Elizabeth knew that Martha had been concerned for her and said to her, "I know that I have been a great burden to you both. I am also aware that you are troubled over my mental state." With a graceful and joyous heart Elizabeth moved over to Martha and gave her a very strong embrace. "I want to ease your mind, and let you know that all is well with my soul," Elizabeth explained. She told Martha of the events that had happened by the pool of Bethesda.

"It would be best that you do not tell Jeru of these matters," Martha said. Martha did not have to explain to Elizabeth why she could not tell Jeru about what happened. Both of them knew how much Jeru hated Jesus because Jesus had claimed to be the Messiah.

Elizabeth agreed with Martha's request and then went back over to the window. Movement on the street caught her attention. She smiled and was glad to see that Jesus was on his way out of Jerusalem, away from the people who sought to kill him.

Later in the evening, Jeru returned with the news that he had obtained employment. It did not surprise Martha, but the look in Jeru's eyes caused her to worry. The smile on his face and the laughter in his voice contradicted with what the windows to his soul revealed. Martha knew far too well that he hid something, but she was also wise enough not to ask about it.

Their relationship was not like many of the other couples that she had known over the years. There were many women who suffered greatly under the domination of their husbands, but Jeru was a fair man. Even with all these fine qualities, she knew that he was still the head of the house. She also knew that her husband knew what was best for their family.

Jeru could tell that Martha knew he had not told her everything. He wanted to tell her about what had happened at the Roman Office, but decided that Martha had enough worries already. With Martha and Elizabeth to consider, he only explained how he had obtained work from private individuals. Jeru knew that he would have to work at a rate lower than what the Romans would have paid. He was glad to have the work that he got, but now they had to exist on a day to day basis. His shop in Nazareth, except for the last few months, always had work assignments. The jobs came in faster than he could produce. His only hope now was to prove himself worthy in this city that was a stranger to him. It was times like these when the voices of the past came to haunt him, "The just shall live by his faith."

CHAPTER X

This was the first time in many, many years that Mashic had missed the Passover feast in Jerusalem. He had planned to go again this year but he had received word from a friend that had passed through Nazareth that his wife needed him. Mashic waited for the hours of darkness to go back into the town, and into his home. It surprised Mashic that Sara had not been startled when he entered the house unannounced.

"I know the sound of your walk. It is a wonder you did not wake everyone in the vicinity with your stomping!" Sara stated.

Their reunion was as beautiful as it was short. With the Passover complete, Mashic knew that he must be leaving again. The news that Sara had revealed to him concerning the family of Jeru troubled him greatly. He was glad that he had this information. "This revelation would be useful in the future."

"Useful for what?" his wife asked.

"I might need to give some advice to a friend in need!"

"Do you think it wise to tell him what happened?"

"I pray that I will know the correct moment to tell Salem of the tragedy that happened to his family after he left Nazareth!"

"Or if you should ever tell him!"

"Yes, that could be a possibility."

"I am so thankful that you have a heart of love."

They kissed and embraced as though it was the first time together, but Sara felt as though it was their last. Sara felt that something was wrong, but she did not know what, and she did not want to ask any more questions. Sara kissed her husband again. The temptation to ask him not to leave again had long been blocked from her mind. She knew he sought the will of their God. There were many things she could do, but to be a stumbling block to her husband was not one of them.

"I managed to earn some money. Please take it!" He knew that she would resist. Mashic knew that Sara knew that he worked very hard to earn even just this small amount. He was no longer a young man, but when you were on the road, you had to work wherever you could. Mashic departed after she finally but reluctantly received the coins, save one.

Mashic hoped that he would not take too long to locate Jesus. Once on the road, he heard that Jesus had gone to the Sea of Galilee, which was called Tiberias. He joined with a great multitude that numbered about five thousand men along with their wives and children and started to walk up into the mountains. Mashic wondered how many of the people that journeyed on this trek followed Jesus because of the miracles that he performed. As the multitude reached Jesus, Mashic noticed that Jesus was seated on the ground with the disciples.

When Jesus lifted up his eyes, and saw the great multitude that came to him, he said, "Philip, where shall we buy bread that these shall eat."

"We do not have enough money to buy food for all these people, not even enough to buy enough for each person to have a little portion," Philip answered him.

Mashic was astonished that he heard Jesus ask Philip that question over the crowd and even more amazed that he heard Phillip's reply. He remembered that he still had one last coin, and he pulled it from the money pouch. Mashic wanted to offer it to help feed the crowd, but before he could offer his coin, someone said, "There is a lad here who has five barley loaves, and two small fishes, but what are they among so many?" Mashic could tell that this man was one of Jesus' disciples.

And Jesus said, "Make these men to sit!"

Mashic's eyes captured yet another wonder of the man called Jesus. The five loaves and two fishes were offered up to heaven, and Jesus gave thanks. The disciples then distributed the loaves and fishes to every person. When all had eaten their fill of fish and bread, Jesus asked for the remainder to be placed in the empty baskets. The fragments that remained filled twelve baskets.

Talk quickly spread through the masses that Jesus was truly a prophet. Many wanted to take hold of Jesus and make him king over all of Israel. Jesus perceived their intentions and departed up the mountain alone.

When Jesus returned the next morning he called his disciples together, and of them, he chose twelve to be his apostles; Simon (whom he later named Peter), his brother Andrew, James, James son of Alphaeus, Judas son of James, Bartholomew, Matthew, Thomas, John, Philip, Simon who was called the Zealot, and Judas Iscariot.

Jesus went down with his twelve and a great number of people from all over Judea, Jerusalem, and from the coast of Tyre and Sidon also. They, like Mashic, had come to hear him. Many others had come to be healed of their diseases. Those troubled by evil spirits were cured. All of the people tried to touch him, because power came from him and healed them all.

Then Jesus looked at his disciples and said, "Blessed are you who are poor in spirit, for yours is the kingdom of God. Blessed are you who hunger now, for you will be filled. Blessed are you who weep, for you will laugh. Blessed are you, because of the Son of man, when men hate you, when they exclude you and insult you and reject your name as evil. Rejoice in that day and leap for joy, because great is your reward in heaven. For that in like manner did their fathers unto the prophets."

Jesus then said, "But woe to you who are rich, for you have already received your comfort. Woe to you who are well fed now, for you will go hungry. Woe to you who laugh now, for you will mourn and weep. Woe to you when all men speak well of you, the false prophets were treated this way by their fathers."

"Never in all of Israel has such a teacher come that said such things," Mashic said.

Jesus continued, "But I tell you who can hear my words: Love your enemies! Do good to those who hate you, and bless those who curse you. Pray for those who mistreat you."

The crowd was captivated by the words of this teacher, this man from the town of Nazareth. "If someone strikes you on one cheek, turn to him the other cheek as well. If someone takes your coat, do not stop him from taking your tunic. Give to everyone who asks of you, and if anyone takes what belongs to you, do not demand it back," Jesus continued. The statement, "Do unto others as you would have them do unto you," left many men confounded, for they had never heard such words.

"If you love those who love you, what reward is that for you? Even the sinners love those who love them. If you do good to those who are good to you, what reward is that to you? Even sinners can do that. And if you lend to those from whom you expect to be repaid, what benefit is that to you? Even sinners lend to 'sinners,' expecting full payment." Many faces displayed the guilt that was in their hearts.

With authority like none other before him, Jesus said, "But I say, love your enemies, do good to them that persecute you. Give to them without expecting to get anything back in return. Then great will be your reward, and you will be sons of the Most High, because he is kind to the ungrateful and wicked.

"Be merciful, just as your Father is merciful. Do not judge and you will not be judged. Do not condemn, and you will not be condemned. Forgive, and you will be forgiven. Give and it will be given to you. A good measure, pressed down, shaken together and running over, will be poured into your bosom. With what measure you use to give, so will it be used to measure for you." The faces in the multitude reflected the change that these words had begun in their hearts.

Jesus also told them this parable: "Can a blind man guide a blind man? Or will they both fall into a pit? A disciple is not above his teacher, but everyone who is fully trained will be like his teacher." Mashic wondered if the twelve men with Jesus could ever be like their teacher.

Jesus began to talk about judging again when he said, "Why do you look at the tiny particle of sawdust in the eye of your brother and yet you pay no attention to the board that is in your own eye? How can you say to your brother, 'Brother, let me take the speck out of your eye,' when you yourself fail to see the board in your own eye? You hypocrite, take the board out of your eye first, and then you can clearly see, to remove the speck from your brother's eye." Many heads nodded with the understanding of such wisdom. It was so simple yet it had always eluded them.

"A good tree does not bear bad fruit, nor does a bad tree bear good fruit. Each tree is recognized by the fruit it bears. People do not get figs from picking in the thorn bushes, nor do they get grapes from the briers. A good man brings forth good things out of the good stored up in his heart. The evil man brings forth evil things out of the evil stored up in his heart. For out of the overflow of his heart his mouth speaks. Why do you call me, 'Lord, Lord,' and do not keep my commandments?

"I will show you what he is like who comes to me and hears my words and obeys. This man is like a man who built a house, who dug down deep and laid the foundation on a solid rock. When the flood

Jeff Frazier

came, the mighty wind and rain struck that house, but it could not shake it, because it was well built. The one who hears my words and does not obey is like the man who built a house on the ground without a foundation. The moment the winds and rain struck, the house collapsed and its destruction was complete."

After he had finished his saying in the presence of all these people, Jesus and some of the crowd went to Capernaum. Some elders of the Jews came to Jesus and told him of a centurion whose servant, whom the centurion valued highly, was sick and about to die.

"The centurion has heard of you, Jesus. He has sent us to ask you to come and heal his servant," one of the elders said.

They pleaded earnestly with him, "This man deserves to have you do this for him, because he loves our nation and has built us our synagogue."

Jesus decided to go with them, but as he neared the house of the centurion, a man approached Jesus and said, "The centurion sent me to say to you: 'Lord, do not trouble yourself, for I do not deserve to have you come under my roof. I did not consider myself worthy to come unto you. But say the word, and my servant will be healed. For I myself am a man with great authority, with many soldiers under me. I tell one, 'Go,' and he goes; and to another, 'Come,' and he comes. I say to my servant, 'Do this,' and he does it."

When Jesus heard this, he was amazed at the centurion and turned to the crowd that followed him and said, "I tell you, I have not found such great faith even in Israel." Then the men who had been sent by the centurion returned to the house and discovered that the servant had been made whole.

Soon after the centurion's servant was healed, Jesus went to a town called Nain. His apostles and a large crowd followed along with him. As Jesus approached the gate of the town, a person who had died was being carried out. A large crowd from the town followed the mother, who was also a widow, as she cried, "My only son. My only son."

When the Lord Jesus saw her, his heart went out to her and he said, "Do not cry." Then Jesus went over and touched the coffin. The ones that carried the body stopped. Jesus said, "Young man, I say to you, arise!" The man who had died sat up and began to talk. Jesus presented him back to his mother.

All who had witnessed this miracle were filled with awe and they praised God. "A great prophet has appeared among us," they said. "God has come to help his people." The good news about Jesus spread throughout Judea and the surrounding country.

CHAPTER XI

The months in Jerusalem had been good for them. Jeru's quality of work proved worthy for the sake of building him a good reputation. He had started with odd jobs, but was quickly recognized as a true craftsman of his trade. Carpenters were easy to find, but excellent craftsman were sought by all who could afford them. The pay he received helped this new family in the City of Peace move from the meager room to one of status.

A very wealthy man had hired Jeru to design and build a fixture that would hold some merchandise for sale. This new assignment made Jeru feel young and useful again. The project was completed well before the scheduled deadline, and he received a generous bonus. When Jeru delivered the fixture to the man, he noticed that a major repair job had started in the home of this man. "Did someone recommend these workers to you?" Jeru asked.

"Well, yes!" the man replied. "Is there a problem?"

"As I entered, I noticed several structural defects in their work. Once it is covered up it could go unnoticed for years, but one day the defect will surface and cost more than the original repairs. You seem to be a man who pays well for what he wants and expects to get what he pays for." The man gave Jeru a look that said to continue. "The materials that they have used so far are of poor quality," Jeru stated.

"Please wait here," the man said as a commandment rather than a request. He disappeared very quickly, and returned just a moment later. "I have investigated your allegations, and found them to be true. The workers were terminated of their responsibilities, and of their payment." The man placed his hands on each of Jeru's shoulders and said, "I surely hope you are not bound by any other agreement, because I want you to be the overseer of this repair. You can hire as many men as you think you will need."

"I do not have any agreements at this time, and I would be honored to accept this task," Jeru answered him.

"It is good for me that you are from Jerusalem," the man commented.

"I am not from here. I am from Nazareth."

"Nazareth?"

The way this man said Nazareth, and the look that appeared on his face, made Jeru feel uneasy, and unsure of this man. "You know someone from Nazareth?"

The man opened his mouth as to say a name, but did not. After the man regained his composure he said, "You have been hired by me and I do not even know your name. My name is Joseph, and I am from Arimathaea."

"My name is Jeru."

"Please, Jeru, come sit outside in the cool shade and tell me how it is that you ended up in Jerusalem."

It was very difficult to tell this stranger of why he was in Jerusalem, and all the circumstances that had brought him to this very house, but he did. "I have not told anyone of these things, nor did I want to tell you!" Jeru said.

"Then why did you tell me?"

"I do not know."

"Thank you for sharing this with me."

"I must go now. My dead son's wife, that we have taken as a daughter, is about to deliver a child."

"Before you go, I have someone for you to meet."

Jeru did not question Joseph of whom he spoke or to where he led him. When he saw that Joseph had led him to the same building where he had gone when he first arrived in Jerusalem, he said, "I have already met these people!" Joseph did not reply, but only opened the door for him.

The man at the desk had his head down when they approached, and it was apparent that he did not notice that someone stood in front of him. After Joseph coughed, the man behind the desk did not look up when he asked, "What do you want?"

"I would like an audience with the governor," Joseph requested.

"The governor is busy–" he started to say, but he stopped when he looked up and saw Joseph. "I will tell him that you are here!" The man exited quickly, and then came back quickly to his post without a word.

"Joseph!" said the Roman high official who had come from one of the adjacent rooms. They greeted each other with a friendly embrace, and talked of trivial matters for several minutes. "What matter is so important that it would take you from your money-making enterprises? Maybe I can settle this, thus we will not disturb the governor."

"I have just hired this man, Jeru, to complete the repairs to your home that I presently reside in." He explained how Jeru had discovered the errors of the previous workers and that he had hired him. "This job would have ended within the next six months, but it should only last four or five months with Jeru," Joseph bragged.

"Jeru?" the Roman said. "I have heard that name before!" "Record Bearer!" he shouted. Almost immediately, a man ran up to the governor. "Many months ago a request for carpenters had been sent out. Check the records and see if a Jeru from Jerusalem is on that list."

"Nazareth!" Jeru interrupted. "I am originally from Nazareth!"

The Roman officer changed his order to the soldier, "Check and see if a Jeru from Nazareth, had been requested to come work in Jerusalem!" he continued.

"I had been required to come to Jerusalem, and did so several months ago. I reported to this Office, but was turned away!" Jeru stated.

"Show me this man and I will have him punished!"

Jeru had recognized the man immediately when he had walked in the building. The scar on the man's right ear could be seen from across the room. The man at the desk did not remember Jeru. After the events had been retold by Jeru, directly in front of his post, the man suddenly remembered the Jew that he had thrown out several months earlier. Jeru pretended to look around the room and then said, "I do not see the man!"

The man's eyes had momentarily linked with Jeru's, and his eyes said, "Thank you."

The three men exchanged farewells. The Roman official said, "Joseph, if this man is as good as you say he is, I will have plenty of work for him to oversee in the months and years to come."

The man with the scarred ear approached the Roman official and whispered privately in his ear. "Great suggestion, I will do it immediately," the Roman official replied. "Here, take this seal. It is proof that you have reported to me. It will take time to check our records and see if a warrant had been issued. In the meantime use this as a symbol of my authority. They will release you without question," he said as he handed Jeru a medallion.

Before Jeru and Joseph got to the door, the man with the scarred ear approached them. "Thank you for your mercy! My name is Cleoiphous. Call on me if you ever need anything." As quickly as he had come up to them, he left.

After they exited the building, Jeru stressed the importance to Joseph that he had to leave, but promised that he would return first thing in the morning with enough workers to complete the job. The impending birth of his son's child was not the only reason that Jeru had to leave Joseph. Jeru had a meeting to attend, one that would change the lives of his whole family.

People with the same thoughts and likes tend to attract one another. It was made evident from the first Sabbath that Jeru had spent in Jerusalem that there were people present that had the same views as his. It had been on that day that he first met them, and these were the same men that he planned to meet today.

It had been very easy for Jeru to be accepted by these men that he had planned to meet this day. Even if all of them did not agree completely on all things, at least they had a common objective. Even in the history of Israel, many nations who had been mortal enemies, joined together to fight a common adversary. They each saw the danger that one man, the one called Jesus, meant to the nation of Israel.

Jeru arrived home a little later than normal. He could not hold in the news of his latest job. Martha was thrilled, but it did not surprise her that Jeru could get such a blessing as this. Martha did not have time to concern herself with such thoughts as to why he had come home so late. She had more pressing thoughts to concern herself with, as it had become more apparent to all that Elizabeth was about to deliver the child.

Since the time Elizabeth had witnessed the miracle at the pool Bethesda, she had lived in a state of peace that her husband's parents misinterpreted as insanity. Martha had always had a problem with worry. With the time of delivery approaching very quickly, Martha was in a state of hysteria. The waiting was testing her patience to its ultimate conclusion. Once Elizabeth stubbed her toe and said, "Ouch."

Martha jumped up and asked, "Is it . . . ?"

"No!" Elizabeth responded before Martha's question was completely asked.

The first birth pang caught her by surprise, and did not go unnoticed by Martha. The waiting was over; the travail of childbirth had just begun. A bright and joyous smile erupted on the face of the older woman. "It will be okay," Martha said.

Preparations were quickly put into place, and the birth stool was brought in. This was not the first such stool that Jeru had made, but it was the first to be used for his lineage. The stool was designed and cut at angles that allowed the forces that pulled objects to the ground to gently help the mother deliver the baby into the world. The stool had been completed for a long time, and with the project completed, so were Jeru's responsibilities for the birth. Due to the traditions of his people, Jeru could not show any concerns for this event, but he had his fears.

"I will greatly increase your pains in childbearing; with pain you will give birth to children," the God of their fathers had told Adam and Eve. Everyone in Israel understood that through Adam, did all sin come into the world. Since the fall of man, men had had to labor by the sweat of their brow and women labored the pain of childbirth.

The pain was no less for Elizabeth, but she worked valiantly to achieve the ultimate prize. The sound of the voice of her newborn child cleansed her memory of all the pain that she had just journeyed through.

"It is a male child!" Martha told her. Martha cleansed the male child, and then placed him on Elizabeth's chest. The child suckled gently and hungrily on the breast of the woman who bore him. Elizabeth smiled with joy because no one could call her barren again. Her joy was quickly replaced with apathy, with the remembrance of Salem.

The child was presented to Jeru for acceptance into the family. He looked down at the reddish-colored and wrinkle-skinned child. Jeru had heard of men that would not accept a child and the child would be cast out onto the rocks. As he looked into the face of the child of his deceased son, he wondered how anyone could cast a child away. The times and customs were not for weak men, and sometimes strong decisions were required. "We shall keep this child!" Jeru proclaimed.

A rejection of this child would have been a rejection of Elizabeth and her husband. The happiness that resulted from Jeru's decision caused brightness in Elizabeth and Martha to glow. The simple expression could not have been purchased with any amount of gold coins.

†

On the eighth day after the birth of Salem's son, the family walked briskly to the Temple. This was the day that the child was to be circumcised. "You know that it is our custom to give the child a name on the day he is circumcised!" Jeru said politely.

"But father, is it not the honor and responsibility of the head of the house to name the child?" she asked.

"The responsibility of announcing the name of a child is customarily bestowed to the father of that child, but in this case I will gladly accept and make the announcement. However, I wanted to make sure that you and Salem had not discussed names for your children in the earlier years of your marriage," Jeru answered her.

"It has been a long time since we have talked of such matters. I know I have had the last eight days to think of a name, but no name seems suitable. To call him BarSalem tears at my heart with the sound of the name, yet I want to honor Salem and my love for him!" Elizabeth confessed.

They entered the Temple in which the child was to have the cutting away of his foreskin, like his fathers before him, to set him apart from all other people. From that time forward he would be a Jew, a child of Abraham, a separate nation.

The screams from the child after the delicate procedure was performed sent chills down the backs of the men, for they knew it would have been painful for an adult male to endure such an operation. Elizabeth's tears flowed freely for the joy of the obedience of the law, and because her son was now officially one of many, a part of the children of Israel. The priest waited for Jeru to speak. Jeru stood and said, "We shall call him Matthew: A gift from God." Elizabeth was joyful with the name that Jeru had selected.

After the ceremony was complete, many of the women went over to congratulate Elizabeth on having such a fine boy. They did not act reserved as the people in Nazareth would have, for they did not know the secret that they kept hidden. "It has been a good thing to move here," Elizabeth told Martha.

It had not gone unnoticed by Elizabeth that many of the people that she had seen at the pool of Bethesda were in the Temple. During this ceremony, like all the others, the men and women were separated, but this did not hinder Elizabeth from keeping her eye on the men that she knew had murder in their minds. She tried not to look at them, but the urge, the temptation was too great. Several of the men talked with Jeru. These men and Jeru departed the Temple and went outside.

"Excuse me, Mother! Would you please watch Matthew while I go outside for a few minutes?" Elizabeth asked.

"Of course, my dear," she responded.

She tried to be sly as she followed them. She tried not to be seen. Several times she had to hide behind vendor booths or pretend to be looking at some of their merchandise. "If you're not going to buy something, get away from my store," one merchant had told her.

The group of conspirators entered what appeared to be a home. By the time she got next to the window to where she could hear what was being said, the discussion had already begun.

"Jeru, tell them what you heard him say," one of the men commanded.

None of the facts were omitted, save one. Jeru had been very thorough in the retelling of the events that had happened in Nazareth, except for the part where they could not throw the man, of whom they spoke, off the cliff.

"This man must be stopped," the same man who had spoken earlier demanded.

Anger grew in their voices as the name of this man was spoken. "How will we do this?" another man asked.

"Let the Romans deal with him!" another man suggested.

"I have the answer," Jeru proclaimed.

Just as Jeru began to reveal the details of his plan, Martha, who carried Matthew, grabbed Elizabeth by the collar of her garment and began to shake her. This commotion caused Matthew to awaken, and he began to scream as though he were the one who had received this scolding. "What are you doing here? Why are you listening in on someone else's conversation?"

The tumult outside the home caused the men to terminate their meeting and exit the room. Jeru was completely surprised when he saw both his wife, who was holding his grandson, and his daughter in a struggle.

"She was spying on you!" Martha stated. "I saw her follow you, so I followed her!"

"Martha, go on home. I will take care of this matter," Jeru stated. She did as she was told. When Martha was out of sight, Jeru grabbed Elizabeth by the hair and pulled her inside the house. The other men followed them inside. The frightened woman stood motionless in the center of the room. She never moved a muscle as Jeru circled her like a lion after its prey. The silence in the room was deafening. Jeru stopped his pacing directly behind her. He slowly moved his mouth close to her ear and whispered, "Do you know the penalty for what you have done?" The words he spoke were only whispered, but it disrupted the silence so suddenly that it caused Elizabeth to jump. "It is a good thing that you have a small child to care for or your punishment would have been greater. A cloth was placed over her mouth to muffle the sound of her screams.

When Elizabeth returned home, she did not even look at Martha when she entered the room. Elizabeth reached down and picked up Matthew. It was then that Martha saw the discolored areas of skin on Elizabeth's arm. She looked at Elizabeth more closely, and repented in her heart for having turned her in. Elizabeth walked toward the door as though she planned to leave.

"Wait!" Martha pleaded. "I am sorry. Please do not leave. I will help you get well, and then help you leave if you choose. Please do not leave. You must consider the life of your child. How will you care for him?"

Without a word, Elizabeth turned around and went to the chair that sat by the window. She offered Matthew the nourishment he needed, and he gladly received it. Martha went to her and asked, "Did they touch you?" Elizabeth did not answer her.

There were two reasons why Elizabeth did not answer her mother-in-law. One was because she knew that Martha should have known the

Jeff Frazier

answer to that question. It had only been eight days since she had given birth and no man who knew her would come to her, lest they become unclean. The second reason was because Elizabeth felt betrayed by the person she admired most. As she sat next to the window and nursed Matthew, she prayed that an opportunity would come that she could leave this household.

CHAPTER XII

One Year Later

The best that Mashic could calculate, it had been almost two years from the day that Jesus stood in the synagogue and proclaimed to the people of Nazareth who he was. Those two years held a lot of memories of the things he saw and heard, and many were considered precious to him. These same two years held much heartache as well. The self-imposed exile from his home, his friend of more than fifty years had become an enemy, and the son of his former friend sentenced to die a slow and agonizing death were just some of the heartaches that he endured. Leaving his wife behind so he could seek an answer to his questions was the one that disturbed him the most. The sad and rejected look on his Sara's face almost caused his heart to tear itself apart. "No more!" he cried. "After I deliver Salem this final message, my Sara and I will be together forever. I care not that they know that I believe that Jesus is the Messiah. They can throw me from a cliff if they so choose, but I am going home." His voice echoed off the walls of the canyon he passed through.

It still amazed Mashic of the many things he had been fortunate enough to have seen. He tried to catalog them in his mind as to which one was the most important to tell Salem. Was it the time Jesus walked on the water? Greater still was the time Jesus calmed the storm. "Who would believe such things?" Mashic thought. He desperately wanted to get to Salem and inform him of the things he had learned and what he had seen.

It had been a long time since Mashic had last seen his friend Salem, and it was most imperative that he see him soon. The months of travel away from his home and wife had taken their toll on his body, but yet he felt young and alive because of the joy in his soul. The words he

Jeff Frazier

had heard Jesus teach convicted him of his own sin, but also comforted him in the knowledge of God's love.

Mashic recalled the words that a man named Nicodemus had told him Jesus had said: "For God so loved the world that he gave his only begotten son, and who so ever believes in him will not perish, but have everlasting life."

Then Mashic also remembered that when he heard those words, a sinister voice whispered in his ear, "Not for you. You do not deserve anything but death for the sin that you have done!"

But he became glad when Nicodemus continued the words of Jesus, "For God did not send his son into the world to condemn the world, but through him the world might be saved." Mashic was glad that he had remembered that saying, because he was only a few miles from the place where Salem now resided.

As he walked up the trail of the unclean, Mashic said within himself, "The pungent odor is not as pronounced as before!" When he was able to see above the crest of the hill that for all practical purposes began the valley of the lepers, Mashic stopped and stared in amazement at what his old eyes beheld. "It is a miracle!" Mashic said. For the first time since he had begun coming to this place of death, he felt compelled to enter. Without thinking or even having concern for his own well being, Mashic stepped into the valley to which his friend was banished.

As he walked, he saw people working, planning for their lives. Most of the people worked so intently on their assignments that they were not even aware of this unauthorized person in their midst. Occasionally someone would notice that the person who walked in amongst them did not have the curse that they had and would shy away from him. They did not act like or appear to be lepers, until Mashic drew close to them, then they would revert back to the way that tradition said they should.

Salem was shocked when he saw that Mashic had entered the camp. Why would any man enter this death pit if he did not have to? A majority of the people who entered never left. Many never left for fear of persecution, many believed that they did not have an alternative, and many more died here. Due to the progress of time, and the curse of leprosy, Salem covered the parts of his flesh that displayed his ailment. He was extremely happy to see Mashic, but all he could ask was, "What are you doing here?"

"I have come to see you, my friend. I have more good news to share with you," the older man replied.

"I expected your soon return to this valley, but to have you actually walk into this tomb is a different matter!" Salem scolded Mashic. "Why jeopardize your own flesh?"

"This does not look like a tomb to me!" Mashic proclaimed, "Besides, neither of us will be here much longer!"

"What are you saying?" Salem asked.

"Jesus has entered Samaria again, and he is on his way to Jerusalem," Mashic proclaimed joyfully.

After the two men celebrated this good news, Salem escorted Mashic around the renovated community. "There was a lot of resistance at first to accept any new way of thinking. They acted as though they were dead because that was the way we all had been taught. Lepers were considered dead and had no hope. Once they saw the life in me, and I showed them the way to obtain life, the response was tremendous. Every man, woman, and child began to live life with all they had. The teaching that you shared with us has strengthened our faith and hope."

The structures were crudely constructed because of the lack of materials and proper tools, but it greatly surpassed their previous condition. "It appears that everyone has participated!" Mashic noticed.

"The weavers wove mats from the palm trees. The carpenters hewed out the boats for the fishermen. The fishermen caught the fish that have added the oils that are important to our diet. All the individual members exist as one. Each member is important for the well being of the whole body!" Salem proclaimed.

The two reunited friends ventured outside the confines of the valley to consume the morsels of food that Mashic had brought. Mashic was almost ashamed to present the offering, because it was so meager. "The quality of food that I have to offer is not as it once was!" Mashic said, as though he was repenting.

"You have nothing to be ashamed of! 'When I was naked you clothed me. When I was hungry, you fed me! When I was in prison you visited me!' Do you remember when you told me those words that Jesus had said?" Salem asked.

Jeff Frazier

"Yes!"

"'If you have done it unto the least of these, you have done it unto me.' I am the least of these." As Mashic wept, Salem reached into his pouch and retrieved a bundle of fresh corn. "This is an offering to you," said Salem. He told Mashic of how the Spirit of the Lord guided him to start the garden, and the building of their town. During the retelling of his story, Salem became keenly aware of the excitement that built up inside his spirit. For Salem, this was just a small taste of the joys of reliving an event. This was the first time that he fully understood why Mashic enjoyed the retelling of such adventures.

When Salem had concluded his version of what had happened in the valley, Mashic began to tell Salem what he had seen and heard. "The blind see, the deaf hear, and the lame walk," Mashic quoted what Jesus had told the disciples of John the Baptist.

Mashic talked well into the first hours of darkness. The joy of sharing the good news of Jesus had strengthened the older man, but even the joyous had to rest. The weariness of the walk and length of his talk seized Mashic all at once. "The look on those when . . ." Mashic said as he went fast asleep. Salem thought Mashic had forgotten what he was going to say, but realized Mashic was asleep when he began to snore.

The sounds of morning gently awoke Mashic, but then the realization of what time it was caused him to bolt upright. "What is it, Mashic?" Salem asked.

"What hour of the day is it?"

"The sun rose two hours ago."

"We have no time to waste!" Mashic shouted. "You must gather up your belongings and follow me!

"Why the sudden rush?"

"I told you that Jesus was coming this way, but I do not know exactly when. I hope we are not too late."

The fear of missing the only opportunity to be rid of this curse flooded his thoughts and Salem ran directly to the room that he had built for himself. He began to survey the items in his room that he had considered vital to his existence, but now with the possibility of leaving this place forever, he decided to only take a warm tunic to wrap up in at night.

"Where are you going?" Bedar asked.

"Jesus is coming through Samaria again!" Salem stated. The words had no more than crossed his lips than he felt sorrow in his heart for not thinking of his friend earlier. "I am sorry, my friend. I should have called you as soon as I found out. Mashic is waiting for me at the crest of the east ridge of the valley. Go quickly and get whatever you need to make the journey."

At first, Mashic was a little annoyed at having to wait for another person, because he knew that the time was short. Even Salem grew weary of waiting for the fellow leper, but he did not let his anxiety show. When they saw nine people walking over the hill, they understood why the delay had been so long. Neither Salem nor Mashic questioned Bedar as to why he had brought the other eight lepers, and Bedar did not offer an explanation. Anyone who might have seen this band of eleven men walking down the road would never have suspected their origins or their destinations.

With each step of every mile, Salem grew more anxious of the miracle that he hoped he would soon be a part of. He had heard of the wonderful things that Jesus had done, and now he might be a recipient of Jesus' power. For him it would be as though he had been raised from the dead. The laws concerning leprosy had been written very clearly, and he knew that his family had considered him dead. These thoughts troubled him now more than they ever had. Had Elizabeth found another man to take as her husband? Had all the possessions that were once called his, now been given over to someone else in a settlement? He tried desperately not to think of these things, but the harder he tried, the more persistent the questions returned.

After they had walked until about midday, Mashic said, "Everyone, please wait here." The band of men stopped at the sound of Mashic's voice. "I will venture to the top of that hill and try to get better a view. I am not sure of the exact route that Jesus will take, but I am sure we are close."

One of the men of the group walked away from the road and sat on the soft green grass on the hillside. Mashic stopped at the top of the hill and began to scan the horizon. He looked in all directions. When he faced the east, he paused as though he had spotted someone or something. It was evident to the ten men that Mashic had begun to shout to someone who was on the other side of the hill, but the group of ten could not hear what he had said.

The attack came swiftly and without a warning or provocation. The man that had suddenly appeared from the other side of the hill pounced on Mashic quickly and mercilessly. The group began to run to the aid of Mashic as fast as they could. The attacker on the hill saw the men coming, and increased the speed of his attack. The sun reflected off of something shiny in the attacker's hand, and Salem prayed that it was not what he thought it was. The hand that held the long knife went up into the air, and back down again. Salem was close enough to hear the sound of the metal as in penetrated through Mashic's woven garment and then through his flesh, but too far away to prevent it.

Salem was the first to reach the top of the hill, and the first to confront the thief who most surely would soon be a murderer. The attacker stood up and pointed the bloody knife at Salem. He started to move toward Salem in an aggressive gesture, until he saw that the would-be rescuer was a leper. The attacker stopped and then looked at Mashic. Salem also looked down at Mashic and said, "Murderer! You are a murderer!"

"I have killed no one, he was only a leper!" the man said.

"He was not a leper!" Salem shouted at the man.

"Then I will be able to keep this," the man said as he tossed a small bag of coins into the air and caught it again.

"No!" Salem screamed and lunged for the man he thought had just killed his best friend.

The man fell back onto the ground and kept the knife aimed toward Salem. With what little strength Mashic had, he grabbed the hem of Salem's robe as Salem stepped over him.

"No! Salem, let him be!"

"Mashic? You are still alive!" Salem said as he knelt down next to Mashic. The attacker seized this opportunity to make a hasty and effective escape.

Mashic took Salem's hand and held it tightly to his crimson, soaked chest. "Forgive me, my friend!"

"You have done nothing to be forgiven of."

"I have kept many secrets from you. I have kept many things

secret from many people," Mashic stalled, coughed and spit some blood out of his mouth.

"Do not talk! Save your strength!"

"What I need to tell you must be said, regardless of my fate. Where should I begin? I will tell you the good news first. Only after you were exiled from your home, was it made known that Elizabeth was with child!"

Salem quickly calculated in his mind at what age the child should be now, "My child should be almost a year old now. Do you know if I have a son or not?"

"I do not know," Mashic answered through a cough. "The reason that I did not tell you sooner was because it was their wish that you did not know! Now, I must warn you not to return to Nazareth."

"Why?"

"Your family no longer lives there!"

"Where have they gone?"

"I think they are living in Jerusalem," Mashic said as blood spat out his mouth. Mashic could see that Salem felt guilty about something. "What has troubled your heart?"

"I realized how you felt not to have a son. We were both the same. Neither one of our wives could bear us a child. Now I feel saddened that you have not ever known this great joy," Salem said.

It had not been hard for anyone who stood around the man whose life quickly faded away, to see that the tears that flooded Mashic's face were from sadness, not pain. Bedar ushered the other eight lepers away from Salem and Mashic.

Salem reached down and lifted Mashic up to a sitting position. His friend was dying, and there was nothing that he could do to help him. "Let us not waste these few precious moments on matters that will bring such great sorrow."

"There is one more thing that I must tell you. We both have a son!" Mashic said, and then coughed again.

"What . . ." was all that Salem could say. Then he asked, "Who?"

"His name is . . . (Cough) . . . Salem . . . (Cough) . . . raised in the household of Jeru!'

Salem became very weak and had to sit down. "You are my father?" Mashic nodded. "How? . . . When?"

"Nine months before the great caravan passed through Nazareth, I passed by the river while your mother bathed. I did not know she was there. I tried not to look, but my lust would not allow me to turn away. She noticed that I watched her. At first she shied away. We seemed to be drawn to one another, and then we committed the act that should have resulted in our deaths." Salem did not know what to say, so he said nothing. Mashic laboriously continued, "She conceived you that day. When Sara never conceived, I knew it was punishment for the sin of adultery. Then when you got leprosy, I cried out to God and said, 'Punish me, not them.'"

Salem felt a great wave of compassion come over him toward the man that he now knew to be his father. "I do not hold you responsible for my present state. I have my own sin that could have brought this plague upon me. There was pride, contentment, false idols, just to name a few!" Salem stated.

Mashic said, "I prayed daily that the Lord God would show me a sign that it was possible to be forgiven. Just before you were born, the great caravan came by. When I learned that they sought the birth of the king of the Jews, I hoped to find redemption. That is why I have sought after Jesus. Jesus is the Messiah. He is the lamb of God that takes away the sins of the world. I needed a savior and his name is Jesus! I regret that I had to tell you this very troublesome news. Please do not hate your mother! Do not let her know that you know. It will kill her!" He coughed a couple of more times then said, "Death is upon me. Goodbye, my son!"

Salem stated, "I am sorry, my friend," he paused, "Father, that I cannot guarantee you a burial according to our customs."

"Worry not yourself of such matters. There have been many things that I have learned in my life, and with the years that I followed Jesus, I have learned one very vital lesson. It is not how this body rests in the earth that is important. Our God told Adam, the father of all men, 'For out of dust thou were taken: for dust thou art, and unto dust thou shalt return.' It is not this body that is important, but the life that I lived. I have lived a life of faith to our Father in heaven." Mashic saw the puzzled look on Salem's face. "These words I heard the Messiah say to his disciples when they asked him to teach them to pray: 'Our Father which is in heaven. Holy is thy name, thy kingdom come, thy will be done on earth as it is in heaven. Give us this day our daily bread. And forgive us out debts, as we forgive our debtors. And lead us not into temptation, but deliver us from evil: for thine is the kingdom, and the power, and the glory forever.'" With the words of Jesus on his lips, the man who forsook all that he had in Nazareth, passed from life into eternity.

Even though Salem had never heard that message before, he said, "Amen." He gently laid the body of his father back onto the green grass. Salem then called the other nine men forward and then led them in the customary prayer of his people for those that had died. Without a word spoken, the ten men prepared the body of their Moses. To them, Mashic had delivered them from the bondage of Egypt. And like Moses, Mashic did not see the Promised Land. After the last rock was placed over the spot where Mashic slept, nine men wept for the friend they had lost, but Salem wept for his father.

"Which way shall we go?" one man asked.

Not knowing for sure of which way to go, "The Lord God almighty will lead us!" Salem had just become their Joshua. He pointed his walking cane to the east and the group of diseased men continued on with their quest.

†

A word had not been spoken for hours, and Bedar decided to comfort Salem. "Salem, what shall you do when we are released from this burden?"

"I will return to Nazareth!"

"But–" Bedar said before he was interrupted.

"I have not forgotten Mashic's warning. He had been a brother and a father to me when all else had forsaken me. I must return to Nazareth and seek out the wife of Mashic and tell her of what has become of him," Salem concluded his statement. With complete understanding, Bedar nodded his head and let the silence that had been broken return.

The band of troubled men stopped along the side of the road to rest. One of the more physically functional lepers walked up to the top of the hill. "There he is! I see Jesus." The nine remaining men did not need another proclamation from their fellow leper to make them speed up their walk to the top of the hill. When the men got to the top of the hill, the man who had originally spotted Jesus said, "There, to the north! Jesus is about to go into that village!"

They began to shout in one voice, "Jesus, Master, have mercy on us!"

When Jesus saw them, he shouted back to the lepers, "Go show yourselves to the priests." And immediately the ten lepers turned and started to walk in the direction of Jerusalem.

"Go show yourselves to the priests?" Salem questioned. "After all this waiting and the life that was lost, all he says is 'Go show yourselves to the priests.'" The thought had no more crossed his mind than he remembered what Mashic had once told him, "Had he asked any great thing of you?" Salem repented from his doubts.

As they walked, one of the men looked down at his hands and shouted, "I am clean. I have been made whole again." He wiggled his fingers as he said, "I have my fingers again! I am clean again!"

"So am I," another one shouted.

"Me too," a different man yelled.

They all began to examine one another and testify that they had been made whole. One of the men disrobed and made a desperate dash for a small lake that was nearby. It did not take long for the rest of the others to join him. They all knew that they had been cleansed from the infirmity, but the need to bathe overwhelmed them. The enjoyment of a bath thrilled all of them. "Clean! Clean! I am finally clean!" Salem said.

As they frolicked in the cool clean water, a young girl walked up to the edge of the water. "What are you nine men doing in my father's pond?" the young girl asked.

"Nine?" Salem thought to himself, as one of the other men explained to the woman why they were swimming in the pond. Salem looked around and he could not find Bedar. "Where is Bedar?" Salem asked the man next to him.

"I do not know!" was the answer the man gave.

"You get out of my father's pond or I will go get him, and then you will pay dearly for this trespass!" the young girl shouted.

"Go get your father!" the man next to Salem shouted.

The young girl stomped away in anger and said, "You better not be here when I get back with my father." After the girl had vanished into the tree line, the men jumped out of the water and retrieved their clothes.

At first, no one wanted to put the filthy rags back on, but when they heard someone coming, they quickly dressed themselves. "The first thing I want to do is to buy some new clothes," one of the men said.

The group of clean men started to walk in the direction of Jerusalem, except for Salem. "Are you coming with us?" one of the men asked.

"No, go on ahead. I want to find Bedar!" Salem responded. The remainder of the group continued on their journey to Jerusalem, but Salem went to find Bedar. "Where could he have gone?" he asked himself. He spent several hours looking, asking for Bedar, but he could not find him. Finally Salem realized that he had wasted precious time. He was in the land in which Bedar lived. Most people would not answer questions from a stranger who asked questions of one of their own. With the resolve that he could not locate Bedar, he turned and headed for Nazareth.

Nazareth was usually busy this time of the day, but silence fell on the streets when Salem stepped into the small town. In small towns usually every eye would turn toward a stranger. Salem was treated like a stranger. Not everyone who saw him realized who he was, but the ones that did cast a judgmental glare at him. They would even turn to the person next to them and whisper when Salem passed by. The ones that knew who he was knew him to be "unclean." They were not aware of the miraculous transformation that had been granted to the man who walked down their street. Most people who returned after a lengthy journey were greeted warmly, but Salem suspected that it would soon be getting hot.

As he passed a store or home, the people would make a frantic move away from him. Salem never looked back as he walked, and was not aware of the mob that had congregated behind him. Salem still did not look back, until he heard the murmuring of the people. When he heard the crowd behind him, he thought, "These people are true to the ways of their fathers! They are still murmuring like they did to Moses." The crowd hushed when Salem turned and began to walk down the street that he had once known as home. He could see the instruments of justice in their hands, but he did not show any fear.

Even before he got to the location where he remembered the shop was, he knew something was wrong. With each step, the revelation of the horrors that had occurred here, by the hand of the people whom he had once called brothers, became more evident. He stopped directly in front of what had once been the shop of Jeru and Salem.

The ashes still remained. The stench had long since vanished, but the scar of what had been done would never be covered. "Who did this?" Salem shouted. "Why did you do this to the innocent?"

He turned to face the people who had delivered this judgment on his family. Salem slowly scanned the crowd. His eyes moved from one person, to another, then another. When his eyes connected with someone, that person would look away.

"Why should we take this rebuke from a leper?" someone from the mob shouted.

With an unquenched wrath, Salem pointed at the man who had shouted at him and shouted back at him, "I know you, and yet I did not judge you! It is your own heart that accused you of this evil deed!"

"Stone the leper," another person said in an angry voice. The ones that did not already have a stone in their hand got one.

"No," cried the voice of an elderly woman. The woman stepped forward from the crowd, into the void that separated Salem from the mob. She walked slowly over to the condemned person. The garment that Salem wore almost tore as she pulled it away to expose his arms. "Do these look like the arms of a leper? They have more color than most of the people here." Her strength surprised Salem when she grabbed his hand and lifted it high into the air and shouted, "Are these the hands of a leper? No! They are whole, and they are strong! Tell these people who obey the law, how it is that you were made whole."

"Jesus healed me," Salem answered almost bashfully.

Again the crowd began to murmur and many whispered, "Jesus?"

"Yes! It was Jesus of this very same Nazareth. It was this same Jesus whom you tried to throw head long off the cliff two years ago. This same Jesus was the one who on his second visit to Nazareth a few months ago replied to your rebuke, 'We have not seen any great miracles,' with the words, 'This town has no faith.' It was this same Jesus who brought this man back from the dead. He was brought back from a place more horrible than death itself, an outcast, doomed to live in daily torment."

Many of those who had held stones in their hands released their grip on them. Small dust clouds erupted within the mass of people as each rock hit the dusty ground. Slowly, the outer perimeter of the crowd began to fade away, and soon there was no resemblance of any organized or unorganized mob.

"Sara," Salem said softly. "I could have defended myself."

"I was in the midst of the ungodly group of unbelievers, and I know that their way of thinking had long since passed the point of reasoning with you. I had to step in to save your life."

Salem thanked the wife of his friend as he brought her close to him. As he released her from this love embrace, their eyes met. "Mashic?" she asked. Slowly Salem closed his eyes and then reopened them. "When I saw that you were alone, I knew that my Mashic had died." He hugged her with a hug a man would have given to a mother that he had not seen for many years. "Come, we will go to my home where we can talk," Sara said as though it was a command rather than an offer. Sara stopped at the threshold of the door and held up a hand to stop Salem. He stopped, as she entered the house alone. She returned with a blanket. "Wrap yourself with this," she said as she tossed it as his feet. When Salem picked it up, Sara demanded, "After you have disrobed! You are not going to wear those rags in my house!"

After he had undressed, covered with the blanket and discarded the last remembrance of his exile into a heap by the side of the road, Sara brought a hot coal from the fire and placed it on the rotten rags. At first only smoke rose from the diseased cloth, but since the cloth was old and rotten, it quickly burst into flames. The flames lapped up the source of its life and then settled down to a slow methodical consumption of the remaining fuel. Soon, all that remained of the clothes that shouted the word to the world that the man who wore them was "unclean," was a disfigured moving mass of ash. A strong gust of wind picked up the fragments of ash and broke them up into smaller pieces as it carried them away.

Salem stood amazed at how quickly the rags had disintegrated. He took it as a favorable sign when he saw the wind remove the ashes of his judgment. "Come inside and bathe yourself. Then we will talk in great detail!"

After he had cleansed himself, he put on the clothes that Sara had set out for him. He examined himself and was amazed that the clothes fit perfectly. After Sara gave him a glass of wine, Salem began to tell her about Mashic's life and ultimately his death. Even though she did not grieve outwardly, he knew she was in torment. Salem abruptly quit speaking when he finished his rendition of the tragic death of her husband, and his friend. The way Salem suddenly ended his speech alerted Sara that he withheld some vital information.

"Is there anything else you need to tell me?" Sara asked.

He avoided the mere chance that their eyes should make contact. Was it just all the women that Salem knew, or was it that all women everywhere, that had the ability to see your deepest secrets by looking into your eyes? One thing Salem did not know, was that when men avoided eye contact after a question was asked, it only pointed to the truth.

"You do not have to burden yourself with the responsibility of telling me that Mashic was your father," Sara said bluntly. She did not have to look at Salem to know that his mouth was open as wide as his eyes.

"He told you?"

"No. He never wanted to hurt me."

"How long have you known?"

"I will save us both some time and answer as many questions as possible without you having to ask. Many, many years ago, I realized that his concern for you was greater than that of a friend of the family. He did not know that I knew. One time he slipped and I think he might have thought I knew, but he never brought it up," she said through her tears. "I still loved him even though he betrayed our oath. Mashic truly repented of his sins and never strayed again. His heart was after the things of God. My heart ached for him when he learned that you had leprosy. It was evident on his face that he felt responsible for the judgment that you received. I could not object when he wanted to bring you the news of Jesus. I did not want to come between a man and his only son."

Salem comforted her, as a son would comfort a mother when she discovered that she was now a widow. Later, Salem told her that he knew that Elizabeth had bore him a child. Then Salem asked, "Have you heard from my family? Have you any information to help me find them?"

After all these years of knowing this kind and gentle lady, Salem had never sat down and talked to her as he was doing this day. He had never realized that she had the same ability as Mashic to recall every detail of events as she had seen it happen. The fact that the details were true made it more grievous to accept. It horrified him at what lengths men would go to when they brought judgment against someone. He understood the initial response of the townspeople, but that should have waned after time proved that the rest of Salem's family was clean. Salem wept several times as Sara told him of what atrocities were cast unjustifiably on his family. He sank heavily onto the floor as she told him that no sooner had his family walked out of the town, than they brought torches to burn their shop and house.

Sara blew the lamp and said, "This day has brought great sorrow to me."

"For me also," he answered.

"That is the reason I want it to end with some good news! Elizabeth had sent word to me, by a messenger, that she has bore you a son!" She listened to the joyous excitement in his reaction, and she mourned silently.

The following morning Salem told Sara that he would take her to where Mashic had been buried, and that he would take her with him to Jerusalem. The offer to go to the grave of her husband was gladly accepted, but she did not give Salem an enthusiastic response about going to Jerusalem. It had not been hard to pack Sara's belongings, for they were very few. "What will you do with your home?" Salem asked.

"This building has not been my home since Mashic departed. I sold it after the last Passover, with the agreement that I could live here until I died, or moved away. They probably thought this old woman would be dead just a few days after the agreement was made, but I fooled them!" Salem laughed softly at the life that still glowed from this elderly, yet beautiful woman.

The nervousness that Salem felt grew more intense as they got closer to the place where Mashic was buried. He thought he had cleverly disguised his uneasy feelings, but knew he had only fooled himself when Sara asked, "What is troubling you?"

"Nothing!"

The breath that Sara let out of her mouth made a sound that let Salem know that she knew that he had lied to her. The look she gave him confirmed that she was suspicious of him. The closer they got to the burial site, the tenser Salem got. The pressure finally forced him to confess to Sara. "I have to tell you that Mashic was not buried in the customs of our people," Salem said as fast as he could.

"Was Mashic aware of the way his body would be buried?"

"Yes!"

"And he had no objections?" The words that Salem then spoke were those of Mashic. She delighted in hearing them. It was not his voice, but they were his words. With the quote complete, Sara commented, "Then neither do I." It relieved Salem to know that he had found favor in this woman's eyes. Now he regretted that he had not told her earlier.

They reverently approached the place in which Mashic slept. Without having to be asked, Salem moved away to allow Sara the time alone in her mourning. The crying he heard was only gentle weeping. He looked in her direction several times to make sure she was okay. She had spread her body over the rocks that covered her husband. She was in this same position several hours later, when Salem came to her. All at once, Salem understood why Sara had refused his offer of going to Jerusalem. Even though it was not their custom, Salem buried Sara next to Mashic, in like manner, as Mashic was buried.

As the last rock was placed on the grave of Sara, a voice from behind the tree cried out, "I heard you were looking for me!"

"Who are you?" Salem responded with a question. The man who had spoken from behind the tree stepped out so Salem could see him. "Bedar," Salem shouted as he ran to greet him. They embraced in a brotherly hug, and they exchanged customary kisses on each others cheeks. "Where have you been? While we bathed, I suddenly realized that you had not joined us?"

"I had more important things to do!"

"I could not find you!"

"Please forgive my fellow countrymen. You had only missed me by several steps that wonderful and glorious day. I have done business with the people of the village that Jesus had entered the day we were healed. The people of the village brought me into their homes when they became aware that I was healed of leprosy. They had seen you pass, and heard your questions. They knew that you were a Jew, and were afraid for me, and answered you not. If a stranger came into your town asking questions about you, would the townspeople answer that stranger's questions?"

At first Salem felt sorrowful that he thought that he now did not have a town to call his own, then he recovered from his momentary depression and said, "Your point is well taken!" Then he asked, "How did you know that I was here?"

"I paid for several boys to watch for a Jew coming from the direction of Nazareth, who might or might not be traveling with a woman great in her years. Just as I heard about you asking for me that day, I was informed that you had come back." He looked in the direction of the piles of rocks behind Salem. "I am sorry about your friend's wife. She must have loved Mashic dearly?"

Salem nodded and then asked, "Why did you leave so suddenly?"

"That, my friend, is an answer that must be revealed over a cooked meal and in comfortable surroundings. Come with me. My house is not but a half day's journey from here," Bedar told his friend. As they neared the house that had been built on the edge of the town, Bedar said, "Here is my home."

He smiled when Salem commented, "It is very quiet here." Salem had no more spoken the words when a roar of excitement burst from the small structure. The occupants of the home must have seen them coming and had been prepared for their arrival, because a jubilant festival began as they neared the home.

Several young ladies ran up to Salem with a large blanket and covered him. The girls began to giggle. Salem remembered when Sara had brought him a blanket to cover up with and he understood why the girls giggled. "I have taken a bath recently!" Salem demanded.

"You do not want to insult your host, do you? Remove those dirty clothes that you are wearing and I will have them washed for you."

Salem did not want to insult his friend and host, so he did as he

Jeff Frazier

was told. After the clothes were removed he realized how dirty they really were. Salem's face saddened as he gazed at the pile of dirt-packed clothes that he had cast off. He had worn dirty clothes before, but this was different. Unlike the dirt in the valley of the lepers, this dirt was a different color. It was the same color as the ground where Mashic and Sara had been laid to rest.

"Come over here, Salem," Bedar motioned. "Here is the bath that we have prepared for you." Salem was ushered to the caldron of hot clean water. After the crowd was moved away by the elder woman, Salem sank deep into the cleansing water of life.

Carrying a large cup of wine and a new tunic and robe, Bedar walked out to where Salem bathed. "Here, this will do your stomach some good, as the warm water works on the outside."

Salem graciously accepted the cup and drank a large gulp. He tried to stand, but the combination of the hot water and cool wine caused Salem to fall back into the water.

"Take your time. Rest your weary bones as I tell you what happened to me the day that we received our miracle." Bedar stood and began with the words of Jesus that Salem had also heard. "When the other nine men went to the pond to bathe, I decided, or rather I knew what I must do. I found Jesus in the village." He paused in his dissertation of the events. His eyes watered at the remembrance of what had happened that glorious day. "Do not be offended at what I tell you next . . ."

"Having been healed of the worst curse known to any man, I ran up to and fell down on my face at the feet of Jesus. 'Thank you, my lord. Thank you. Praise be unto the God of Israel. Thank you for showing your mercy on this unworthy Samaritan,' I cried."

"And Jesus answered unto me, 'Were there not ten who were cleansed? Where are the other nine? There are none found that returned to give glory to God, except this stranger.' And then he said unto me, 'Arise, go your way, your faith has made you whole.'

"After he told me to arise and go my way, I returned home."

"Why did he call you stranger?" Salem asked.

"I do not know?"

"I know why. Jesus has demonstrated that he knows the hearts of all men. You were a stranger to him because he had never met you before. Yet, Jesus knew that I was no stranger to him, for we were both from Nazareth. Jesus knew that I was one of the other nine! Salem stood up in the water and grabbed the robe that Bedar had given to him. "What a fool I have been! I must find Jesus and tell him that I, too, am thankful."

"You can begin your quest in a couple of days. First you must finish your bath, get some rest and regain your strength," Bedar told him. Salem sank back down into the comfort of the warm water.

After Salem finished his bath, he entered the main room of the house. Salem noticed that the large feast that had already started just rose in its intensity. "Come, my friend," Bedar said as he stood up. "This is for you!" They ate and drank until late in the day, and the merriment could not be contained within the confines of the house. The joyous festivities flowed out into the streets of Sychar.

"This feast sure has lasted a long time!" Salem proclaimed.

"This feast started when I returned home, and was only rekindled with the news of your arrival," Bedar replied.

"I did not know that your success as a merchant was so great," Salem commented about his observations.

"I, like you, was considered dead. All of my belongings were granted to my heirs. Praise the God of Israel that they have done very well. They brought me back into my family, and established me as the head of the household, as though I had never left." The sons of whom he spoke smiled brilliantly at the words of their father's praise.

The younger children danced to the music that the older children made. Sadness filled Salem's heart when he remembered that he had a son, a son that he had not seen. Bedar noticed the weariness in Salem's eyes and face. He clapped his hands together and made a circular motion with them immediately after. Salem had never seen obedience as quick as this as when everyone left the room without a moments hesitation. "It is time we talked! You yearn for your own family, do you not?"

Salem nodded and said, "Having seen your family, and the great works of your sons, the desire to see my son has increased! The longing in my heart to see his face is causing me pains! I must go to Jerusalem and find my family!"

"That is a good thing. While we are in Jerusalem looking for your family, we might cross paths with Jesus, and you can tell him of your thankfulness."

"I do not understand. You made your comment as though you had all the intentions of going with me!"

Laughing while he talked, Bedar said, "And he has understanding as well as good hearing! I cannot let you make this journey alone. You admitted to me while we were in the valley of the lepers that you did not make very many of the religious trips to Jerusalem. Did you not tell me this? I have connections in Jerusalem both with the Roman Authorities and with some wealthy merchants. I will tell my family that I am going to conduct some business in Jerusalem."

"Will your business suffer with your absence?" Salem asked.

"Oh, my no. My sons run the business anyway. They have actually done better without me. Being the head of the household is only a title. Come now, let's get some sleep."

†

Bedar's sons had generously provided the two friends with ample supplies to travel to Jerusalem. Bedar went over to the tree where a young colt was tied. He loosened the ties and brought the colt over by the two asses that Salem and he were intending to ride.

Salem had been accepted by Bedar's family as one of their own, and the children played with him. Salem accepted their hospitality, and joined in the children's games. The younger children wanted to keep playing even up to the moment that Salem and Bedar had planned to leave. Caught up in the joyous atmosphere, Salem picked up the smallest child and was about to put him on the young colt.

"No!" Bedar shouted. Salem put the child back on the ground, and was confused at the sternness in his friend's voice. "Forgive me for shouting at you, but this colt has never been ridden. The child could have been injured."

"I do not mean to question your motives, but why bring an animal that will serve no purpose?" Salem asked.

"We are like these dumb animals to our God. We need to be looked after or we will hurt ourselves. Even when we are young and untrained, there is purpose for us in God's plan. Like this colt, we must be led on a rope to a destination that we know not, to accomplish an unknown mission."

"You are quite a philosopher."

"That was just something my father's father told me many years ago.

"Then why bring it?"

"We are like these dumb animals to our God—"

Salem interrupted him as he smiled and said, "Okay, I get the message," and walked away.

After their journey to Jerusalem finally began, Salem asked, "Do you think I will be able to find my family?"

"If they are in Jerusalem, we shall find them! It is a wonderful thing the way our God of Abraham works amongst his people. If it had not been for Mashic's death you would have never returned to Sychar, and I would have never told you the words of Jesus. Had it not been for the need of carpenters in Jerusalem, your family would not be there as well. There must be a great purpose for all of these events to happen at the same time. I praise his holy name that I can be a witness of such things."

"Has your family accepted your faith in Jesus as the Messiah?" Salem asked.

"Many in my family had never believed, but the ones that had, still remained true to their confession. However, many things have changed in Samaria since the first visit by Jesus to Samaria two years ago. There has been a seed of dissention planted in the hearts of our people. Many religious people have talked with evil words against Jesus. They have spread lies to change the hearts of many."

Salem shivered at the remembrance of his father's own hatred of Jesus. "I know of such hatred, and close to my own heart!" S i l e n c e crept over them like a dark and menacing cloud. They said not a word for the next several miles of their journey.

CHAPTER XIII

Death had become a very familiar entity to Elizabeth. The more death presented itself to her, the more she accepted it. The thoughts of death no longer threatened or scared her. Even though she feared it not, she did not seek it. She had once been so full of life, but with the exile of her beloved, she entertained it daily. It has always been there, but until her Salem left, she had never met that vile creature.

Elizabeth shook her head to clear her mind of such depressing thoughts. From the time of Salem's announcement of leprosy, she had lived in a valley of darkness. Her only purpose in life was to ensure that Salem's child would be healthy and live with dignity and honor. She had doubts of her ability to accomplish the goals that she had set for herself until she saw Jesus heal that man at the pool of Bethesda. This man called Jesus displayed a sincere hope for life. This revelation had changed her.

She scolded herself again because she had allowed her mind to fester over such depressing matters, but then once again slipped back into the same low mental state when she remembered the reason for her going to Bethany. Lazarus, the brother of Martha and Mary, had died four days ago and the two sisters of Lazarus were still in mourning. A lot of Jews spent time with them, but failed to comfort them.

As she walked the two miles from Jerusalem to Bethany, she remembered the first time she met Martha in the market. Matthew was only a few months old and many people would come up to her and compliment her for having such a beautiful baby. Martha had been one such person.

Most of Elizabeth and Martha's conversations centered on Jesus. Except for the hatred that Jeru had expressed, and of the miracle that she actually witnessed, Elizabeth knew little of Jesus. She had not grown up in Nazareth like Salem had. She had been raised in Jericho and the thought of moving to the small, insignificant town of Nazareth did not appeal to her. She was but a child when her marriage to Salem had been arranged. The love that had grown over the many years of their life together did not start out so smoothly, but it quickly grew.

At first Martha did not talk about Jesus, until Elizabeth revealed her innermost feelings concerning the man called Jesus. Elizabeth laughed openly at the remembrance of the first story Martha had told her:

†

"Jesus came to visit us one day," Martha said. She continued, "I was always the type of person who would be up working. It was no different this day. I was cleaning and preparing a meal for Jesus and the men that followed him. Many times as I would pass the door, I would see that my sister Mary just sat at his feet and listened as Jesus taught. Finally, my temper could not be controlled, so I burst into the room and said 'Lord, don't you care that my sister has left me to serve alone? Tell her that she should help me!'"

"What did he say?" Elizabeth asked.

"Martha, Martha, you are concerned and troubled about many things, but one thing is needful. Mary has chosen that good part, which shall not be taken away from her," Martha quoted Jesus.

†

The wails and cries could be heard coming from the house of Martha and Mary. Elizabeth wished that she had left Matthew in Jerusalem, but he was her responsibility, no matter what. Matthew woke up when they got to Bethany and Elizabeth had hoped that he would not disturb the sisters in their time of mourning.

Just as Elizabeth stepped onto the street that led to the house of Martha and Mary, she saw a man enter their house. The man had no more entered the house, than a woman exited and walked in the opposite direction from which Elizabeth approached. When Elizabeth got to the door, it opened, and she saw the man who had just entered.

"Excuse me, but I am on my way out!" the man stated.

"Please forgive me," she said as she moved to one side to allow the man to pass. The man walked past her, and then she said, "Wait!" The man stopped and patiently looked back at her. "I have come to express to Martha and Mary my sympathies at the loss of their brother, Lazarus." The man acknowledged her concern with a slight nod of his head. "I saw one of them leave a moment ago, but I could not tell who it was, is the other sister in?"

"Martha just left, but Mary is still here," the man replied.

"Can you tell me where Martha has gone?" she asked.

"Martha and Mary had sent for Jesus to come to Bethany when Lazarus first got sick. They waited, but Jesus did not arrive. We were told that Jesus was coming and she has gone out to meet him," the man explained.

"Thank you!" Elizabeth stated, and then entered the home.

The degree of mourning had not diminished from the moment of Lazarus' death. The sisters truly loved their brother. Murmurs spread through the congregation in the house.

"Had not these sisters sent a message unto Jesus saying, 'Lord, behold he whom you dearly love is sick'?" Elizabeth overheard one man say.

"Then why did he tarry?" the woman asked. "I truly think they mourn because they believe that Jesus could have healed their brother, but did not show up on purpose."

Piece by piece, Elizabeth began to put the puzzle together. These women were equally as hurt from the loss of their brother as they were from the fact that Jesus did not come heal him. Just when Elizabeth thought she had all the answers to this troubling scenario, Martha entered the home and went straight to Mary. Martha discreetly went over to Mary and whispered something to her. Elizabeth could not hear what was said. Mary rose up hastily and went outside with Martha. It became apparent that Elizabeth was not the only person who had noticed what was going on because everyone began to follow after Mary.

"She is going unto the grave to weep there!" someone said.

Having a small child to deal with can hinder many of the personal decisions a mother might make. Following after the crowd to the grave of Lazarus was what Elizabeth wanted to do, but Matthew's insistence on getting some nourishment halted that. When Matthew was finished, she forgot what the man at the door had told her. She went directly to the last place that she heard mentioned, where Lazarus' body had been laid. When she saw no one at the tomb of Lazarus, Elizabeth said quietly, "Surely they would not have left so soon!"

She was about to turn away and return home when she heard the crowd coming. In the midst of the crowd, she could see Martha, Mary, and a man who was not with them earlier. "Jesus! It is Jesus! They went to meet Jesus!" Elizabeth said excitedly to Matthew. "We better get down there!" she said. The crowd arrived at the tomb just as Elizabeth walked up.

"Take away the stone!" Jesus said.

Martha said unto him, "Lord, by this time he stinks, for he has been dead four days!"

Jesus answered her and said, "Did I not say unto you, that if you would believe, you should see the glory of God?"

The men rolled away the stone from the tomb. The sound of the rock scraping against rock sent shivers down the spine of most of the women, and men. Several people began to back away in case a very strong and pungent odor came from the tomb.

Jesus lifted up his eyes and said, "Father, I thank you that you have heard me. I know that you always hear me, but because of the people which stand around me, I said it, that they may believe that you have sent me." After he finished his prayer, Jesus cried with a loud voice, "Lazarus, come forth!"

The silence that fell over the crowd was as though everyone there had died. Every eye was cast in the direction of the tomb's entrance. No one could have expected the silence to intensify, but it did when the grave cloth-wrapped Lazarus appeared at the tomb's exit. The hole in the tomb from the beginning of time had always been an entrance only, for those who had been carried in, but not on this day. At this time, at the command of Jesus, it became an exit. The man who was dead came forth, bound hand and foot with grave cloths. His face was bound with a napkin. Jesus said unto them that stood about, "Loose him, and let him go."

Many of the people who came with Mary and had seen these things which Jesus did believed in him. Not since the time when Elizabeth realized that she had conceived and when Salem was with her, was she ever this happy. She was happy for Martha and for Mary. She was happy for Lazarus, but she was the happiest for herself. For on this day, she believed that Jesus was the Messiah, sent from God.

Everyone was excited and praised God. Everyone was excited except for several men at the far edge of the crowd. They had joined the crowd somewhere between Bethany and the tomb of Lazarus. They gave each other a quick glance and departed the area. Having taken precautions to cover his face, Jeru made sure that Elizabeth did not see him in the midst of the crowd.

Jeru and the other men went their way from Bethany. They were on their way back to where the Pharisees were. With each step that Jeru took, the anger within him increased. Hatred had not always been a part of him, but like an unattended sore, it festered and became worse. The events that played themselves out in Jeru's life caused him to choose the bitter road. He had a choice, and he chose bitterness. Hatred and rage so filled Jeru, the men that walked with him noticed that his face was contorted.

"Jeru, are you feeling okay?" one of them asked. He only responded with a snort, and no one else dared to ask him any more questions.

CHAPTER XIV

This being the first day of the week, meant it was six days before the Passover. Jesus went to the house of Lazarus. Elizabeth had never sat in a room with a man that had once been dead, but now lived. She laughed at herself at that thought, because there are not that many people, if any, who could also say they ate with a man who had once been dead. They had made a big supper for Jesus and his disciples. Elizabeth had to laugh again silently when she noticed that Martha, as usual, served the meal.

Then Mary, unprompted by anyone, took a pound of a very costly spice called spikenard, and anointed the feet of Jesus. Elizabeth noticed that one man gave Mary a disapproving look and then he came near to faintness when Mary wiped the feet of Jesus with her hair. The fact that the same man protested and said, "Why was this ointment not sold for three hundred pence and the money given to the poor?" did not surprise her.

"Who is that man?" Elizabeth asked of Martha.

"Which man?" Martha asked.

"The man with the money bag," Elizabeth emphasized.

"That is Judas, Judas Iscariot, the son of Simon," Martha answered and continued to serve.

Then Jesus said, "Let her alone. She has kept this unto the day of my burial. For the poor you will always have with you, but me you will not always have."

The following morning Jesus departed the house of Lazarus to enter into Jerusalem and the crowd followed after them. When Jesus neared the Mount of Olives, he told two of his disciples to journey over to a certain village. He told them that a colt would be tied up and to bring it back to him.

They asked, "What if the owner refuses?"

"Tell them the Lord has need of it!" he answered.

†

Jeff Frazier

Salem and Bedar were glad to see the village that was just outside of Jerusalem. They knew that when they came to this village, they were very near to their destination. Bedar made arrangements with a local farmer for them to make camp and for a place to tie up the colt. Salem secured the colt and began to prepare their camp.

It had gone unspoken, but Salem would be very happy to be rid of this young wild animal. This creature had caused several days delay in their trip. It would not bother Salem if he never saw this animal again.

They asked the owner of the pasture if he knew of Jesus of Nazareth. They laughed at the man's response of who has not heard of Jesus. The man also told them that he had seen Jesus leave Jerusalem not too many days prior. The land owner said that Jesus might have gone to Jericho, but he was not sure. This news upset Salem to the point of distress. Bedar and Salem decided to break bread and dine near a fig tree. As they sat in the shade, Bedar became aware of Salem's discomfort. "Do not let these things hinder your faith, but let it be an obstacle for our God to overcome," Bedar encouraged his friend. "Do you want to search for your family first or continue on your original quest?"

The struggle in Salem's mind was evident to Bedar. Then a peaceful look came upon Salem's face as he said, "I must find Jesus first, then I will locate my family!

Salem shouted the word, "Stop!" so loud and expectantly that it almost caused Bedar to drop his meal. Before Bedar was even aware of what was happening, Salem had already jumped up and began to run toward the place where the colt had been tied up.

As Bedar ran after Salem, he could see two men as they untied the colt from the post that it was secured to. He arrived at Salem's side just as he heard Salem ask, "Why are you taking this colt?" One of the men said, "The Lord has need of it!" From that point, neither Bedar nor Salem protested the action of these men.

"Why do you let your feet remain fastened in one place?" Bedar asked. Salem was only able to give his companion a bewildered look instead of an answer. "The Lord that they speak of is Jesus. If we follow them we can find Jesus." They quickly gathered up their belongings and set a course in the same direction as the men who were doing the work of God.

As they walked away, Bedar quoted what he himself had said at the beginning of this trip, "We are like these dumb animals to our God. We need to be looked after or we will hurt ourselves. Even when we are young and untrained, there is purpose for us in God's plan. Like this colt, we must be led on a rope to a destination that we know not, to accomplish an unknown mission." Salem did not respond to this gentle, yet truthful reminder.

The two men took the colt over to Jesus. They placed their cloaks on the back of the young colt and Jesus set himself on the back of the colt. A large crowd had already gathered around Jesus by the time they got to where Jesus was. "Calm yourself, Salem. If it is God's will, you will be given an opportunity to give your thanks!" The crowd began to move toward the East Gate of the city.

Even with Matthew in her arms, Elizabeth joined in with the crowd and pulled down palm branches as Jesus came down the street as he rode a young colt. The branches were spread over the street for the colt to walk upon. With one great voice the people began to cry, "Blessed be the King that cometh in the name of the Lord; peace in heaven, and glory in the highest." All that were there to see Jesus praised and rejoiced in the name of the Lord for the mighty works that they had seen Jesus do.

There were those who had a watchful eye cast toward Jesus. They waited for the opportunity to accuse him of some wrongdoings. The Pharisees that walked amongst the multitude cried out, "Master, rebuke your disciples."

Jesus answered, "I tell you that, if these should hold their peace, the stones would immediately cry out." When Jesus came near the city and beheld it, he wept.

The mass of people continued to follow after Jesus. Even more people joined the parade as they ventured further into the city. Some of them just wanted to see what was going on, while others were captivated by the excitement of the time. With the Passover feast nigh unto them, the excitement level had already been high, but now the intensity increased significantly. When the crowd came within several blocks of the Temple, Elizabeth realized that it was time for her to go home. She made a hasty exit down the next street she came to.

Salem and Bedar's progress through the mass of people was hampered by the numbers that increased. As they passed a certain street, Salem shouted above the noise of the crowd, "I wonder when I will be able to speak to Jesus?" He thought that his loud voice had fallen on deaf ears, because Bedar only shrugged his shoulders.

The words he shouted shot from the crowd, traveled down the nearly empty side street and echoed off the brick walls. The sound of his voice entered softly in the ear of Elizabeth. At first she thought that a child had whispered from one of the many entrances that led into a home or shop along the street. That voice sounded very familiar to her. When she realized who had spoken those words, she spun around to face the direction from which she thought the voice had come. Elizabeth noticed that only a few people were on the street now from where she had just come from. Her eyes darted from one person to another, but she did not recognize any of them. The bottoms of her shoes clapped loudly on the stone road as she ran back to where she had left the crowd of people. Again she looked from one person to another, but still there was no one that matched the face she looked for.

"Could it really have been him? Could it have been Salem?" she finally whispered in a low voice. "How could he have come back from the place he has gone?" Elizabeth questioned herself. The question had no more than entered her mind and she remembered Lazarus. "Jesus could have brought him back from the dead!" she said excitedly to Matthew. When she remembered where she was headed, she said to her young son, "If Salem is indeed healed, let us give thanks unto our God, but let us pray that he is not in Jerusalem!"

It surprised both of the men how fast this large mass of people moved through the streets of Jerusalem. These men with a specific goal flowed along with the crowd as though they were just caught up by the joyousness of the event. It had always amazed Salem how many people could get in the Temple. As large as this building of worship was, it had its limits, and that is why a large crowd remained on the steps. Jesus taught the people into the evening, and when he concluded his teachings, he departed unto Bethany.

The two strangers to Jerusalem followed in the distance behind Jesus and his disciples. Salem knew that Bedar was tired and he waited for him. They lost sight of the group that followed when Jesus passed through the gate of the wall that encompassed the city. As they walked back to where they were to camp, Bedar said, "I should have called on my friend this night, but it is late. Besides, we need to be where we can see Jesus in the morning."

"Sleeping in the open is not a problem for me," Salem commented. They both laughed at that statement. In the previous two years, neither man had slept in a comfortable bed inside a warm house.

†

The sound of the animals as they began to stir aroused both of them before the sun had even shone the first light of day. They cleansed themselves and packed their bundles. Even before Jesus had reached the place that Bedar and Salem had camped, a large congregation of people had already gathered around him. Like the day before, Jesus went to the Temple.

They had decided to wait until the majority of the crowd passed by before they joined the procession. As they walked along the way, someone in the crowd asked, "Why did Jesus curse that fig tree by the side of the road?"

Salem was not sure who it was, but he thought it was one of Jesus' disciples who answered, "Because it did not have any fruit!"

Just as Bedar and Salem reached the first step that lead up to the Temple, the whole congregation halted abruptly. "What is happening?" Salem asked.

"There appears to be some trouble in the Temple!" the man in front of Salem replied.

The sound of tables being overturned and metallic sound of the coins that rolled on the floor could be heard. Animal noises quickly added to the confusion. From deep within the tumult, the voice of Jesus could be heard.

"It is written, My house shall be called a house of prayer, but you have made it a den of thieves!" Jesus shouted with authority. The crowd quickly parted as the guilty persons exited the sacred building. Salem remembered that Mashic had told him that Jesus had done this once before. When were these corrupt vendors going to learn not to peddle unjustly in the house of God?

Jesus began to teach the people in the Temple the things of God. Salem slowly edged his way closer to where Jesus sat. The teachings so captivated the mind and spirit of Salem that he almost forgot the reason that he was there. He found a place to rest and listen. The words that

Mashic had brought to him during his time of exile were as cups of fresh water in the desert. To hear the words from Jesus was like having a river of living water brought to him. The words that Mashic had delivered unto him gave to him the taste for life. But the words he heard now were life itself. It was a wonderful thing to meet the Master and to hear the words from God.

As Jesus finished his teaching, Salem decided that this would be a good time to give thanks unto God for what the Lord had done for him. Just as Salem stood up, the sick people in the crowd began to move forward like a flood of rushing waters. At first Salem felt indignation toward them, until he saw the desperation in their faces. These people needed hope, and the hope was before them, the same hope that he at one time needed and sought after.

In the midst of the onslaught of the sick and lame, Salem saw that a blind man was being moved by the tide of other sick people moving toward Jesus. The helpless blind man could not guide his own steps, and was tossed about like a ship without a sail in torrential seas. The push to the front of the Temple caused the blind man to stumble. Salem caught the man before he fell heavily onto the floor. "Thank you!" the man said very graciously. "You are very kind!"

Salem acknowledged the man's thankfulness, and set him in the direction that he would receive him. When Salem looked over at Bedar, Bedar had the largest grin that Salem had ever seen on any man's face.

Bedar said, "It appears that Jesus will be busy for some time now. Come; let us go meet a friend of mine. He will help you find your family, of this I am certain."

Salem said, "I must speak with Jesus!"

"The Passover is approaching, and that is why he is here. You should have several opportunities to speak with him," Bedar replied.

As they walked out the front door of the Temple, Salem asked, "How will we know where he is?"

"For a man who is smart, talented, and needful, sometimes I wonder if you use the mind the Lord God Jehovah gave you," Bedar said laughingly. "Just look for the crowds and you will find Jesus." They departed the Temple and ventured into a section of Jerusalem that they had not been to earlier.

Just moments after Salem and Bedar had left, several men set foot on the steps of the Temple. Just a few steps separated Jeru, his lawyer companion and Salem and Bedar. Jeru had seen the two men leave the Temple, but they did not cause Jeru to bring any attention to them. His mind was on other important matters.

"Jeru, we have selected several men who have shown themselves to be of high standard. The time has come for you to prove yourself before the high priests that you are opposed to Jesus and his teaching," the lawyer stated.

"Why not arrest him right now? He is in the Temple as we speak!" Jeru stated.

"We could not afford to bring attention upon ourselves at this moment. A public riot would cause unnecessary pain and suffering to many innocent people, and bring a quick and dreadful response from the Roman Government. There are also many among us who secretly believe in Jesus of Nazareth, but have not revealed their faith in Jesus publicly for fear of scrutiny, and of being put out of the synagogue," the lawyer answered.

"What is it that you require of me?" Jeru asked.

"He has always taught for several days in whatever city he was in, so we know that he will return. We need a person who is not, should I say, that is not in a position of authority that could mix in amongst the people and ask him questions that would entrap him. We need you to monitor his movements around and in the Temple. Let us know when Jesus is coming to the Temple."

Jeru acknowledged his task as they walked up the last few steps. They stopped when the crowd began to exit the Temple. Jesus passed through the mass of people and went down the street from which he had entered. As Jesus and the crowd passed by the two conspirators on the steps, two of Jesus' disciples were overheard saying that Jesus and the disciples were going out to Bethany. Jeru returned home and watched the street that led to Bethany and waited for the return of Jesus.

†

The knock on the door was answered by a young girl, who by her clothing appeared to be a servant rather than a family member. "The master of the house is busy at this moment. Please forgive any inconvenience," she said as though she had the words memorized rather than knowing exactly what it was she said. The accent to her words revealed that the girl was from a different country.

"I am Bedar from Sychar," Bedar announced as though he were Caesar himself, "and this is Salem, my partner."

"Wait here," was all she said, and then she closed the door. The huge door looked monstrous compared to the small girl, who seemed to have no trouble closing it. Most doors that size hung heavily and required special levers and braces to be moved so effortlessly, but this door seemed to be perfectly balanced, despite the very intricate designs on its face. Salem studied the craftsmanship on the door when he suddenly found himself looking directly into the face of an old, white-bearded nobleman.

"Bedar, my old friend," Joseph said joyously. The bearded old man moved past Salem with such speed that it almost caused Salem to fall over. The reunited friends grasped each other with such fervor that anyone, besides Salem, who watched, would have thought that the two men were in a physical struggle. They exchanged salutations and Joseph escorted both men inside his home.

They talked for hours about the days of old and of the many pranks that they had pulled when they were younger. Joseph had a large meal prepared for his guests and they dined in a leisurely atmosphere. After they had eaten a very delicious and fulfilling meal, Joseph asked, "I had heard that a terrible thing had come upon you about two years ago. Are the rumors true?" That question changed the mood of their reunion.

With a serious and less jovial mood, Bedar answered, "They were!" The look on Joseph's face did not show fear, but confusion. The expression on his face simply implied for Bedar to explain further. Bedar started his reiteration of his life as an outcast from the day that he discovered the leprosy up to the day that Salem entered the valley of the doomed. "My friend can tell you the rest of what took place," he said as he turned to look at Salem.

Salem, who had sat silent for most of night, was suddenly hurled to the center of attention. The sudden shift of attention to him caught him unprepared. "I do not know where to begin," he said as though each word were a stumbling block. He quietly stood up and paced in a circle as he gathered his thoughts. "I cannot continue at the point that you have paused at in this incredible story. I must begin in Nazareth,"

Salem stated. He talked about his family, his wife, his mother, his father, and of Mashic. Salem spoke of Jesus' return to Nazareth and of the night the hot ember fell on his hand. Despair emanated from his voice as he relived the night that he departed from his family and home.

The more Salem spoke, the more Joseph and Bedar held back their tears. Bedar had heard this sad tale before, but hearing it anew quickened his emotions to the point of melancholy. Bedar knew all too well of the horrors of living as a leper. The gloom was lifted from the room like fog dissipated by the heat of the sun, when Salem told of how the words of Jesus were brought to him by his friend, Mashic. Salem then told of his conversion. The thought had never occurred to Salem that Joseph might not be a believer until it was already out of his mouth. Salem stopped in his story to try and get a feel of how Joseph had related to his conversion. Joseph never responded to the good news that he had just been told, but something in Joseph's eyes told Salem that there would be no harm if he continued with his recitation of events. By faith, and sheer excitement of what had happened to him, Salem told all that he believed in Jesus.

The telling of events went back and forth, from Salem to Bedar, as they retold the events that both of them shared. It had become a game to them of who could tell the most of the details. Neither man purposely interrupted the other, but they would seize an opportunity if the other person faltered or stumbled during their turn to speak. Joseph had caught on to this even before the two tellers of these stories were aware of what was happening.

The scene turned somber again as Salem told of the death of Mashic, but was lifted up when they told of their healing. To demonstrate the actions they had done that day and the desire to be rid of the filthy rags that they wore, Salem almost disrobed during his reenactment of that glorious occasion.

Bedar expounded on the details of how he had gone back and thanked Jesus, while Salem sat quietly on a beautifully embroidered pillow. "And that is why we are here! Salem wants to give thanks to Jesus!" Bedar explained.

"I need to find my family as well!" Salem interjected.

"I see. I have many connections in this town and I think I will be able to help you!" Joseph proclaimed. "But it is very late and we must get our rest!" He clapped his hands together and almost immediately a servant appeared. "Arrange for some sleeping accommodations for my guests."

"They have already been prepared!" the servant stated.

"Good! Show my friends to their sleeping quarters!" Joseph ordered. Just as the procession reached the door, Joseph called out, "Bedar! May I see you for a moment in private?" Salem followed the servant down the elegant hall of this warm and friendly home.

Joseph sat down and patted the cushion next to his, to imply to Bedar that he wanted him to sit close by. When Bedar sat down, Joseph stated, "I already know where your friend's family is and what has become of them. As your friend told me of his life, I was able to deduce who his family was. I will make a valid attempt to find them, but–"

"If you already know who they are it should be easy to find them!" Bedar proclaimed.

"You do not understand. It is very imperative that he does not find his family, or at least delay it as long as possible," Joseph stated. He explained to Bedar the circumstances behind his reasoning. Joseph concluded his statement to Bedar with, "It was Salem's father, Jeru that I hired to do the repairs on my home. I was amazed that Salem did not recognize his father's style of craftsmanship on the front door."

"That was the reason he studied the door so closely when we first came to your home," Bedar said retrospectively. Then Bedar agreed to help in the hindrance of Salem's quest.

It had been a long and exhausting day, yet Bedar could not fall asleep because of what he had learned. "How can I deceive my friend? Yet it is vital for his well being that I do so," he mumbled to himself before he finally went to sleep.

†

The noise the crowd made as they came down the street caught Jeru's attention long before he saw it. He did not wait to look out the window to see the hordes of people. Jeru knew what was happening. After he left his room, he went to inform the chief priests. After the information was passed on to the proper persons, Jeru went to the Temple.

Having made important connections with members of the Sanhedrin, Jeru knew of several back rooms and hallways that allowed him to get close to the spot where Jesus would be teaching from in the Temple. All he had to do now was to wait for the appropriate time to ask the preplanned question that they had given to him.

As Jesus walked in the Temple, there came to him the chief priests, the scribes, and the elders. They asked of him, "By what authority do you do these things? And who gave you the authority to do these things?"

Jesus answered and said to them, "I will also ask of you one question, and if you answer me, I will tell you by what authority I do these things. The baptism of John the Baptist, was it from Heaven, or of men? Answer me!"

The chief priests, scribes, and elders gathered together and reasoned amongst themselves of how they should answer Jesus' question. "If we shall say, from Heaven; then he will say, why then did you not believe him?" one man said.

"But if we say, of men; the people will revolt for they count John to be a prophet indeed!" another man said.

"Then we must tell him we cannot answer his question!" one man said. The group of men informed Jesus that they could not give him an answer.

"Neither do I tell you by what authority I do these things!" Jesus answered them. He spoke unto them a parable. "A certain man planted a vineyard, and set a hedge around it. He dug a place for the wine press, and built a tower, and leased it out to stewards, and went to a far country. And at harvest, he sent to the stewards a servant, that he might receive the fruit of the vineyard. They caught him and beat him, and sent him away empty handed. He sent to them another servant, but they threw stones at him. They wounded him in the head and sent him away shamefully. And again he sent another servant, but the stewards killed him. Many others were sent, some were beaten, and others killed. The man had yet one son, whom he loved. He sent him also unto them, saying, 'They will reverence my son.'

"But those stewards said amongst themselves, 'This is the heir. Come, let us kill him, and the inheritance shall be ours.' They took the son, and killed him, and cast him out of the vineyard. What shall the lord of the vineyard do? He will come and destroy the stewards, and give the vineyard to others. Have you not read this scripture: The stone which the builders rejected has become the chief cornerstone? This was the Lord's doing, and it is marvelous in our eyes?"

Many of the men in the religious order became very angry because they knew that Jesus had spoken this parable against them. The men who tried to entrap Jesus wanted to arrest him immediately, but the others persuaded them that it would be best to wait. "Remember, we can not provoke the people unto wrath where they may riot," one of the elders said. The hunters left the Temple without their quarry.

"Master," Jeru shouted from amongst the crowd, "we know that you are true, and that you guard no man above another, but you teach the way of God in truth." Jesus turned to the man who had addressed him. "Is it lawful to give tribute to Caesar or not?" Jeru asked.

"Why do you tempt me? Bring me a penny, that I may see it," Jesus demanded. Jeru brought a coin forward, and Jesus asked, "Whose is this image and inscription?"

"Caesar's," Jeru answered.

And Jesus answered and said unto him, "Render to Caesar the things that are Caesar's, and to God the things that are God's." And all that were there marveled at this saying.

The contempt in Jeru's heart against Jesus increased when he realized that he had lost a perfect opportunity to ensnare his foe. Having been publicly humiliated by the man whom this crowd held in awe prompted Jeru to make a hasty retreat. As Jeru exited, he ran into the man that had sent him on his mission.

"You did not do very well, did you?" the man asked of Jeru.

"You are the lawyer! You go and ask him a question!" Jeru retorted, as he left.

Then came one of the Sadducees, who asked, "Master, Moses wrote unto us that if a man dies and leaves his wife behind, and has no children, that man's brother should take his wife and rise up seed unto that man. Now, there were seven brothers. The first took a wife, and died with no children. The second brother took her and died, and left no seed. And the third man did likewise. This continued to the seventh brother, and he died, and last of all, the woman died. Therefore, in the resurrection, when they shall rise, whose wife shall she be, for the seven brothers had her as a wife?"

"You do surely err. You do not know the scriptures, nor the power of God. For in the resurrection they neither marry, nor are given in marriage, but are as the angels of God in Heaven. But as touching the resurrection of the dead, have you not read that which was spoken unto you by God, saying 'I am the God of Abraham, and the God of Isaac, and the God of Jacob?' God is not the God of the dead, but of the living." And again, the multitude was astonished at his doctrine.

The lawyer that had spoken to Jeru asked Jesus, "Master, which is the greatest commandment in the law?"

Jesus said unto him, "You shall love the Lord thy God with all your heart, and with all your soul, and with your entire mind. This is the first and great commandment. And the second is like it, you shall love your neighbor as yourself. On these two commandments hang all the law and the prophets." At this, they asked him no more questions.

Then Jesus said to them, "How can they say that Christ is David's son? David himself said in the book of Psalms, 'The Lord said unto my Lord, sit thou on my right hand, till I make thine enemies thy footstool.' David therefore called him Lord, how is he then his son?" Jesus then talked to his disciples in the audience of all the people, "Beware of the scribes which desire to walk in long robes, and love greetings in the markets, and the highest seats in the synagogues, and the chief rooms at feasts; which devour widows' houses, and for a show make long prayers. The same shall receive damnation."

Jesus looked up and saw the rich men as they cast their gifts into the treasury, but when he saw the poor widow cast in her two mites, Jesus said, "Of a truth I say to you, this poor widow has cast in more than all of those. For they have given out of their abundance, but she gave all that she had."

"My Lord, this Temple is adorned with goodly stone and gifts," one of Jesus' disciples proclaimed.

Many people arrived late, and one of them was Elizabeth. Elizabeth berated herself for not arriving at the Temple sooner, but she could not find anyone to watch Matthew. Normally she never left him with anyone else, but she did not want to miss any word that Jesus spoke by having her young son moving all around.

"These things which you behold, the day will come, there shall not be one stone left upon another," Jesus warned the people of Israel. Jesus went on to warn them of false messiahs who would say 'I am

Christ.' He told them that there would be "wars and rumors of wars, but do not be terrified, for these things must first come to pass; but it is not the end." Jesus told them, "Nation shall rise up against nation and kingdom against kingdom. There will be great earthquakes in various places, famines, pestilences, fearful sights and great signs shall come from heaven. They shall lay hands on you, persecute you, deliver you up to the synagogues, and to prison. You will be brought up before kings and rulers for my name's sake."

Elizabeth did not like to arrive late. It was hard to understand a person's comment when you only hear the end of the message. The first words she heard Jesus say, "They shall lay hands on you, deliver you up to the synagogues and to prison," disturbed her. She questioned if she had missed Jesus saying when these things were to happen. The words he used, like "abomination of desolation, then will the end come, let them in Judea flee unto to mountains, woe unto them that nurse their young infants, " only added to her fears. What had this prophet prophesied?

†

Because Salem, Bedar and Joseph had stayed up late to converse with one another, they slept longer the following morning, more than they really had intended. Salem was the first to wake up and was surprised to see a servant waiting for him to arise. The servant ushered him to a special room where he could bathe and prepare for the first meal of the day.

The sun shone brightly through the window and was quite warm for this time of day, Salem thought. Salem went to the window and shielded his eyes from the sunlight. He could tell that it was almost midday and he had wasted most of the day. Salem quickly cleaned his body and called for a servant. "Are Joseph and Bedar awake yet?" Salem asked.

"Yes, they are getting ready for the day as you are!" the servant answered. "I was instructed to bring you to the dining room when you are finished," the servant continued.

The servant escorted Salem as he had been instructed. Salem sat on a pillow and waited for his friends. He had only waited a few moments, but he had already become restless. As he was getting up, so he could pace around the room, his friends arrived. Salem continued to get up, in order to show respect to his host.

"Please be seated, Salem," Joseph said. "You too," he said as he looked at Bedar. After they had seated themselves, Joseph made himself comfortable. He looked at Salem and asked, "I hope you slept well?"

"Too well," Salem replied. The laughter that broke out eased Salem's apprehension.

"Enjoy the meal, and then we will turn our intentions and efforts toward finding your family!" Joseph proclaimed. As they nibbled on the fruit that was common to this region of the world, Joseph declared, "I have many friends in the religious, financial, and government offices, and I am sure that they will be glad to assist you. I will arrange a meeting for you, and then you will be on your own. I am much too old to trek around the city all day, but I am sending you my most trusted servant to go with you. Please do not steal him from me, Bedar!" They laughed at the remark from the generous old man that they called their friend.

They walked briskly down the street. Their guide would point in a certain direction, and they would go that way. He would point in another direction, and they would go that way as well. Several times, Salem thought that Joseph's servant had gotten them lost. Salem was glad to finally see some buildings that he recognized. As they passed in front of the Temple, Salem stopped to get better look at this wonderful and historic building.

Bedar stopped to see what Salem was doing. "Solomon, wise King Solomon, and many more kings of Israel walked up and down these steps. One day the greatest king of all time will walk up these steps," Salem prophesied.

"He already has!" Bedar proclaimed. "And from the crowd that is here now, I would say that he is in the Temple right now!" Bedar motioned for the servant to come to where he stood, "While we are in this sector of town, I need to see a man to cancel a reservation for tonight!"

The servant acknowledged with a nod and replied to Bedar, "Lead the way and I will follow." The three men went out toward Bethany. Bedar cancelled the reservations of his and Salem's camp site. The land owner still held a deposit because the remaining asses that Bedar and Salem brought were still in the man's barn. Bedar turned to the servant.

"Do not let your master know that we spent our first night in town under a tree. He would never forgive me!" Again, the servant acknowledged with a nod of his understanding of Bedar's request.

They started toward Jerusalem, when Salem said, "Wait! There is something that I would like to see while I am here!" The other two men did not question him, but followed after him. It had been very easy to find the fig tree along the side of the road, because it was completely dried up. "Could this have been the tree that we heard of that Jesus had cursed yesterday morning?"

"It is!" came a voice from behind them. The three men turned to see who it was that spoke to them. "I was present when Jesus cursed this tree yesterday, and I was present this morning when he explained to his followers what had happened to the tree!"

"Please tell us what happened," Salem almost demanded of the stranger.

The man said, "Yesterday as Jesus and his followers came by this tree, Jesus went over to get some fruit off of it. There was no fruit on it. Jesus cursed the fig tree, and this morning the fig tree was dried up, even the roots. When his disciples asked how Jesus made it happen, Jesus said, 'Have faith in God. Verily I say to you, that whoever says unto this mountain, be thou removed, and be cast into the sea, and does not doubt in his heart, that those things that he said shall come to pass; he will have whatever he said. Therefore I say to you, whatsoever things you desire, when you pray, believe that you receive them and you shall have them. And when you stand praying, forgive, if you have ought against any, that your father also which is in heaven may forgive you your trespasses.' And then he went to Jerusalem," the man said.

"Thank you!" Salem proclaimed and they went back to their initial task.

The streets were filled with people scurrying to and fro and it made travel difficult. The servant led them to a Jewish building that the Romans now occupied to conduct their governmental duties, and pointed at the front door. He handed Salem a message that was embossed with the emblem that Salem had seen at Joseph's home and said, "Give them this message, and they will help you!"

"Are you coming in with us?" Salem asked.

"No. I will wait outside for you," the servant answered. Salem assumed that since the man was a servant he would not be allowed to enter this Roman building.

"You can go now. We will be able to find our way back." Salem reassured him. At first the servant was reluctant to leave, but Bedar reminded the servant that Joseph had told them they would be on their own after Joseph had arranged this meeting. The servant departed.

It surprised Salem and Bedar when they entered the building. There seemed to be more traffic in this building than in the streets. They walked over to an official and handed the rolled up papyrus to him. The official looked at the seal and then got up from his desk. He carried the message to another office. A few moments later, a man who seemed to have a higher rank of authority than the other man came out and greeted Salem and Bedar.

"Cleoiphous here," the higher official said as he placed his hand on the arm of the man that Salem had handed the message to, "will help you in any way that he can. Now, how long ago did your family come to Jerusalem?"

"Just over a year ago, and a few months," Salem answered.

"Cleoiphous, give these men a list of all the carpenters that have come to Jerusalem seeking work in the last year and a half!"

"Yes, my lord!" the man replied.

Speaking to Salem, the official said, "I have other duties that require my attention, so please excuse me for leaving so soon." Salem and Bedar nodded and bowed slightly.

"It will take some time to sort through all these papers. Could you come back tomorrow?" Cleoiphous asked.

Salem was disappointed and it showed in his answer, "Yes, we can come back tomorrow!"

The two requesters of help exited the building. The higher ranking officer approached Cleoiphous' desk. "How did you get rid of them so quickly?"

"I told them that it would take at least a day to sort through all this information. They will be back tomorrow!" Cleoiphous answered.

"Joseph is a very wise man. Had he not sent a messenger to warn us that Bedar and Salem were coming and not to give them the information that they sought, we surely would have done so," the high official stated.

"How could Joseph have been sure that the other messenger would have gotten here first?" he asked.

"Knowing the craftiness of our Jewish friend, Joseph of Arimathaea, he would have sent a guide with them, who would have taken them on a longer route," he answered and then left.

Throughout the day Salem and Bedar journeyed from business to business to ask if they knew of any carpenters that had come from Nazareth. The constant walking tired Bedar out. Knowing that he labored with the deception to keep Salem from finding his family added to his own weariness. "I wish I was as young as you!" Bedar commented.

"I am very thankful that you decided to come with me. You were never under any obligation to make this journey. I am honored with your presence and I appreciate your financial support. I would understand if you decided to go back to Samaria, even though I would miss you terribly," Salem said.

"Have you forgotten that I invited myself on this trip? I intend to see it to its end!" Bedar replied.

"And for that I am very thankful, but at least go back to Joseph's home and rest for a few hours," Salem suggested.

Through a weary yawn, Bedar responded, "That sounds refreshing! Please do not continue to search for your family without me."

"I will use this time to go back to the Temple and try to complete my first task there!" Salem responded. Bedar was about to respond, but Salem said, "I promise that I will wait for you before I start the search for my family again!"

With a smile and a nod, Bedar said, "Wise choice, my young friend. You do not need the help of an old Samaritan to give thanks unto God," as he patted Salem's back, and then turned to leave.

It relaxed Salem when he took a casual stroll back to the Temple, instead of the chaotic pace that had been established earlier that day. This slower pace allowed him the time to reflect on what he needed to do, and what his God had done for him. His quiet inner solitude was shattered as a large group of people left the Temple.

As usual, many people accompanied Jesus wherever he went. Salem could see Jesus, the usual twelve men who were trained by him, and some women. Salem recognized Mary, Jesus' mother. He did not know the other women who were with Jesus. He felt like a spectator who watched a parade go by. Scores of people moved in the same direction. Salem had a difficult time standing in one place.

Then he saw her! Could it really be her? Where was the child? Where was their child, their son? Salem tried to run along the side of the moving mass, but he fell as he tried to call out the name of the woman he loved, "Eli . . ." His voice had been smothered by the shouts of the people, and she never heard her name called out. The ones who heard him thought he had called out to God for help.

In the panic of trying not to be trampled to death by the stampede of followers, Salem crawled under a table of a vendor who sold fruit. By the time he could climb out safely, the majority of the crowd was gone. Salem finally found the direction that the crowd had gone, and he caught up with them. His heart sank in despair when he could not see his beloved Elizabeth. Elizabeth was with the entourage out to Bethany. She felt weird. It was hard for her to tell why she was troubled. The feeling that thrust itself on her the day before had returned. It was as though someone was close by that she should have seen, but did not.

Salem followed them out to Bethany. He watched the crowd as they came to a certain street. There were many homes on that street and Salem could not tell exactly which house the crowd stopped in front of. Soon, early in the evening of that day, the crowd had begun to disburse. Salem could tell by the reactions on the people's faces, and the comments made, that everyone had been sent to their homes. He still did not see his Elizabeth.

In deep desperation, he let his back fall heavily on the wall of a shop. With the strain of what he missed, and the physical exertion that his body had suffered, Salem let his weary body slide down the wall until he was sitting on the ground. Salem wept. Where had she gone? Had she gone down a side street? It had been such a long time since he had envisioned her beauty, and like a vapor, she was gone. The despair of missing this perfect opportunity and the soreness of his body did not allow him to continue. His spirit yearned for her, but Salem could not move. With a body succumbed by fatigue, Salem went to sleep where he sat.

Inside the home of Lazarus, Elizabeth surveyed the scene before her. The disciples relaxed and ate a hearty meal and Jesus slept. Elizabeth considered herself blessed that Martha and Mary had allowed her

Jeff Frazier

to come into their home as often as she did. She knew that Jesus was the Messiah, and it meant a lot to her to be close to him.

The hour had come that Elizabeth had to leave, for the arrangement for Matthew's care was about to come to its end. She excused herself from the house, and thanked Martha for inviting her back again. After she exited the house, she closed the door and began to walk home. She saw the man asleep in the shadows, but decided to leave him be. It would not proper for a woman to walk up to an unknown sleeping man. Besides, he might be drunk.

The sound of the door opening behind her caused Elizabeth to stop and turn around. At first she did not notice who it was coming out of Martha and Mary's house. Once she knew who it was, she hid in some nearby bushes. The man walked past her hiding place and only looked around to see if anyone had followed him.

She thought about following him, but the sudden remembrance of what had happened the last time she followed a man to a secret meeting caused her to shiver. There was something wrong and she knew it. With all concerns for her own well being cast aside, she began to mimic the movements of the man she pursued. If he went left on one street, she went left down the same street. It had been very easy to follow this man. Elizabeth had already calculated how many steps he would take before he would turn around and look to see if anyone was following. "Thirty six, thirty seven, thirty eight, hide," she would say quietly to herself.

She offered a short and thankful praise to the God she loved, when the man entered a home that was far from where Matthew was. By the time she was able to get into a position that she could hear what was being said, the men had already started talking. Panic flashed through her body when she heard the voice of someone else coming. She quickly hid herself before this latest arrival could see her.

As soon as the latest arrival was in the house, Elizabeth returned to her original observation post. She had found the perfect spot. Not only could she see what happened, but she could hear what was said as well. The light was dim, but she still could see the person who had just gone through the door. Elizabeth was able to see that some of the people were some of the chief priests.

"I am so glad that you could make it!" the man who owned the meeting place stated.

"What do you have for me this time?" one of the priests asked.

"There is someone I want you to meet," the man said as another man walked up to the priests.

The panic she had felt only a moment earlier was mild compared the absolute fear that engulfed her. Of all the people in Jerusalem, this face was the one that she wished she would never have seen again. The coldness in that man's heart made her blood run cold through her body. For the second time this night, her body shivered, even though it was not cold. Elizabeth had concluded a long time ago, that the man that she was looking at did not have a heart of compassion, but of stone.

"You do know Jeru, from Nazareth?" the man asked.

"Yes! Yes! We have met." the priest answered as though he was annoyed.

"He has found a man that he wants you to meet!" the host stated. "Since Jeru was the one who found him, I will let him introduce him to you!"

Jeru motioned for the man in question to come where they stood. When the man was near them, Jeru said, "This is Judas, Judas Iscariot." They moved away from the spot where Elizabeth could see them, and she could not hear their conversation. She waited patiently and prayed that they would not leave the house soon.

After about half an hour of not being able to see or hear anything, the men appeared again in the place where Elizabeth could overhear what they said. Then one of the priests said, "Here is the money, thirty pieces of silver. The Passover is nigh, and we must take care of this problem before the Passover. Remember, you must deliver him into our hands within two nights."

"What if I do not have the opportunity to leave?" Judas asked.

"Make one if you have to!" the priest snapped back. "Are you certain of the location?" the priest asked Judas.

"Yes, he goes there often to pray," Judas answered.

"He must be alone, or with as few people as possible. We do not want the multitudes to turn on us when we arrest him," the priest said and then the priests started to walk toward the door. The first priest who got to the door scanned the adjacent streets, but he saw no one, and then they left.

Elizabeth practically ran all the way home. She knew that the woman that watched Matthew while she went to hear Jesus would be very angry with her. The woman was not calmed by any apology that Elizabeth could offer. After the woman left, Elizabeth slowly rocked Matthew. Her son was asleep before she had picked him up. The rocking motion was used to comfort herself, as well as her young son.

†

Salem awoke the following morning with a severe pain in his head. There had been too much information, problems, difficulties, and failures for him to deal with. He tried to remember the facts that he had so calmly gathered the day before, but it only caused the pain to worsen. Sleeping in an awkward position all night did not help matters. Slowly and purposefully, he made his way back to Joseph's home.

Immediately upon entering the room, Joseph and Bedar knew that Salem was in pain. Joseph offered Salem a long green vegetable that would ease the pain in his head. The crunchy noise of this food sounded like an echoing horn blast in Salem's head and he put the food aside. The food would have normally been very flavorful, but today it was tasteless.

"Forgive me. The food is good, but I am not well!" Salem stated. He tried to explain what had happened the day before, but most of his words were indistinguishable.

"You need to rest today. We can begin the search again tomorrow!" Bedar commented.

Joseph concurred with Bedar's statement and said, "I will have a messenger go to the Roman Office and retrieve any information that they might have gathered."

Jesus taught in the Temple again this day as he had done since arrival in Jerusalem. As usual, the crowd gathered to listen to him.

Elizabeth did not leave Matthew today because she had stayed away too much the day before. It had also been an unbearable night for her. "Where were they going to meet? When?" And the toughest question of all, "Why?" she asked herself throughout the night.

This new morning had not relieved her of any of the anxiety that she felt. It was torture for her, knowing that some people were plotting to arrest Jesus and she was helpless to prevent it. For what? She knew something terrible was about to happen, but she was powerless to do anything about it. This day to her was endless. Just to complete the simplest of tasks required extreme effort.

Elizabeth longed for the days that she had spent with Salem. She longed for the days when Martha and Jeru were her family. It was in the past and there was nothing she could do to regain them, so she had to do what she must to provide for her Matthew.

The lawyer and Pharisee that was Jeru's liaison from the Temple offered Jeru a task to gather a select group of people for a raid. That offer was gladly accepted by Jeru. The servant of the high priest had been selected as well. At first Jeru thought that the high priest's servant had been sent along to keep an eye on him, but he knew that the arrest would just further his stature with the council, the Pharisees, and the priests. Jeru spent the majority of the day gathering participants for the raid to arrest Jesus. No one knew the years that Jeru had waited for this moment.

As each hour passed, Jeru cursed Judas silently. "Where is he?" he shouted several times that day. Many of the volunteers thought Jeru had lost his mind for shouting the question without notice or reason. It angered Jeru that this day ended without an incident.

CHAPTER XV

The rest that Salem had gotten the day before revived him. It still amazed him how much he had slept. The whole day and night before were only a dim memory to him. He remembered seeing Elizabeth, falling down, and talking to Bedar and Joseph, but that was all. Having obtained a much needed rest, Salem woke before the sun rose. "I want to get out early, before the streets become crowded and Jesus gets to the Temple," Salem told the young servant who had questioned him as he left. He exited the house quietly.

Salem's plans had started to work according to his calculations. He wanted to get to the Temple early. Salem would wait for Jesus to enter the Temple and give his thanks to him, no matter how large the crowd was. He could only hope that Elizabeth would be with Jesus. Then both of his goals would be completed in one quick moment.

Later that morning, as the man servant of Joseph was about to walk out the door to go get water in the pitcher that he carried, Bedar stopped the servant and asked, "Have you seen Salem?"

"Yes, he left quite early this morning. He wanted to get to the Temple early," the servant answered. "His health seemed to have improved greatly!" the servant said. "There is some fruit and bread set on the table for you both," the servant stated. After Joseph and Bedar went to the table to eat, the servant went to complete his assigned tasks.

Bedar and Joseph were pleased that the servant had told them that Salem looked well, and rested. As they ate, they talked of what they should do about Salem.

"I should go help him!" Bedar stated as he walked toward the door. Bedar opened the door, stopped and looked at what was happening on the street. Bedar looked at Joseph to make him aware that something did not appear to be as it should be.

Joseph asked, "What is it, Bedar? What is it, my friend?" Joseph asked as he rose to go to the door.

"Your man servant is being followed by some men," Bedar answered just as Joseph walked up and stood beside him.

The man servant walked up the steps to the house and the calmness on his face told the two onlookers that the servant was unaware that he was being followed. The servant paused momentarily when he noticed Joseph and Bedar, but continued on after Joseph motioned for him to continue. The two strangers that followed the servant continued on up the steps.

Grave concern of who these men were was about to take hold of Bedar's spirit, until he looked at Joseph. Bedar could tell that Joseph knew these men. Then Bedar realized that he had seen these men before, but he could not remember where he had seen them.

"The Master instructed us to come into the city, and that we would see a man bearing a pitcher, and we were to follow him. And whatsoever house he should enter in, say unto the good man of the house, 'The Master saith where is the guest chamber, where I shall eat the Passover with my disciples.'"

"He sent us two to make it ready," one of the men stated.

Quickly, without another word or hesitation, Joseph showed the two men the room that they would be using. The two men began to prepare the room for the Passover meal. Bedar decided that this would be a good time to go look for Salem. Joseph instructed him to be back before the evening, because the customary meal would be served at that time.

People had begun to fill the streets, but no organized crowd had shown up. The hours slowly crept by, and Jesus did not come to the Temple this day. Frustration increased within Salem as the time evaporated. It surprised him when he saw Bedar walking toward him. Bedar walked up to Salem and gently placed a hand on his shoulder.

"Our God is a strange and wondrous God, is he not?" Bedar asked.

The nature of the question took Salem completely by surprise. It shocked him to the point that Salem could not answer. When Bedar saw the bewildered expression on his friend's face, he said, "We search and strive to mold the circumstances around us to fit our personal needs. Here you are seeking the Messiah in a Temple, yet he is not here."

Salem realized that the Samaritan was playing one of the word games that were common to his people. "What are you trying to tell me?" Salem finally asked.

"You seek Jesus here, but he will be going to the home in which you lodged!" Bedar stated as though he had just given a very expensive gift to a friend.

Excitement erupted from Salem. "Let's go and wait for him there! The crowd will not hinder me from talking to him!" Salem said very excitedly.

Without moving from the rock that he had just sat down on, Bedar stated, "There is time, my friend! His disciples are preparing the upper room as we speak, but Jesus will not be there until the evening hour."

Calmer now, Salem said, "Then we will have time to search for my family! I know they are here. I have seen Elizabeth with my own eyes, but I was unable to reach her."

"I will help you!" Bedar quoted his original offer to this Jew.

They toured the streets for several hours and they stopped to rest. The city was large, the streets full, everyone was moving about, and still they did not find whom they sought. "I just saw her two days ago with Jesus. Surely she should be here somewhere!"

"Let us stop here and eat! I have bread and some delicious fruit of the vine," Bedar proclaimed. "Then we can continue," Bedar pointed toward a certain street, "down that street."

Wearily, Salem sat down and accepted the bread and wine, but he looked suspiciously in the direction that Bedar had pointed. He studied the scene for several moments then the anger began to build up within him. "Do you take me for a fool?" Salem shouted.

Bedar coughed with the food in his mouth and tried to speak, but could not.

"How long were you going to deceive me? Any child could tell that we have been down that street several times. You and Joseph have tried to keep me from a certain section of town. Were the Roman Officials involved in this as well?" Salem shot the accusations at his friend.

Shame engulfed Bedar so deeply that he could not hide the sadness that clothed his face, because he had kept the truth from his friend. "I am sorry that I have kept the truth from you, but we thought that it would be best not to tell you, until your faith was much stronger," Bedar admitted.

Angrily, Salem grabbed Bedar, "Tell me of my wife, my son, and my parents!"

"There is so much to tell," Bedar spoke. "Please calm yourself down first. I know where Elizabeth lives and I will take you to her."

"How long have you known?" Salem asked.

"Since the first night at Joseph's house. Joseph told me all about your family," Bedar answered ashamedly. "Please do not be angry with us, for we knew this would be too hard for you to bear. At first Joseph did not know who you were. Your father only told Joseph that you died. It was not until you told your story, that he become aware of who your family was."

"Is there some terrible news about my family that you could not tell me?" Salem asked.

"Yes, but I think it best that Elizabeth tell you." Without any words spoken, Bedar led Salem to the house where Elizabeth lived. "There," Bedar said as he pointed at the door of a small home, " . . . is where you can find her."

At first Salem only stared at the house, then Bedar said, "I am sorry that I have deceived you. I will leave you now. If you choose to never forgive me, I can understand." Salem began to walk toward the home, but Bedar stopped him. "After the Passover is complete, I will return to my home in Samaria. You are always welcome there."

Again Salem walked toward the door, but Bedar did not hinder him now because he had already left. A nervous sickening sensation built up in Salem's stomach. What would he say to his wife that he had not seen for almost two years? The large hand of the man who once worked as a carpenter, gently knocked on the hard wood door of the small home.

For the last several hours Elizabeth had paced back and forth in her home. Her feet were sore from the constant nervous walk she had tortured herself with. This was the second day that she endured the agony of what she had overheard the men plot to do their evil deed. Today had to be the day, because the Passover would start the following day.

Tension accumulated in her breast as the hours passed. The worry that someone had seen her leave the area of the secret meeting only fueled the flames of uncertainty that drove her body into a frenzy of panic. When someone outside knocked on the door, the already tense

Jeff Frazier

woman screamed as she jumped at the sound. She waited for several moments, and hoped that whoever was at the door would leave, but the knock returned. Finally she gathered the courage to open the door.

When Elizabeth opened the door, Salem spoke only one word, "Elizabeth?"

What she saw caused her to crumble to the floor like a discarded rag. Over and over again, like a dream, she heard someone call her name, "Elizabeth! Elizabeth!" She awoke to see the face of a man that she had not seen in a long time. The face belonged to a life that had passed away. Those joyous memories had gone away from her. If those memories were no longer a part of her, then why were they here and why were they staring at her with the warm, gentle eyes of the man she knew as Salem?

"Elizabeth, are you all right?" Salem asked.

She had been lying down, but she shot up straightway and tried to move away from the man that had once been her life. "Do not be afraid!" Salem said, but she continued to move away from him. "I am clean," he said as he rolled up the sleeve of his garment to expose the arm that had once been leprous.

The reality of what she had seen finally seeped into her mind, and she totally engulfed Salem within her grasp. "Praise the Lord. Praise the Lord God of Israel," she said very loudly. She began to whisper his name affectionately over and over.

It had been a lifetime since someone had held him in such a manner, but then he felt her enthusiasm diminish. He pretended not to notice at first. Then without warning she withdrew forcefully from his embrace. "What is wrong?" Salem asked.

The embarrassed woman hid her face as she turned away in her grief. "I have married again."

"Married?" Salem asked.

"Timothy has been extra kind to us," Elizabeth said as though Salem had asked if her husband had been good to them.

"What a fool I have been. That is why my friends tried to keep me from finding you!"

"I had no choice! I could not take care of Matthew by myself," she stated.

"Matthew? That is what you named our son?" Salem asked.

"Yes! Your father gave him that name. He is such a fine child!" Elizabeth answered.

At first Salem thought she meant Mashic, and then he realized that she meant Jeru. The thought came to Salem to ask her to see Matthew, but he knew that it would be painful for all of them, so he rejected that notion. "Did Jeru not accept Matthew into the family?" Salem asked painfully.

"Yes, he was accepted, but I moved away immediately after your mother's death," Elizabeth answered.

"My mother is dead?" In the twinkling of an eye, Salem was flooded with a torrent of emotions. His heart grew heavy for the death of his mother, but he was relieved to know that he would not have to see her. Salem knew he could not judge his mother for what she had done, but he could not look into her eyes. He did not hate his mother for what she had done, but he was afraid that just as Sara had seen into his soul, so could his mother. He had truly wanted to look upon his mother's face again, but he did not want her to know that he knew the truth about his real father.

"Yes. I am sorry, I thought you knew! Since you were the one that found me, I thought you knew."

"Please tell me about my family!"

"I can only tell you of what I know!"

Elizabeth began her recollection of events that started shortly after Salem had left. His ears burned with agony as he heard how his family was persecuted in Nazareth, and why they moved to Jerusalem. The words that he heard about the ability of Jeru to obtain good work did not surprise Salem, but the fact that Jeru had worked for Joseph startled him. Salem remembered the fine art work that he had noticed on the door to Joseph's home.

From time to time Salem would stop to question her. He wanted to make sure that he got all the facts straight. His emotions would rise and then fall according to what Elizabeth said. Love and joy flooded him as she told of Matthew's birth, yet he was overcome with great sorrow for not being there.

When Elizabeth paused momentarily with her rendition, from the expression of pain on her face, Salem knew that she had reached the event of his mother's death. "Please tell me all that you know," Salem demanded.

She sighed, and then said, "When I left for the market that morning, they were arguing over finances. I knew that Matthew and I were becoming a burden on them since only one man provided the income now. As I arrived back from the market with some fresh bread and leeks, I heard a commotion coming from the building that we resided in. I saw this woman hanging from the outer ledge of the building. I saw the hands of a man reach out and grasp the woman in peril. At first I thought he was going to lift her up to safety, but it looked like he intentionally dropped her. I rushed to the scene, and that was when I discovered that it was your mother. I looked up at the window from which she fell, and Jeru looked down at me. His eyes were cold and dark. There was no sadness, no remorse, nothing. He just simply returned to the seclusion of the room. Martha had fallen on a large water pot. She was motionless, her stare was vacant. Matthew had begun to cry from all the jostling that he received. I ran to the apartment to confront Jeru. He was already being challenged by the men from the area. I overheard him tell them that she had tripped over a rug and fell out the window. At the first opportunity Jeru found, he leaned over to me and said, "You are next.""

Salem wept bitterly as she told him of the horrible death of his mother and of what Jeru had done to his wife, to his sweet Elizabeth.

"I left that day and never returned," Elizabeth concluded her story. "Joseph took us into his home. Jeru did not know we were there. If it were not for Joseph we would have suffered a much more terrible fate."

The anger that had built up in Salem toward Jeru grew into hatred after he heard the evil Jeru had done. "He will pay for the evil that he has done against you and my mother!" Salem prophesied.

"Salem, don't let this knowledge cause you to hate. One day I heard Jesus say that vengeance belongs to God, and he will repay!" she tried to reason with Salem. She could feel the rage that had come over him. In an attempt to lessen the effect of that anger, she asked, "Salem, please tell me how you were delivered from your affliction."

After Salem was calm enough to speak, he told her about the children that he had run into after he left Nazareth. It delighted her to hear of Mashic's love and devotion toward Salem. Mashic had indeed been a great missionary to the needy. It was Elizabeth's turn to cry when she heard of Mashic's murder. For the sake of the wonderful memory that Elizabeth had for Mashic and for Martha, he did not tell her that Mashic was his father.

"What a horrible way to die for any man, but for a man who loved God it is worse," she commented.

Elizabeth rejoiced at how Salem had been healed. The news that their home and the carpenter shop had both been burned down saddened her. Happiness swelled up within her as Salem told her of how Sara came to his aid, but she winced when she heard of Sara's death.

Salem delighted her with the news that Bedar had come to find him at the place Mashic and Sara were buried. Then his voice cracked with sorrow when he told her of how Bedar had told him that he had gone back to thank Jesus. She felt his sorrow for not having thanked Jesus for the healing that he had received. "That is one of the reasons that I have come to Jerusalem," Salem stated.

Elizabeth did not ask what his other reasons for coming to Jerusalem were, for she knew that she and Matthew were the reason. Then she suddenly remembered what had kept her emotions at the state of insanity for the last two days and she said loudly, "Jesus, we must find him."

The loud proclamation that came from her caused Salem to jump. "I know where he is and I have time to find him," Salem stated.

"No, you do not have much time! Your father has conspired with the chief priests and one of Jesus' disciples, Judas Iscariot, to deliver him unto death."

"That is impossible! Jesus is at Joseph's house to partake of the first night of the Passover feast."

"I do not have time to explain what I know. You will have to trust me. Jesus is in danger. This is the night that they must arrest him."

Salem did not hesitate to return to Joseph's house. He was breathing hard when he reached the front door. Everyone was startled to see Salem enter the room in such a panic. "Where is Jesus?"

"He has already left," Joseph answered. "Is something wrong?"

"They are going to arrest him!"

"What is the charge?" Bedar protested.

"I do not know! We must find him and warn him!" Salem demanded.

"Jesus already knows!" Joseph stated. "After their feast was complete, I overheard the disciples talking. One of them said that Jesus told them that one of the disciples was going to betray him."

"How could he know?" Salem asked.

"Have you forgotten who he is?" Joseph answered.

"I cannot stand here and do nothing while an innocent man is arrested," Salem yelled. "Bedar, are you coming with me?"

Bedar was not sure of what to do. He deliberated in his mind for a few seconds then walked over to Salem. "I will go with you."

"One of the disciples said that Jesus and his disciples were going to the Garden of Gethsemane," Joseph informed them. Salem walked to the front door. Bedar followed, but as he passed by Joseph, Joseph said, "Maybe you can keep Salem from being arrested as well!" Bedar nodded and continued on out the door.

Normally, Salem would have been exhausted from the distance he had already run, but the current situation caused him to exceed his human abilities. Bedar, however, could not keep up with the younger, more agile man. Periodically Salem would slow down to wait for Bedar to catch up.

"Go on ahead," Bedar said breathlessly. "I know where the garden is. I will meet you there!"

"I hope that I am not already too late!" Salem said and then quickly ran down the street and turned down a side street.

When Salem vanished around the side of the dark building, Bedar said to himself, "I pray that you are not too late."

Salem reached a spot outside of the city where he could see the garden. Horror consumed him when he saw that a large mob of men with lit torches were descending toward where three other men were. Knowing that he was too late to warn Jesus, Salem climbed up a tree to get a better look.

With the light the torches gave off, Salem was able to see some of what happened, but it was impossible to hear anything at all. As he watched the mob move toward Jesus and the other two men, he heard someone call his name, "Salem? Salem? Where are you?" It was Bedar at the base of the tree.

"I am up here!" Salem shouted.

"What is happening?"

Salem paused to look at the scene that unfolded in the garden. "Jesus just woke up two of his disciples.

"Where are the other disciples?" Bedar asked.

"I do not know. The mob has reached Jesus now. They appear to be talking. Someone just kissed Jesus. They have laid hands on Jesus and have arrested him. Wait! One of the Jesus' disciples just drew his sword! The disciple just cut off the ear of one of the men that came to arrest Jesus. Jesus appears to be scolding his disciple."

"What are they doing now?"

"You are not going to believe this, but Jesus just put the man's ear back on!"

"I believe it!" Bedar truthfully said.

"The disciples that were with him fled!" Salem stated. "The ones who arrested Jesus are leading Jesus away now." With nothing more to see, Salem climbed down from the tree. The mob with torches, swords, and staves passed in front of Salem and Bedar. "I am glad that Mashic is not here to witness this travesty," Salem moaned.

"What shall we do now?" Bedar asked.

"I do not know," Salem answered.

The mob was completely out of their sight and they just stood by the tree. The shock of what they had seen stunned them out of their placidness. The sound of men coming broke them from the trance that they were in. "I have seen these men before," Salem admitted.

"Are they Jesus' followers?" Bedar asked.

"I am not sure, but I think so," Salem answered. "We should follow them and see where the others have taken Jesus."

"Why follow those men? It would seem wiser if we were to follow the band of angry men who took Jesus. Surely we will get there faster," Bedar suggested.

"You are correct," Salem admitted. "What do you think they will do to him?"

"It really depends on who is mad at Jesus. If it is the religious leaders, the penalty could be severe. If the Romans have any ought against him, it could be terminal. I have no way of knowing. I cannot see anything that Jesus has done that would deserve death."

As they walked at a much slower pace than their quick pace to the garden, Salem said, "Forgive me for my rudeness. I know now that you only tried to protect Elizabeth and me. Surely she had consoled her spirit that I was indeed dead, which allowed her to marry again. Now she must live with the agony that she might have made the wrong decision, and could be living in sin."

"It was not easy for me to hide the truth from you!" Bedar said. "It is I who should ask for forgiveness." Salem and Bedar followed the band of men to a certain house. Everyone that was in the band did not enter into the house. As Salem and Bedar approached the house, Salem asked, "What place is this?"

"It is the house of Caiaphas, who is the high priest this year," a person answered, whom Salem did not know.

Bedar began to walk toward the front door and Salem asked, "Where are you going?"

"I want to see what is going on inside," Bedar answered.

Salem chose not to go in, but he did not hinder his friend from going inside. It was cool during the night hours, so several of the servants and officers had made a fire of coals to warm themselves. Salem warmed himself next to a fire. As he stood near the glowing heat, another man approached the fire. Unlike the man who had answered his question several minutes earlier, Salem recognized this man. The man appeared to be very frightened. Salem knew he should not reveal the man's identity, if he was truly who Salem thought he was. Salem could not help but stare at this frightened man, until his attention was drawn to the man who walked up the steps to the house. Salem was sure that the man who went up the stairs and the man who was warming himself by the fire were the same two men that he had seen with Jesus in the garden.

Then a damsel said to the man that had just come and stood by the fire, "Are you also one of this man's disciples?"

The man who Salem was sure to be a follower of Jesus answered, "I am not, and I do not understand what you are talking about."

After Bedar entered the house of the high priest, he managed to find a place to sit, and he tried to look important enough to be in this place at this time. As he watched the preceding, another man that had just entered came and sat next to him. Bedar remembered seeing this man. The man that sat next to him was one of the men that had been at the Passover meal with Jesus.

The high priest said, "Jesus, tell me of your disciples, and of your doctrine."

Jesus answered him, "I spake openly to the world; I taught in the synagogues, and in the Temple, where the Jews always resort; and I have said nothing in secret. Why ask me? Ask them which heard me, what I have said unto them: behold, they know what I said."

And after Jesus had spoken, one of the officers which stood by struck Jesus with the palm of his hand, and said, "Why answer the high priest in such a manner?"

Jesus answered him, "If I have spoken evil, bear witness of the evil: but if well, why did you smite me?"

The chief priests and all the council sought for witness against Jesus. They wanted to put him to death but could not find any person who could truthfully bring charges against him. Many false witnesses were brought up to speak against Jesus, but their charges did not agree. Bedar saw two certain men rise to bear false witness against Jesus.

Bedar had no way of knowing that the man he saw and heard speak had been Jeru, the man who had raised his friend who was still outside. As Jeru pointed to the man who stood with him, he said, "We heard him say, 'I will destroy this temple that is made with hands, and within three days I will build another made without hands.'" The other man spoke but neither of their statements matched.

The high priest stood up in the midst of the crowd and asked Jesus, "Are you going to answer? What about what these witnesses have said against you?" But Jesus held his peace, and answered nothing. The high priest asked Jesus, "Are you the Christ, the Son of the Blessed?"

And Jesus said, "I am: and you shall see the Son of man sitting on the right hand of power, and coming in the clouds of heaven."

Then the high priest tore his clothes, and said, "What need we any further with these witnesses? You have heard the blasphemy: what do you think?" They all condemned Jesus to death, for they believed Jesus to be guilty.

Bedar could hear the men make a gurgling sound in their throats just before they would spit on Jesus. One man came up from behind the accused and covered his face with a cloth that prevented Jesus from seeing what was happening. The accusers were like hungry jackals. They had tasted blood and now they wanted a kill. Bedar recoiled at the sound of the slap that was delivered venomously across the face of Jesus. Someone mocked Jesus and said, "Prophesy which one of the servants struck you." The grief-stricken merchant from Samaria departed the building a sad and discouraged man.

As the man who Salem knew to be a follower of Jesus stood and warmed himself, another person asked him, "Are you one of his disciples?"

Peter again denied that he was a disciple of Jesus by saying, "I am not!"

Salem had managed to remain quiet during the last several hours while the exchanges between the accusers and the man who was being accused occurred. It took several hours to watch the events unfold. "What could be happening inside?" Salem wondered. "Something must happen soon, it is almost daylight." Salem's attention was drawn away from the conversation at the fire, when he saw Bedar exit the building.

Just as Salem was about to leave, he heard the servant of the high priest, ask, "Did I not see you in the garden with him?"

Again, the man who Salem knew to be a disciple, denied that he knew Jesus and he began to curse and to swear, and said, "I know not the man," and immediately a cock crowed. Salem saw a disturbed expression emerge on the man's face. Sure the hour was late, but how could the sound of a cock crow upset anyone?

Immediately after the cock crowed, all eyes were drawn to the front door as they led Jesus from Caiaphas' home. Salem could see that Jesus' eyes had connected with the eyes of the man who, in the last several hours, had three times denied knowing him. The man that had been by the fire started to weep and ran away.

Quickly Salem ran to where Bedar was. When he got to his friend, he asked, "What has happened?"

Bedar replied, "It is not good! They have charged him with blasphemy."

"Why?"

"He claimed to be the Christ!"

"What are they going to do now?"

"They are taking him to the Hall of Judgment called Praetorium."

"Who is in charge there?"

"Pontius Pilate!"

The reality of the circumstances and the seriousness of the charges moved over their souls like a thick menacing fog. The religious people wanted Jesus dead, but could not kill the accused themselves. It was so convenient to have the Roman Government accomplish this murderous task for them. This carpenter from Nazareth had claimed to be the Messiah. The Messiah would deliver his people. The Roman Government would have to do something about a man who had claimed to be a king, or, as in this case, the Son of God.

"What should we do?" Salem asked.

"You can wait here if you want. I am going back to Joseph's home to wait. Let me know if you hear some news," Bedar answered.

CHAPTER XVI

"Cleoiphous!"

The sleeping man moaned, "What?"

"Cleoiphous!"

More awake now, Cleoiphous responded to the slave that called his name, "What is it?"

"The Governor wants you at the Judgment Hall immediately!"

"Pontius Pilate?" Cleoiphous asked.

The slave nodded his head as he brought the water basin forward. Cleoiphous liberally washed his face and then dried it with the towel that the slave handed him.

"Do you know what the trouble is for him to summon me so early in the morning?"

"A man has been arrested and the Governor wants you to scribe the transcript!"

"What was the man arrested for?" Cleoiphous asked as he put on a clean garment. The slave only raised his shoulders slightly. "I know slaves hear more than they let on. Tell me what you know!"

"This man who was arrested was delivered by the priests and scribes."

"Surely Pilate should know that this is a religious matter since the priests and scribes delivered this man to be judged," Cleoiphous stated and did not really expect a reply from the slave.

"They say the man has claimed to be some sort of king and they are prepared to have this man put to death," the slave said with his head bowed low.

"That sheds a different light on the whole subject. Is the Governor already in the Judgment Hall?"

"Yes! He wants you to get there before he starts the proceedings."

"I hope he is not angry that I have kept him waiting!" the Roman clerk admitted.

"May a slave say what is on his mind?" the slave asked.

"Proceed," announced Cleoiphous.

"The impression I got was that the governor wanted to stall in hopes of letting this matter settle down," the slave stated.

"Thank you. Is my horse prepared?"

"It is being prepared as we speak. It should be at the front by the time you have gotten your materials together."

As quickly as he could, Cleoiphous gathered up what precious paper he could, and a writing utensil to record the trial that waited for his arrival. Even though he was in a hurry, Cleoiphous stopped at the door and looked back at the slave. "Who was the man that was arrested?"

"Jesus," answered the slave.

A loud sigh escaped from Cleoiphous' lungs even though he really did not want to show any emotions. The reins of the horse were handed to him by the horseman as soon as he closed the door. In one move he was on the back of the horse and was en-route to the Judgment Hall.

The cool morning air combined with the speed of the horse created a chilly breeze over his whole body. A cool breeze had evaporated any sleepiness that had tried to hold onto him. He was thankful for the cool air that slapped at him as the horse galloped down the street in Jerusalem.

Cleoiphous knew that he would have to be as alert as possible, for he had heard many things concerning the man called Jesus. A day had not gone by that he had not heard of that name. Cleoiphous was only a clerk, but he was an excellent one. His position allowed him to be in rooms where many heated discussions about Jesus had taken place. A few people even defended the man. He remembered when one said that Jesus had healed this man's servant with just his words. Others did not speak so highly of Jesus. Somehow Cleoiphous knew that this day was inevitable, and that the decisions made this day would affect this country for many years to come. As much as he dreaded it, this day had arrived there was nothing he could do to prevent it.

The sound of the horse's hooves colliding on the stone road warned many of the people that had awaken early that the individual approaching was in a hurry. The garb on the horse would alert everyone who saw it that this was a Roman official on important business, and he should not be hindered.

Surely everyone heard him coming, unless one was deaf. Even the deaf should have seen him coming. Everyone scurried out of the path of the on-coming horse, except for one man. He was not blind, nor was he deaf. This man was preoccupied with his own thoughts. Cleoiphous shoved his heels deeply into the horse's side. The horse let out a loud warning snort to the man in his path. The sound of the horse broke the man from his apparent trance, but it was too late for him to move.

An arm of a man that Cleoiphous had not seen pulled the startled man away from the almost certain death that quickly galloped toward him. The side of the horse brushed against the man just as he was pulled to safety. The sound the hooves made as they hit the stone street did not change in the slightest as it barely brushed past the now distraught man.

Salem had seen the horse bear down on Bedar, and had responded as quickly as he could to come to the aid of his friend. With anger in his voice, he said, "That man could have killed you with his horse!"

"That is true. I thank you for your help and for saving my life. I will never be able to repay. I thought you were going to stay at the Temple?" Bedar asked.

"I reasoned with myself that it would be best that I come with you. From the looks of things, I am glad I did," Salem stated. "I could not be a witness to the travesties that my fellow countrymen are doing. I, too, have decided to return to the house of Joseph."

The two friends started to walk toward the home that they hoped would bring some peace in this time of madness. The sound of the thundering horse had completely disappeared, and was being replaced with the sounds of morning activity.

Cleoiphous was off the horse before the servant that waited for him in front of the Judgment Hall could grab the reins. He ran past the religious officials outside the hall. They only looked at the Roman as he ran up the stairs.

As Cleoiphous entered the room, he could see Pilate seated in the seat of the judge. As he walked toward the Judgment seat, Cleoiphous scanned the room. He noticed that the only Jew in the room, other than himself, was the accused. The remaining people were all soldiers. He had his pen ready, when he got to the side of Pilate. "I got here as quickly as I could," he confessed.

"Fret not yourself!" Pilate said.

Cleoiphous scanned the room one more time and asked, "My lord, where are this man's accusers?"

"You did not see them outside when you arrived?"

With a nod Cleoiphous answered, "Yes, but . . ." Before he could ask the question, Pilate raised his left hand to stop the clerk of the court from asking his question. He motioned for Cleoiphous to come closer.

When Cleoiphous bent over and was close enough for Pilate to whisper to him, Pilate said, "They find it sufficient to have us here to complete any task that their laws or customs forbid them to do, such as putting a man to death. Yet, because of the Passover feast, they would not dare defile themselves by entering this place." Pilate repositioned himself in his chair. His present posture signified that he was prepared to proceed with the case before him. Cleoiphous stood up straight again.

Pilate began to talk to Cleoiphous while he was still in his thoughts and he missed some of what Pilate had said. ". . . . make sure that all aspects of this trial are recorded accurately." Pilate motioned for Cleoiphous to lean close to him again. He whispered, "I do not want history to record the wrong version of what is about to happen in this room today."

The Governor stood up and said to Cleoiphous, "Follow me!" He turned to the soldier and said, "Bring him with us!" The Governor, the clerk, the soldiers and the accused went outside. "What accusation do you bring against this man?" Pilate asked the religious officials.

The accusations came so quickly that Cleoiphous had a hard time writing down all the things that they said. He recorded what one man had said that Jesus perverted the nation, and forbade them to give tribute to Caesar, saying that Jesus himself claimed to be Christ the king!" Cleoiphous looked up from his work to see the face of the man that had made this claim. The man who put forth the words that he dutifully recorded was Jeru, the carpenter that had spared him from suffering the shame and punishment for not doing his duty.

Tensions had been very high for several days, and when Jeru remembered the incident where Jesus had made him look foolish in the Temple, just two days prior, it justified in Jeru's mind the reason that he lied about his accusation. Jeru had heard Jesus say, "Render unto Caesar what is Caesar's and to God what is God's," but a slight revision of the truth would work nicely in his plans.

The fact that Jesus did not respond to the charges of the men that wanted him dead truly amazed Pontius Pilate. Many men had stood in this same spot with the same possible sentence before them. Some had denied their guilt; others begged for mercy, and the more sinister boldly defied their accusers with their guilt. Yet this man was different. It was as though he knew he was innocent, yet he must die. "Die for what?" Pontius Pilate thought. He instructed that Jesus should be taken back inside the Judgment Hall. He told the Jews, "You take and judge him according to your own laws!"

They responded, "It is not lawful for us to put any man to death."

Pilate turned and started to walk toward the Judgment Hall. Cleoiphous followed without having to be told. "Cleoiphous! Did I not tell you why they brought him here? They want me to kill this man for them."

Pilate sat back in the seat of judgment and asked of Jesus, "Are you the King of the Jews?"

Jesus asked Pilate, "Do you say this on your own, or did others tell this of me?"

Pilate answered, "Am I a Jew? Your own nation and the chief priests have delivered you unto me. What have you done?"

"My kingdom is not of this world; if my kingdom were of this world, then would my servants fight, that I should not be delivered to the Jews. But now is my kingdom not from here," Jesus answered.

"Are you a king then?"

"You have said that I am a king. To this end was I born, and for this cause came I into the world, that I should bear witness unto the truth. Every one that is of the truth hears my voice," Jesus answered.

Pilate asked, "What is truth?" After he asked the question that all men have asked, Pilate went out again to the Jews and said, "I find no fault at all in this man!"

A voice from the accusers shouted, "He has started trouble from Galilee to this place."

Pontius Pilate turned to Cleoiphous and asked, "Is Jesus from Galilee?"

"Yes, my lord, he is. Jesus is known as the carpenter from Nazareth."

"Good. This Jesus falls under the jurisdiction of Herod. Send him there." He took Cleoiphous to one side and said, "Let Herod know what has transpired here and for the reason that I sent Jesus unto him."

"Yes, my lord!"

The soldiers delivered Jesus to be questioned by Herod at his palace.

†

The night that had just passed had been like an eternity for Elizabeth. The torture of knowing that an innocent man was about to be betrayed and she could do nothing about it only added to her agony. One misery was compounded on another when Salem reappeared in her life. The hardest and cruelest task she had ever done was when she told the man who was no longer her husband, that his mother had suffered a cruel death at the hands of his father, and that she was now remarried.

She had confided in Salem what his father was up to concerning Jesus. As quickly as he had returned to her, he was gone. Now the sun was up and she had still not heard from Salem or from anyone about what had happened to Jesus.

Elizabeth's new husband, Timothy, was not a cruel man. He even took notice of her dilemma. At first she could not bring herself to tell Timothy that Salem had returned, but he had been so good to her, and she did not want to be unfair to him. After Timothy offered to watch Matthew so she could see to whatever it was that troubled her, she gave him a brief description of what had happened the night before. She told him about Jesus, Judas, and Salem. He had already known that she followed after this teacher named Jesus, but the news that Salem had returned, shocked him. Timothy had been told by Joseph when he agreed to take Elizabeth and Matthew in that Elizabeth's first husband was dead.

After Timothy had allowed her to leave, she wondered if he had really believed that she went to help Jesus instead of meeting with Salem. Her husband had not given any indication that he was jealous. Even though she cherished her family dearly, and she especially loved her son, Elizabeth had never felt this relieved to be out of the house. She moved gracefully through the crowd to get to the Temple.

When Elizabeth got to the Temple, she heard the news that Jesus had been arrested. This upset her greatly, but she was relieved to learn that no one else had been arrested. She had also learned that Jesus had already been questioned by Pontius Pilate, and was now being interrogated by Herod. Many of the religious leaders had already gone back to the Temple, yet others remained to receive word concerning the finding of Herod. She almost panicked, when her eyes saw Jeru, but she stood firm. She waited for him to notice her. The left side of Jeru's mouth only curled up slightly when he saw her.

Jeru nudged the lawyer that he had done most of his dealing with, and pointed at Elizabeth. She knew that he only tried to scare her, but she refused to be frightened away like a young girl. She was determined to stay and see what they planned to do to Jesus. The man who had caused so much pain in her life would not scare her anymore.

After he was sure that she had taken her eyes off of him, Jeru stealthily made his way through the crowd. It startled Elizabeth when she felt a man come up from directly behind her. "What are you doing here?" Jeru asked.

She whirled around and looked squarely into the face of the man she knew she hated. "I want to be a witness!"

"Witness to what?"

"To the truth!" she responded. "I want to be a witness of what you and these other people are doing," she repeated her proclamation.

That statement only made Jeru laugh, but his laugh made her shiver. This was no longer the laugh of a man, but of a wild animal. She drew what courage and faith she had and stood up to the evil beast in front of her. Jeru only laughed harder when she called him an evil man. He responded with the charges that Jesus had been charged with and stressed no man had a greater evil than to call himself equal with God.

"No matter how you want to record this travesty of justice based on your version of the law, I will tell my son the truth!"

"Your son," Jeru said while he laughed. "Could you be talking about the boy who is the son of a leper?"

"And that would make you the father of a leper as well!"

"I am the father of no one," he said as though it were a curse.

"Is Salem not named in your lineage?" she asked.

"His name is mentioned in my lineage, but his blood and lineage is of another man!"

"Is your heart so full of evil that you would speak this blasphemy of your dead wife?" Elizabeth asked.

Elizabeth did not move when he leaned close to her ear. She was determined to stand up to this wicked and perverse man. The heat from his breath singed her ear when he said, "The reason that I know that I am not Salem's father is because Martha told me just before she died. Let me rephrase that statement. She told me that Salem was Mashic's son just before I pushed her out the window where she fell to her death."

"But you told everyone-"

"I know what I told everyone else," Jeru interrupted her question. "She admitted to me that Mashic was the father of Salem. In a fit a rage I hit her in the face, she tripped on the rug and she fell out the window. Even though Martha had done something worthy of death, and hid it from me for many years, I did not want anyone to know that I was so stupid not to notice something so vile. I told everyone that it was an accident and they believed me. I knew you suspected, and that is why I had to scare you."

"I will tell–"

"You had your chance to tell. Besides, whom are you going to tell?" he interrupted her again. "You will need two witnesses, and that you do not have. Besides, who are they going to believe: you, a stupid woman who believes that the pathetic man called Jesus will save her, or me, a man who is respected by the high priests and the council?"

Her strength succumbed to the strain, and she bolted away from Jeru and away from the crowd. Even though she quickly departed the Temple, she could clearly hear Jeru's hideous growl laughter that rose up from the bowels of hell. She could think of nowhere else to go but to Mary and Martha's home. She prayed that her friends would be home and that they could tell her what was going on.

†

As Salem and Bedar approached Joseph's house they knew something was different. Unlike the mornings that they had spent at the home of their merchant friend, today was drastically different. All the occupants of the house appeared to be in mourning. The windows were covered, as to prevent the light of day's entrance. It seemed as though Joseph had already received the news of what had happened to Jesus.

After they entered, it took several minutes for their eyes to adjust to the darkened room. Very few words were spoken, and the ones that were uttered, were faint. The agony of what had unfolded before them was felt deeply in their souls. They had no need to tell each other of how they felt, for the grief was a part of them all.

"Is Joseph here?" Bedar asked the servant of the house.

"He is not here, but he should be back any moment!" the servant responded.

Even though his eyes had adjusted to the darkened room Salem still had to squint to see the man that sat in the corner of the room. Slowly but purposefully Salem made his way over to the man that cowered in the far end of the large room. The man had looked up several times as Salem made his approach, and tried to convey the message that he did not want to be disturbed, but Salem would not be daunted. When Salem finally stood directly in front of the man, he was certain that he recognized him. Salem asked, "Were you the man at the fire at the chief priest's house?"

He did not lift his head as he replied, "I am the one!"

Salem was not sure, but he thought that the man spoke through a veil of tears. "Who are you?"

"I was called Simon, but Jesus called me Peter," the voice beneath the shroud said. "Jesus told us that we all would deny him. I told Jesus that I would never betray him, and Jesus told me that I would deny him three times before the cock crows, and I did. He told us all that we would flee when the shepherd was smitten. Jesus told us that Judas would betray him, even unto death."

Compassion replaced the indignation that Salem had felt toward Simon Peter. He lowered himself onto the cool, smooth floor, and crossed his legs as he patiently listened to the man, whom Jesus had named Peter, as he retold the events that had led up to this moment.

Peter started his oration with, "Now when the even was come, Jesus sat down with us, the twelve. Then Jesus said that his spirit was troubled, and testified, 'Verily, verily, I say unto you, that one of you shall betray me.' All of us looked at one another, and wondered of whom he spoke. Now there was one that leaned on Jesus' bosom, John, whom Jesus loved. I beckoned to John that he should ask who it should be of whom he spoke that would betray him. Then John, who lay on Jesus' breast, asked, 'Lord, who is it?' Jesus answered, 'It is he, to whom I shall give a sop, when I have dipped,' and when he had dipped the sop, he gave it to Judas Iscariot. Then Jesus said unto Judas, 'What ever you do, do it quickly.' Now no man at the table knew what Jesus intended when he spake this to Judas."

As Peter continued with his statement, Salem noticed that the whole household of Joseph had gathered around to hear the words of this very sad man. Peter was not aware of the crowd that had grouped around him, as he continued, "For some of us thought, that because Judas had the money bag, that Jesus had said unto him, 'Buy those things that we have need of against the feast; or, that he should give something to the poor.' Judas then having received the sop went immediately out into the night. And we did eat; Jesus took the bread, blessed it, broke it, and gave it to us. Then Jesus said, 'Take, eat: this is my body which is broken for you.' And we ate it. Then he took the cup, and after he had given thanks, he gave it to us, and we all drank of it. Jesus said to us, 'This is my blood of the new testament, which is shed for many for the remission of sins. Verily I say unto you, I will drink no more of the fruit of the vine, until that day that I drink it new in the kingdom of God.'"

Everyone was captivated by the words that Peter spoke. They dared not breath too loudly and miss one single spoken word by Simon Peter. Never had these people in that house heard of such things. One servant felt sorry for Peter and offered him a glass of wine to drink. When he saw the wine, Peter wept bitterly. The act of kindness and duty to a guest in his master's home only brought rebuke upon himself. The servant backed away, but came again to hear the rest of Peter's words.

After Peter had composed himself, he said, "Then Jesus said to us, 'All of you shall be offended because of me this night: for it is written, I will smite the shepherd, and the sheep of the flock shall be scattered abroad. But after I am risen again, I will go before you into Galilee.' Then I said to Jesus, 'Though all of these men shall be offended because of thee, yet will I never be offended.' Then Jesus said to me, 'Verily I say unto you, that this night, before the cock crow, thou shalt deny me three times.' And again I said to him, 'Though I should die with you, yet will I not deny you.' Likewise also said the rest of the disciples." Salem remembered when Peter had left the high priest's palace. The cock had just crowed and Peter had denied Christ for the third time that night.

Peter said, "Then Jesus took us to a place called Gethsemane, and told us, 'Sit ye here, while I go and pray yonder.' And he took me, and the two sons of Zebedee with him and Jesus became very sorrowful."

As Peter continued his story that Salem had witnessed the night before, Salem ushered Bedar away from the group. "Jesus told the disciples that he would be betrayed, and it happened. Jesus told Peter that Peter would deny that he knew Jesus three times before the cock that crowed. To all these facts, I am a witness. If everything else that Jesus said was true, Jesus will be put to death today."

"Surely the people will revolt against Jesus being put to death. Have we not heard many times during the days in Jerusalem that the Pharisees and Sadducees were afraid of what the people would do if they arrested Jesus?" Bedar answered Salem.

"I believe what Jesus has said and I must talk to him before he is murdered. I will give him my thanks unto God, even if I have to shout it from amongst the crowd," Salem responded and then turned to walk toward the door. Bedar knew Salem must fulfill his quest, and that Salem must go alone.

†

"Tell me, Cleoiphous, how did it go with Herod?" Pontius Pilate asked.

Referring to what he had written, Cleoiphous said, "My lord, Herod was quite pleased that you sent Jesus to be questioned by him. He seemed as though this could be a peace treaty between you and him!" It had been common knowledge amongst the workers that Pontius Pilate and Herod did not agree on many issues.

"Yes, yes! We have been at odds for some time now. Tell me of this purple robe Jesus is wearing."

"Well, my lord. After the chief priests had stated their charges, the soldiers took immense pleasure in mocking him. They called him, the King of the Jews," Cleoiphous replied. "And then Herod sent Jesus back to you!"

Pontius Pilate did not respond to what Cleoiphous had told him, but he did rub his hand on his chin, as to give air that great thought was being given to this matter. And Pilate called together the chief priests and the rulers and the people, and he said to them, "You have brought this man unto me, as one that perverted the people: and, behold, I, having examined him before you, have found no fault in this man of those things whereof ye accuse him. No, nor yet had Herod: for I sent you to him; and, surely nothing worthy of death is done unto him. I will therefore chastise him, and then release him."

The crowd refused to accept Pilate's decision. Pilate did not want to start a riot, nor did he want to appear weak in the eyes of the Jews. Cleoiphous came near to Pilate and said, "My lord, these people have a custom, that on the Passover they should release one man whose fate is death. There is another man sentenced to die, his name is Barrabus. Surely these people will let Jesus go and sentence the guilty to his rightful fate." Cleoiphous did not have to explain to Pilate that if he put Jesus' life in the hands of the people, it would relieve him of all responsibility. Pilate simply nodded at the suggestion that the skilled scribe had given.

†

The pressures and tensions that had drifted into Elizabeth's life over the last several years were only a snow storm compared to the avalanche that had quickly and suddenly engulfed her. Salem's return had startled her. Jesus' arrest frightened her, and the hate she felt from Jeru petrified her very soul. Not being able to find either Martha or Mary only fueled Elizabeth's hysteria. Who was she going to turn to? Who was going to help her? With her head hung, she appeared to be a woman with great shame rather than a person in deep grief.

The heart of the city of Jerusalem pulsed around her, yet she was not aware of the life of the city around her. Unaware of where she had wandered, she had drawn near the Judgment Hall. The very vocal sounds that the people emitted broke Elizabeth from her lethargic composure. As she lifted her eyes to see where she was, the man that had met with Jeru several nights back passed in front of her eyes. There was no mistake on her part as to who this man was. "Judas," Elizabeth whispered to herself.

She wanted to hate this man for what he had done. The angry woman felt contempt toward the man until she saw his face more clearly, then her disgust miraculously turned to compassion. The last time she had seen his face, Judas had looked confident, purposeful, but now he looked dismayed, disoriented, confused. She could see the tunic that he wore move up and down as he breathed. Yes, this man was still alive, yet his demeanor said that he was a man on the verge of death. How could

Elizabeth condemn him? Judas Iscariot was already condemned. The attention she awarded the man to whom she knew as a traitor was drawn away when Pilate stood to address the crowd.

Pilate said unto them, "Who do you desire that I release to you? Barrabus," as he pointed toward the condemned man, "or Jesus which is called Christ?" For Pilate knew that because of their envy of Jesus the chief priests had delivered Jesus to him. The chief priests moved through the crowds and began to persuade the people in the way they should vote. The chief priests and elders persuaded the multitude that they should ask for Barrabus' release, and to have Jesus destroyed.

The governor asked them, "Which of the twain do you desire that I should release unto you?"

The multitude responded, "Barrabus!"

Pilate saith unto them, "What shall I do then with Jesus, which is called Christ?"

They all said to Pilate, "Let him be crucified."

And the governor cried aloud, "Why? What evil has he done?"

His appeal only made the crowd cry out the more, saying, "Let him be crucified."

When Pilate saw that he could not prevail, but that rather a tumult was made, he took water, and washed his hands before the multitude. Then he said, "I am innocent of the blood of this just person. See you to it."

Then all the people answered, and said, "His blood will be on us, and on our children." With a movement of Pilate's arm and hand, Barrabus was released to them. With great disgust, Pilate departed from the hall of judgment. The murderer walked away and the innocent man was led away.

Never had Elizabeth mourned with tears of sadness as she did when she heard the sentence of death proclaimed against a man, who to her was blameless, a spotless lamb, a sacrificial lamb. A burning desire to hate rose within her breast as she contemplated what she had just witnessed. She turned to cast an evil stare at the repulsive man who had set the grinding wheels of injustice into motion, but the man was no longer where she had last seen him.

As Salem approached the Judgment Hall, he heard the crowd call out, "Let him be crucified." Surely they did not plead for Jesus to be crucified, Salem thought. Again he heard the words shouted by the multitude. Just as Salem turned the corner on the street that would allow him access to the Judgment Hall, a man ran into him, and both men almost fell to the ground.

After Salem recovered from the accidental assault, he looked directly into the face of the man that had collided with him. "You! You killed my father!" Salem shouted.

The man froze for an instant, and then Barrabus remembered the face of the man that accused him of murder and took a step back. "You were that leper that was out on the hill side . . . ?" Barrabus asked with a stutter.

"Yes, it is I." Salem stated as Barrabus began to recoil from him. "I was a leper whose skin has been cleansed by the hand of the Son of God," Salem responded.

Barrabus stared intently at Salem for several moments, and then asked, "Who was the one that cleansed you?"

"Jesus. Jesus of Nazareth!" Salem proclaimed pridefully.

"This Son of God of yours, Jesus of Nazareth, does not have long to live!" the freed man stated. "He has been sentenced to die in my stead."

What Salem had heard the crowd vocalize, and what the vile man that stood before him had just revealed, sent his mind into a very turbulent confusion. So great was this tumult that Salem did not notice that Barrabus had already fled. "How could this be?" Salem repeated over and over to himself as he walked down the street. Salem stayed in this stupor until he heard someone call his name. He looked up into the beautiful, yet mournful face of Elizabeth. They spoke not a word to each other as Elizabeth fell limply into his arms.

After several minutes of dreadful mourning, Elizabeth asked, "Do you know what the people have done?" Too choked up to answer, Salem only nodded his head. Elizabeth only wept more. The angry multitude that left the Judgment Hall did not take notice of the couple that mourned together on the side of the street.

Gently, Salem lifted Elizabeth off her feet and into his strong arms. He remembered where her house was and he had decided to take her home. All of his senses were numb and he was not aware of the burden in his arms. As he walked down the stone street, the pain in his legs called out for relief but went unanswered because Salem's mind did not even hear the plea. Time was an unreal object to him. How long did it take to walk from the Judgment Hall to her home? How long had he walked? An hour? A day? A year? A lifetime? It did not matter to Salem, for time had stopped for him. He was a man without purpose. All he wanted to do was to thank the man who healed his body, yet he had been denied every time. Salem had berated himself often for not being thankful from the start. It had to be revealed unto him, a Jew, by a Samaritan, to give thanks to the Son of the Hebrew God!

The house was small, and it frightened Salem to make the journey up to the front door. What would Elizabeth's new husband think when he saw her in the arms of another man. It had never crossed Salem's mind to just place her at the door and leave. Salem knew he was doing the right thing, and knocked on the door. The look of shock on the man's face was almost humorous when he saw Salem holding his wife. The shock on his face turned to wrath when he realized that another man held his wife. The wrath then turned to compassion when he saw that Elizabeth was not in her proper mind. The man of the house relieved Salem of the responsibility of the care for Elizabeth as he took her from Salem, then carried her inside. Salem did not follow him inside, but turned to walk away.

"Wait!" Elizabeth's husband said. Salem turned back toward Timothy. "Thank you for bringing her home. She has been very troubled these last few days," he said to Salem. "I should not have let her leave today," he directed at himself rather than at Salem. "You must have been in quite a dilemma, if you should bring her home or not? How could you know how I would respond? Thank you for not leaving her alone on the street, where she could have been violated. My name is Timothy, and you must be Salem," he said as he offered Salem his hand. The shock that Salem expressed was easily perceived by Timothy, who ushered Salem inside his home. "Elizabeth told me that you had returned. Joseph had told me that it was told to him by your father, Jeru, that you were dead."

"According to the law of Moses, I was dead, but I have been raised from the dead," Salem told Timothy. Salem was not sure exactly how much Timothy knew about him, so he let his statement end there. Some people probably would not even accept an ex-leper.

The fact that usually the guilty start to explain their actions before being questioned was what prompted Salem to hold back his explanation of events. Once Timothy asked, Salem started the explanation of events that led up to the reason why he carried Elizabeth home. Had it not been for his physical exhaustion, Salem would have completed his dissertation in just a few minutes. His mind was cluttered with thoughts of confusion that made it difficult to just sit and talk. When Salem finished his story, he rose to his feet, walked to the door, and said, "I must be going! I must know what has happened to Jesus."

"Thank you. The information that you have given me will be useful in the healing of Elizabeth's mind! May peace go with you!" Timothy said.

Salem hoped it was possible, but doubted that it would.

CHAPTER XVII

The soldiers escorted the accused back inside the Judgment Hall. Cleoiphous accompanied them for the sole purpose of recording the actions against the proclaimed King of the Jews. Unlike the Romans that he worked for, Cleoiphous was a kind and gentle man. Most Roman men thrived on the brutality that they administered. The more cruel the punishment, the more content the men became. It sickened him to record what he watched.

Before every execution, prisoners would be tortured first. Jesus was no exception. Their punishments were increased if the condemned were rich or royalty. It was not too often that these soldiers got the opportunity to torture a king, so they were determined to extract every enjoyment at the sake of Jesus. The act used to humiliate a captured king of an opposing army would be to strip him of his clothing, thereby stripping him of his dignity. This first act on the King of the Jews had been done with great ease. One by one the soldiers mockingly knelt before the King, then stood, and would either spit on or bludgeon the man known as Jesus of Nazareth with their fists. Each took their turn and administered their version of punishment. Some of the men towered over the smaller Jew and brought forth much wrath. An officer of the squad said, "If he is a king, give him a robe to wear!"

A purple robe was brought and placed on Jesus' shoulders. Purple fabrics were designed and assigned for royalty or the very wealthy. To the Romans, Jesus was neither wealthy, nor royalty.

"All kings need a crown!" one soldier shouted.

Cleoiphous was amazed at the speed with which these executioners weaved their craft. The soldier had no more suggested a crown, than a man with lesser rank appeared with a hand full of brush. The brush contained a great number of large thorns. They wove the thorns into a crown and shoved it sharply down on the head of Jesus. Blood ran down his head from his pierced scalp by the long, sharp thorns.

"Hail, King of the Jews!" one soldier said as he offered the customary Roman salute.

The most diabolical instrument of torture, except for the ones designed for a long cruel death, was then brought forward. The Romans had claimed that it was a deterrent against crime, but Cleoiphous knew that most of the people who received the force of this instrument did not live to commit other crimes. Everything that had a name had a reason for that name. The cat of nine tails earned its name respectfully. It had nine leather straps connected to one wooden handle. Tied to the end of the leather strap was a piece of metal, rock, or other hard object that would tear into the victim's flesh. If the deliverer of judgment operated the cat of nine tails properly, the sound of the whip would be like the scream of a large cat. The objects fastened to the end of the tails would sink deep into the flesh of the judged like the claws of a lion.

The robe was removed from Jesus' back and the cat of nine tails was lifted high into the air and was about to be delivered to the accused, when Cleoiphous yelled, "Wait!" A look of puzzlement came over the face of the disappointed executioner. "Remember, only thirty nine stripes!" Cleoiphous stated. After the man's puzzled look did not subside, Cleoiphous said, "Criminals who are scourged receive forty lashes. Pontius Pilate did not find him guilty of any crimes!" The man simply nodded his head, and by the duty that was required of him as a Roman soldier, gave Jesus thirty-nine lashes with the cat of nine tails. Jesus' back had been shredded like an old discarded piece of cloth, ripped asunder as rags, and blood ran freely down his back.

†

Since Jews were not allowed inside the Judgment Hall, Jeru went to the Temple. Pilate assured the high priest that he would be notified when Jesus was to be delivered to be crucified, so they could be present. Jeru had no more walked into the Temple, than someone else entered. Jeru was the first to see that it was Judas who had entered and warned the priests when he said, "Judas approaches." The room hushed as Judas came near the chief priests.

With great sorrow in his voice, Judas said, "I see that Jesus is condemned." No one responded. He reached inside his tunic and brought out the thirty pieces of silver that he had received for the betrayal of Jesus and said, "I have sinned, in that I have betrayed innocent blood."

And they said, "What is that to us?"

In ire disgust Judas cast down the thirty pieces of silver in the Temple. The coins landed noisily on the hard floor, yet there was little or no response detected on any face in the room. As quickly as he had entered, Judas left the Temple.

One of the members of the council walked up to Jeru and said, "Follow him. Let us know what he does!" Without a word, Jeru followed after the man who had betrayed the Son of God.

One of the servants picked up the coins and brought them to one of the chief priest and asked, "Shall we put these in the treasury?"

"No! It is not lawful for us to put that money in the treasury, because it is the price of blood," the priest responded.

"What shall we do with it then?" the servant asked.

"We will wait and see what events unfold!" the priest answered.

†

Salem had not been gone long from the house of Timothy when Elizabeth had awakened from her trauma-induced sleep. Timothy reassured her that Salem had departed in good physical health, but that Salem's spirit seemed to be troubled. He also told her what Salem had told him. He did not have an answer when she asked about Jesus. Timothy became angry when Elizabeth insisted on going out again.

"It is a matter of life or death!" she insisted.

"From what Salem has told me that matter has already been decided. You have known for several days of what was to be, and you were powerless to stop it. What makes you think you can do something now?"

"I do not know why I must go, I just know that I must!" she proclaimed through her tears.

"Since I brought you and that son of yours into my house, I have suffered as you pranced around the city every time the name of Jesus was whispered," Timothy shouted accusingly.

"Please do not torture me so!" she cried.

"A time will come when everyone that followed after Jesus will be sought out. I am not willing to suffer for the memory of a condemned man."

"He is not dead!" she emphasized.

"Not yet! But soon!"

"Your words are evil," she whimpered.

"I have just told you the facts. Once a death sentence is pronounced on someone, the Romans take extra pleasure in fulfilling the orders of the court," he said as she continued to cry. "You can stay, or go, but it is my desire that you remain. If you leave now, take your son, and return not to this place ever again."

†

It was not hard for Jeru to follow Judas down the street. Jeru's target did not seem to notice or even care if anyone followed him. Why should he, Jeru thought, the deed had already been done. Jeru watched as Judas acquired a length of rope from a local merchant on his way out of the town. Jeru saw him climb into the tree and fasten the rope to a large limb. Judas tied the rope around his neck and leapt off the limb. A sick snapping sound echoed through the area as the weight of Judas' body reached the end of the rope and it became taut. Even though the rope was tight, the body of Judas swayed back and forth.

Jeru nervously came near the dead man. A strong smell of human waste greeted Jeru's nose before his eyes could see the contorted face of the man who had betrayed his own teacher. The lower part of Judas' legs and garment were stained from the waist down. It appeared to the witness of this death that the suicide had caused a release of Judas' intestines. Jeru knew that Judas was dead. After Jeru returned to the palace of the high priest, he informed them of what he had witnessed concerning Judas.

"Are you sure he was dead when you reached him?" one priest asked.

"His bowels had spilled out!" Jeru said. He did not have to explain to the other men present the details of what happened to a person's body when it hung from the end of a rope.

Upon hearing the news of Judas, the chief priests took the silver pieces, and repeated what they had said earlier, "It is not lawful for us to put the coins into the treasury, because it is the price of blood." They took counsel, and decided they would use the silver coins to buy a portion of the potter's field. The potter's field was used to bury strangers in.

"We shall call the place that we bury Judas 'The field of blood,'" they said.

†

Word had been sent to the religious leaders in Jerusalem that Jesus would be brought out for the final phase of his punishment. It seemed as if the whole city of Jerusalem had vacated their homes and shops to watch the event of a lifetime. This being the week of the Passover feast, many people from all over Israel were still in the city this day. There were even people from various parts of the world.

As the cat of nine tails was the most vicious torture, crucifixion was the cruelest form of execution. Sometimes the condemned would hang for days on the instrument of death. Every man destined to die on this day, would die upon a cross. Persons condemned to die must carry their own instrument of death to the place to where they would lose their lives. On this day, Cleoiphous recorded that three such persons would bear the wooden death instruments on their backs. Cleoiphous had not scribed for the court during the other two cases, but he had heard that the other two men had been convicted of theft.

Three crosses were carried by the three men who were condemned to die. They began their one-way journey to the place called Golgotha. Golgotha was interpreted as, "The place of the skull," which was located just outside of Jerusalem. It seemed apparent to Cleoiphous that Jesus had been the only person who suffered torture prior to the death march. He presumed that the soldiers had spent so much time on Jesus, that they neglected the other two men. It had pleased Cleoiphous that they had dressed Jesus back in his own clothes before they left the Judgment Hall.

As the parade proceeded down the stone-covered street, Jesus' knees buckled under the weight of the cross. One soldier struck Jesus and commanded him to get up. The Roman soldier realized that Jesus was too weak because of the beating that he had endured. The solider quickly pointed at a dark-skinned man in the crowd. "You! What's your name?"

"Simon, I am a Cyrenian," the man responded. The Roman soldier pulled Simon from the crowd and made Simon carry the cross for Jesus.

Because of the crowd, Salem could not see what happened at the far end of the procession. He followed after the crowd because he knew that what he feared most had come to pass. As he walked behind the crowd, he wondered how many of these same people had, just one week earlier, shouted, "Hosanna, Hosanna, Glory to God in the highest," and meant it. How many of these people had heard Jesus speak, and were amazed? How many of these people had heard or even witnessed Lazareth being raised from the dead? How many of these people were his disciples?

"Salem?" someone called from directly and near to him.

After he heard his name, Salem turned around and said, "Bedar? What are you doing here?"

"I have come to help Joseph acquire a very precious object before the hour that the Sabbath begins."

"Is Joseph not concerned with what has happened to Jesus?"

"With this matter, he is very concerned! This precious object is the body of Jesus. Joseph and several of his influential friends have gone to Pilate to get permission to retrieve Jesus' body!"

Even though Salem knew in his mind that Jesus walked toward his death, Bedar's statement shocked him to his very core. Bedar ushered Salem over to a side street and helped him to sit down, but Bedar did not sit down. Salem could not admit it to himself that Jesus had to die. "Jesus is not dead yet, and why do you seek to bury him?" Salem said.

"Joseph wanted to make sure that Jesus' body is prepared as to the customs of the Hebrew law," Bedar stated.

Bedar said, "I knew that you knew the truth. By the confession of your own mouth, and with words that your ears have heard, prior to the actual sentence passed against Jesus, that Jesus would die. Let me tell you what another of Jesus' disciples told us after you left the house of Joseph:

This disciple told us that he had not always followed Jesus. This disciple had first followed John the Baptist. He had heard John the Baptist speak many times of how one would come that was greater than he, whose shoes that he was not worthy to untie. Then one day, Jesus came nigh unto the place where John baptized people. John the Baptist said, 'Behold the Lamb of God, slain from the foundation of the world that takes away the sin of the world.' Jesus had asked to be baptized, but John wanted Jesus to baptize him instead. Jesus persisted and said, 'That the scriptures must be fulfilled.' Also we have received word from the Judgment Hall that Jesus had told Pilate that it was for this cause that he came into the world. Our God, Jehovah, had intended for this day to come, from the beginning of time."

"I cannot understand the purpose of why the innocent has to be slain!" Salem cried.

"Why must a Samaritan teach a Hebrew his own heritage? This is the Passover; an innocent lamb must be slaughtered so that death would not touch the house of Israel. As it was on the first Passover, the blood of an innocent lamb was shed. The blood must be shed so the people can be set free. Jesus is that lamb! Just as Jesus told John the Baptist that the scripture must be fulfilled concerning his baptism, so must the Passover lamb be slain.

"No! No! I cannot accept it!" Salem shouted as he got up. "How can the death of one Jew set the whole nation of Israel free from the Romans?"

"The nature of man is truly inbred in all men. You were once blind to the truth, and then the truth was revealed to you. The truth you accepted was alive and well. Now you are unsure of that truth, so you revert back to your sightless ways." Bedar grabbed Salem's shoulders and turned him so he could look squarely into his eyes. "John the Baptist said, 'Behold the Lamb of God, slain from the foundation of the world.' The death of Jesus is to set mankind free from a force greater than Rome. Jesus will set men free from sin. Jesus is not just any man, as you had stated earlier; Jesus is the only begotten Son of God."

Salem broke away from the Bedar's grip and ran down the street that the crowd had headed down earlier. Bedar did not follow after the confused man, nor did he call out for Salem. Bedar departed the area as well.

†

"Martha? Mary?" Elizabeth shouted as she pounded heavily on the door. "Are you home? Please help me!" The fear and tension in her voice caused Matthew to cry. Elizabeth cried and Matthew squalled as they fled from the house that yielded them no comfort. There was no one to tell her what had happened. There was no one to help her. There were several places that she could have gone to, but she did not know if they would turn against her, since she followed Jesus. Some of the people that she saw that cried, "Crucify him," were some of the same people who had cried, 'Hosanna," earlier that week. She was desperate! Alone! Fearful! What was she to do?

It was now the sixth hour of the day, yet a vast darkness quickly consumed the land. Elizabeth was just one poor Jewish woman in a city in the nation of Israel, yet she knew that this darkness that she experienced was felt across the whole world. Somehow the hopelessness that invaded Jerusalem seemed to be universal. Could what happened to Jesus, who called himself, "The light of the world," be the cause of this sudden and lifeless dark scene that enveloped her? What has happened to Jesus? If only she could find someone to answer her questions! Had this evil and corrupt world extinguished the light that had come to save the world?

†

Jeru used the light from the fire that the soldiers had lit to look up at the man that he had perceived to be the creator of all of his troubles. "Finally, I have seen the end of this trouble maker!" he muttered to himself. "His death will be a victory cry for the people of God!" Jeru said. Jeru laughed at the women that mourned for Jesus. Every man that walked by would curse at Jesus. "Where are your disciples now, Jesus?" Jeru asked as he stared directly at Jesus.

The time of the Sabbath was near and the bodies needed to be removed. Jeru asked one of the chief priests if they could petition Pilate to have the legs of the guilty men broken so it would speed up their death. It would have pleased Jeru all the more to make Jesus suffer longer than he did now, but he set his personal pleasures aside to make sure one prophecy about the Messiah would not come true. Jeru, like many good Hebrews had heard many prophecies that related to the Messiah. One such prophecy said, "There were found in him no broken bones." Jeru did not want the disciples of Jesus to come back at a later date and testify that Jesus fulfilled all the prophecies of the Messiah. The chief priests went to Pilate and Pilate granted their request.

Jeru had convinced himself that Jesus was not the King of Israel, nor was he the Messiah. All the years that Jeru had lived with the thoughts that Jesus blasphemed God, were only a minute speck in time to what he witnessed today.

There, hung before all to see, were the blasphemer and two thieves. It made Jeru happy when people would come by and mock the man nailed on the cross. Even the two thieves that hung on each side of Jesus cast their insults at Jesus.

One of the malefactors which were hanged with him said, "If thou be Christ, save yourself and us also."

The other man rebuked the first man, and said, "Do you not fear God, can you not see that you are in the same condemnation? And we indeed justly; for we receive the due reward of our deeds: but this man hath done nothing amiss." He then turned to Jesus and said "Lord, remember me when you come into your kingdom."

Jesus said to the repentant man, "Verily I say to you, today you shall be with me in paradise."

"You will be nowhere but the grave," Jeru whispered as he looked directly at Jesus.

†

Though Bedar had not followed Salem, the words of the Samaritan hammered mercilessly in Salem's ears. In a vain attempt to block out the words, Salem covered his ears as he ran, but the words persisted. Salem knew that the truth that he heard came from within his soul, instead of his ears. He could only guess how long he had wandered around the streets outside the wall of Jerusalem. One hour? Two? One day? A week? Who knows? What did it really matter? All seemed lost.

No stars shone from above because it was still day. The darkness that had come over the earth was darker than any night. Out of the darkness leapt a beacon from a hill outside the city. Salem knew what travesties occurred in the deceitful light. He did not want to go there, yet his feet moved at a steady cadence toward the light. Like a moth drawn to a fire, Salem was compelled to walk to the hill known as Calvary.

With each step he dreaded what he would see. His mind warned him to stop. His heart threatened to burst under the stress, yet his feet inched forward. By the time Salem was close enough to see what he really did not want to see, it was almost the ninth hour. Just as the ninth hour approached, a mighty earthquake shook the ground. Had God begun the destruction of the world because the world killed his son?

The first person that Salem saw was a Roman soldier whose face showed a great fear. Salem realized that it was not fear he saw on his face, but awe, when the soldier said, "Surely this must be the Son of God!"

It had only been three hours since the mob had taken Salem's hope away. It had been three hours since the darkness came. Salem had to remind himself that he was not the one condemned to die, yet he felt as though he was the one who had suffered a great loss.

Salem's head hung low, as he approached the location that spewed out a great horror of injustice. No one noticed the new arrival on this scene, and why should they notice him? The main attraction was held up for the whole world to see. Time moved slowly as Salem absorbed the horrible scene before him. Except for a voice here or a voice there, all other sounds had ceased. It was as though he only heard the words that he needed to hear, and all others had been voided. His first observation was a man on the cross. This was not Jesus. What had this man done?

A quick glance at the cross and Salem read the message that had been written and posted above the guilty: "A thief." "This man was a thief," Salem whispered to himself. The condemned man on the cross would push his body up and then he would exhale, then inhale and relax. The thief would have to use the spikes that were driven through his hands and feet as leverage to raise his body up to breathe. Each breath meant excruciating pain in his feet and hands that would convulse through his whole body. This torture continued several more times as Salem watched. Agony erupted on the man's face each time he used the spikes as leverage to raise his body up. This man was in pain, yet his face was peaceful. Salem was truly puzzled.

"Move!" thundered the voice of a large Roman soldier with a very hard club in his hand, as he pushed Salem to one side. The giant stood just to the left of the man who was nailed on the cross. The soldier lifted the large wood club into the air and positioned it for the most effective strike to the man's legs. He moved the club several times as he adjusted the projected path of the lethal weapon. Salem could see the solider calculate at what angle he would have to strike to generate the most effect with his delivery.

Whoosh, went the club as it sliced the air and sailed toward its target. A loud, sickening crack shot out from the thief's legs as they shattered. The wooden instrument destroyed both of the legs that it collided with. Thump, went the body as it fell downward under its own weight because the broken bones relinquished all of its support. The flesh ripped from the man's upper wrists and shoulder joints as they tore from the dead weight of his body.

Never in all his life had Salem heard such a horrible sound. The devastation that hit the man was equal to that if he had been struck by lightning. Each portion of this scenario added to the drama of this ordeal. The man desperately tried to get even an ounce of air, but was unable to raise himself. The last gasp of air the man consumed prior the collision with the tool of death, had been his last. This was a painful, yet spontaneous death. The smell of the human waste mixed with blood lingered ominously around the dead man. Salem had not even seen such repulsive things in the valley of the lepers.

Salem's eyes followed the huge soldier as he walked past the man in the middle and over to the man that hung on the far cross. The sign above him said the same thing as the man who had been executed. The man on the far cross had seen what had happened to the other condemned and began to panic. The same deadly blow was administered to the other thief as well. This man was just one more silent man, dead on a cross.

There were three crosses on this hill. Because of the law, two of those men deserved the punishment they received. If what Bedar had told Salem was correct, then by the law, Jesus must die as well in order to fulfill it. Two died because of their own sins, one would die for sins of the world.

"Look at the Son of God, numbered among the accused!" Salem heard one man say.

Then Salem's eyes followed the executioner as he walked up to the man that hung in the middle. The soldier assumed the same stance as he had twain. Just as the force was about to be released on the condemned man, an officer yelled, "Stop!" The officer moved closer to the man in the middle. "This one is already dead!" Without another word spoken, the solider took a spear and thrust it into the side of the man that hung between heaven and earth. Blood and water spewed out from the chest of the pierced body of Jesus.

Time seemed to have stopped for Salem. He moved closer to the body that had been pierced. Is this Jesus? Salem thought. Even Jesus' mother could not recognize him now. It has to be him! He was scheduled to die here today! With closer scrutiny, Salem examined the body. Is this really Jesus? I know Jesus! We grew up together in Nazareth, Salem thought. The man Salem looked at was not the man he remembered.

This man's body was bruised, and bore many stripes. Blood covered his face because of the crown of thorns. Even the beard of this man had been plucked out. What flesh was visible, had turned black because he was bruised. Each hand had a spike driven through it to fasten him to the tree of death. One rusty nail held both of his feet to the cross. This man was dead.

Behind the cross, Salem saw the men who had gambled for his clothes. He heard the people as they bragged of how they had taunted this man. They bragged of their question how he could save others, when he could not even save himself. Salem heard them mock the very words of the accused.

"Father forgive them, for they know not what they do," they laughed as they repeated his words. One man laughed as he told of how he had taunted the man on the cross with guile and vinegar after he had said that he was thirsty. Salem smelled the vinegar and noticed a discarded sponge on the ground. All of these facts bombarded his mind, but he refused to accept that this was Jesus on the cross.

Salem looked above the dead man and noticed the sign that read, "The King of the Jews." It had been written in many different languages, but Salem only understood the Hebrew words. Everything Salem had heard, everything Salem had seen, everything Salem had learned about the Christ caved in on him. This was truly the Lamb of God. Jesus was dead.

"Unclean! Unclean! Unclean!" Salem shouted as he fell heavily to the ground. Several people that had stood close by moved away when they heard Salem's cries. "Unclean! Unclean! Unclean!" Salem repeated his oration. "Woe is me! For I am undone; for I am a man of unclean lips, and I dwell in the midst of a people of unclean lips: for mine eyes have seen the King, the Lord of Host," Salem quoted Isaiah. He wept bitterly. He wept not because of the death of an innocent lamb that had been sacrificed, but because of the sin in his heart that caused the innocent one to be slain. It was at this moment that Salem truly understood all the words of the prophets. The prophets had all spoken of Jesus. They had known who had sent them to make ready the Kingdom of God, and that he, Jesus, would be sent to save the world.

"Thank you! Thank you! Thank you!" repeated Salem with tears on his face as he looked up at Jesus on the cross. Salem did not thank Jesus because he had healed him of leprosy, but because Salem had been forgiven of his sins. In an instant, everything that he had ever learned about his God, his religion, his customs, was revealed to him because of the man he saw on the cross. Salem saw on the cross the babe that was born in Bethlehem, the son of a carpenter, the teacher of God's word, the healer of the afflicted, the Lamb of God that took away the sins of the world, the Savior of all mankind.

Just as the first perfect lamb had been slain in Egypt to set God's people free, so was this perfect Lamb of God slain. Every drop of blood was shed to set all people free by the remission of their sins. Salem knew that Jesus hung there because of the sin of the world and that whosoever believed on him, Jesus, would be saved. Salem believed and accepted the precious gift of forgiveness.

Several men pushed by Salem and approached the cross to which Jesus was still fastened. A soldier tried to prevent them access to the cross but the leader of the men handed the soldier something. The soldier examined the article as the man explained, "We have permission from Pontius Pilate to prepare the body of Jesus for burial. It is the ninth hour and the Passover Sabbath is near. We do not have much time to prepare his body."

The soldier motioned with his hand indicating to the men who made the request that they could proceed. Salem was glad to see that one of the men that took the body of Jesus down from the cross was his friend Joseph. Jesus' back revealed the scourges from a hideous weapon that he had endured before he made his journey to the Golgotha. They carefully placed a clean linen cloth over the face of the crucified lamb. Spices and herbs were religiously administered to the exposed flesh of the body. Then the rest of his body was wrapped with a cloth made of linen.

The aroma of frankincense and myrrh drifted up to Salem's nostrils as the spices were applied to the body of Jesus. This smell of these spices reminded Salem of the many times Mashic had told him of gifts that the wise men from the East had brought to the King of the Jews that had been born. The words, "For this cause came I into the world," echoed in Salem's head.

Salem stood up and was about to follow the procession of the dead, when a strong and rough hand clamped tightly on his shoulder. "Salem? What are you doing here?" asked the man that was behind him. It had been a long time since that voice had entered Salem's ears, but he knew to whom the voice belonged. The voice had changed; it was older, meaner, and lonelier! It was the voice of Jeru.

"Jeru," Salem said, "Why did you touch me? The last time you saw me I was a leper? Why would you touch a leper?" Salem asked before he turned around to look at Jeru.

"I saw you from the front a moment ago."

Salem turned to look at the man that had raised him. "Do you know the reason that I am clean now?" Jeru only shook his head. "The man whom you have crucified, the man you knew as Jesus of Nazareth, is the one that healed me! He is the reason that I can now say, 'I am clean!'"

"Jesus was a heretic!"

Salem raised his arms and pulled down the sleeves of his garment to expose his arms. They were as perfect as they were before the affliction. "Could a heretic do this? Can a blasphemer give sight to the blind?"

"You speak as a man who has been deceived. I have waited for many years to see Jesus put to death. I do not care what sort of magic he cast on you to deceive you, but the man is dead and there is nothing you or anyone else can do about it," Jeru said. "I saw your antics as you fell on your knees earlier. When I heard you cry "Unclean," I realized who you were. I came over to you, but you knelt before a dead man. What I saw repulsed me more than when you were a leper!"

"Then why did you confront me?"

"I just thought–"

"You just thought that if I saw you face to face that I would renounce Jesus and come back with you! You are an evil man. Your heart is cold and eaten up with hatred." Salem admitted openly his hatred of the man he had once called father. "You are a murderer!"

"I have killed no one!"

"What about my mother?"

Jeru took longer to reply to this latest accusation. "I had no hand in the death of anyone that did not deserve it."

"What did my mother do that deserved death?"

"I did not want to tell you this," he said as he looked around, "but your mother was unfaithful to me. She committed adultery and deserved death."

"I know of the sin of my mother. Mashic told me just before he died." Salem saw the satisfaction in Jeru's face when he heard that the two people that had betrayed him were both dead. "Mashic lived in torture all those years with the knowledge that I was his son, yet he had to be called childless. Mashic repented for that sin and begged God daily to be forgiven of his sins. When he heard that the Savior had been born, he knew that one day he would be truly forgiven of his sins. He prayed every day that the Lord God Jehovah would show him a sign. All looked good for him until I came down with leprosy. He blamed himself for my infirmity. He believed that God had sent judgment, for the sin of the father had been placed upon the son."

"Just as the women who wept before the cross of Jesus did not touch me, neither did this miserable excuse of a story touch me! No one has been put to death that did not deserve it!" Jeru repeated.

All the frustrations that Salem felt were suddenly released from him like pressure released from a covered pot with a fire under it. Salem vented all of his anger that had built up in him since he had learned of the death of his mother, and what this evil man had done to Jesus. In one quick and forceful move, Salem thrust both of his hands around the throat of Jeru. Jeru fought back, but Salem's sudden burst of anger caught him unprepared, and he fell, taking Salem with him.

The onlookers began to bet on who the winner would be. Some thought the younger, stronger man would prevail. Others thought that the old man was wiser, craftier, and tougher, even though he was a smaller man. The pair rolled in the dirt and mud.

Salem prevailed over his adversary and was able to get a large rock in his hand. With the rock lifted high in the air Salem said, "No one will be put to death that does not deserve it!" He aimed the rock toward Jeru's head. As the hard piece of earth plummeted toward the face of Jeru, Salem heard yet another voice return to his mind, "Forgive them, for they know not what they do!" Just as quickly as the rock had sped toward Jeru, it was diverted away. The rock made a thudding sound as it hit the ground.

"I forgive you!" Salem said. He rose to his feet and walked away.

Jeru breathed heavily as he laid in the dirt and mud at the foot of the cross. "I will find you and I will see to it that all who have trusted in the name of Jesus will be put to death!" Salem heard what Jeru had said, but he paid no heed to a man so full of hate. Jeru stood up and brushed his tunic off as he watched Salem walk off into the darkness. "I will catch up with you later, Salem," Jeru shouted. "But right now I have other prophecies to prevent," Jeru said to himself.

†

Elizabeth did not have to be told that Jesus was dead. She knew it when she saw a procession of Joseph, one other man, Mary, Martha, Jesus' mother and several other women. They mourned as they walked toward the place where they were to bury the dead man. She joined the procession of tears and mourned with them.

After the body had been properly prepared and the tomb secured with a large stone, Joseph and the other man returned to their own homes, while all the women went to Mary and Martha's house. It was at this house that Elizabeth heard all the horrible details of the death of Jesus. Her heart loved Joseph all the more when she heard that Joseph owned a tomb that no man had ever been laid in, and gave it so that the body of the Messiah could be laid in it.

†

The chief priests and Pharisees came together unto Pilate and said, "Sir, we remember that the deceiver said, while he was yet alive, 'After three days I will rise again.' Command therefore that the sepulcher be made secure until the third day. Should his disciples come by night, and steal him away and they say to the people, 'He is risen from the dead,' the last error shall be worse than the first."

Pilate said unto them, "You can have a watch over the tomb. Now go your way, make it as secure as you can." So they went, and made the sepulcher secure. They sealed the stone that had been rolled in front of the tomb. A watch had been set over the sepulcher. The Roman soldiers that had been hired to guard the tomb had been told that they would be put to death if the sepulcher were ever breached.

†

The next day did not bring any relief for any of the believers. From Bethany, where Mary, Martha, and Lazarus lived, to the other side of Jerusalem where Joseph's house was, many people mourned. The ones that mourned did so silently, for fear of discovery and reprisal from the Jewish leaders. The disillusioned disciples moped around. Peter, the more outspoken of the bunch, had suggested that he might return to his old trade in Galilee. The other disciples thought that they might join him on his boat to help catch fish. Elizabeth and the majority of the other women cried most of the day. Salem and Bedar sat silently in their rooms at Joseph's house. Very little food had been eaten by any of them.

Bedar had become very concerned over Salem's despondency and talked with Joseph of this matter. Everyone felt the pain that Salem suffered, yet Salem's agony seemed different. Bedar went to talk to his friend from Nazareth. "Salem!" Bedar said, as he gently touched Salem's shoulder. "What are your plans now?" Bedar asked.

"I do not know yet. I have not decided. To stay here would be painful, because of Elizabeth. To return to Nazareth is not an option either. My thoughts have returned many times to the people that we left behind in Samaria. I have contemplated returning to the valley of the lepers, to help those poor souls," Salem said passionately.

"That would be a noble gesture, but the severity of such a decision should be calculated very carefully," the Samaritan wisely offered his advice.

"It was just a thought, and only a faint one at that. I feel the need to wait." Salem could see that Bedar was about to ask him a question, so he quickly raised his hand up to stop Bedar, "Do not ask me how I know that I must wait, I just do!" His friend nodded his head to show that he accepted Salem's statement even if he did not understand.

"While you wait to make a decision, consider this offer. Joseph needs two men to travel to the village of Emmaus to conduct some business for him. Now that today is the Sabbath, you will have to wait until the first day of the week to go," Bedar said.

"Tell Joseph that I consider it an honor to do him this service. Will you go as well?" Salem asked.

"No!" he answered with a laugh. "Unlike you, I do have a place to go. I have fulfilled my mission here. The mission to help you accomplish yours is complete, even though it did not come out like we desired and hoped. On the morning of the first day of the week, I will return to my home in Samaria. Know this one thing: you are always welcome in my home."

The realization that he would soon lose the company of a brother in like faith saddened Salem. He decided that this time should be used to glorify the God of Israel, instead of weeping and being sad.

"Besides, Joseph already has someone to go with you. I would like you to meet Cleopas!" Bedar said as the man approached.

They exchanged greetings, and Salem gave the man a strange glance. Salem noticed the scar on the man's left ear. He thought he recognized him from somewhere. "Do I know you?" Salem asked.

"Cleopas is the name my parents gave me, Cleoiphous was given to me by the Romans," Cleopas stated. "I was the man that greeted you in the hall of records the day you and Bedar came to look for your family."

"I remember now," Salem replied to Cleopas' statement.

Since Salem was unfamiliar with the area, Cleopas explained to Salem on how to get to Emmaus and the business that they would conduct there. They talked and came up with a time that would be best for the both of them to leave on the first day of the week.

It made Bedar happy that, even for just a short time, maybe, just maybe, Salem could get his mind off of what had happened. Bedar did not fool himself to think that anyone who had heard, or been through the horrible things that had been done, could ever completely forget. Bedar knew that he could not forget!

CHAPTER XVIII

It had been an uneventful night for the hired guards. They had agreed to take this job for two reasons. The first reason was because they had reasoned amongst themselves that it would not be that hard to guard a dead man. The second reason was the extra pay that they would receive. Their pay came from the Roman system of taxes that were levied against this conquered nation, yet a special job like this offered extra benefits directly from the ones who requested the watch. They also knew that the Jewish religious leaders had a lot of money.

They had been warned that the followers of the man in the tomb might try some strong arm tactics, and remove the body from its grave. Each man was armed with swords and spears and had been properly trained in the essentials of battle. They did not fear the Jews, and why should they? Their so-called king had been put to death and his followers, except for a few women, fled like birds that were flushed from their hiding place.

Their fire had not been rekindled because the first light of the morning had begun to appear in the sky, yet they were still in darkness. One of the men mentioned that their task was just about over when he saw the dim glow of the sun in the East. Some of the watchers that had fallen asleep had begun to rise.

Elizabeth knew that it was considered an honor to take part in this latest task even though she was tired, but she dared not complain. She knew that Mary Magdalene, Joanna, Mary, the mother of James, and the other women were as tired as she was. To mourn the way that they mourned exhausted anyone.

Death, like life, has requirements that must be accomplished. One such requirement was the reason that these women were on the road at the dawn of the first day of the week. The women had prepared spices to anoint the body of Jesus. They talked amongst themselves of who would roll the stone away for them.

The man in charge of the watch saw the women as they approached.

He alerted his men to be ready. Then it hit. No warning. No preparation. A mighty scream rose from the ground as it shook from the tremor of the earthquake. None of the watchers were asleep now. The movement caused them to struggle to stay on their feet, but when the light that was as bright as lightning appeared, the men fell on their backs as though they were dead.

"The stone has been rolled away," one of the women shouted.

At first, no one wanted to advance any closer to the tomb. Then Mary Magdalene ran forward to the opening of the tomb. Elizabeth had frozen in her steps as Mary Magdalene entered the tomb that contained the body of the man that had died on the cross. The commotion that erupted after Mary had entered the tomb caused Elizabeth's knees to shake harder than when the earth had moved just moments ago.

"His body is not here! The body of my Lord is not here!" Mary shouted from inside the tomb.

All of the other women moved forward to investigate. Some went inside, while the others remained just outside the entrance. Two men clothed in a brilliant light suddenly appeared before the women, as they stood motionless in and outside of the tomb, The women were afraid, fell to their knees, then bowed down their faces to the earth.

The men clothed in the radiant garments said to the women, "Why seek ye the living among the dead? He is not here, but is risen. Remember how he spoke unto you when he was yet in Galilee, saying, 'The Son of man must be delivered into the hands of sinful men, and be crucified, and the third day rise again. As they left to go tell the disciples of what they had just heard, they talked amongst themselves of how they remembered what Jesus had said unto them concerning his death and resurrection.

After the Roman guards awoke from their stupor, they saw the two men that appeared to be clothed in light, yet carried no lamp, talking to the women. They saw the women as they ran away from the tomb. The man with the highest rank recognized the expression in the faces of his subordinates as fear, because he himself was engulfed by it. He motioned for them to get up and leave the area. They likewise started to run toward Jerusalem. The men ran faster than they had ever run before.

†

Jeff Frazier

Salem had learned more about the men known as the eleven, who had once been the twelve, just in the short time since Jesus had been crucified. He learned that there had at one time been up to seventy disciples and they were called apostles. Salem wondered if any of them would call themselves apostles now. He also learned how each man had counted what they had lost. There were two of these men who were brothers and they wanted to sit, one on Jesus' left and one on Jesus' right, when Jesus brought his kingdom into maturity. Now these brothers had no place to sit. The fisherman, who Jesus said would be a fisher of men, did not have a net. The one that Jesus loved did not feel loved.

Never had the desire to sleep come over Salem as it did at this moment, but sleep had not been an option for anyone in the house. They had mourned and wept continuously since the Messiah had been put to death. Only occasionally would someone fall into a weak slumber, but the sleepers would awake suddenly at any noise.

The household had just begun to settle again after the quake occurred at the dawn of this, the first day of the week. Then the sudden calamity at the front door startled every occupant in the house. Some were fearful that the mob that had arrested Jesus had come to arrest them. Their tension had been quickly released when someone looked out a window and said that it was Mary Magdalene who banged on the door. The person said that some other women were on their way up the street as well. The door was unbolted and they ushered her inside. One by one the women were also allowed to enter as they came up to the door.

As each woman would enter, Salem would look to see who it was that entered. Some of them he had seen before, with Jesus. The other women he did not know. The door was closed for what Salem thought was the last time, but just as it closed, it reopened to allow another inside. The woman removed the cover from her head and instantly a flood of emotions flowed over him. Her eyes met his eyes and Salem could tell that Elizabeth still desired him.

Salem walked over to her and asked, "Are you okay?"

"Yes, I am fine, but something has happened!" Elizabeth said. "Let Mary Magdalene explain it. They both turned their attention toward Mary Magdalene.

Some of the men tried to scold Mary Magdalene for her sudden appearance because they were still in mourning. No matter what rebuke anyone tried to place on her, she simply ignored them. It was evident that her excitement could not be smothered by the men who mourned.

"They have taken his body and I know not where!" Mary Magdalene wailed. "We have seen a messenger of the Lord God Almighty. He told us that Jesus had risen from the grave!" Joanna said.

"His grave clothes were still there, but his body was gone!" Mary stated.

It was evident to Salem and Elizabeth, by the response of the apostles, that the apostles did not believe what the women had said. Salem found it hard to believe such a thing also. He had been healed, but who would heal the healer. He had heard of the dead that had been raised, but who would raise the one that raised the dead. Confusion and arguments mingled throughout the room, and no one was immune to their effects.

It shocked many of the people in the room when Peter rose up and ran out of the house. John, the apostle that Jesus loved, and Mary Magdalene followed after Peter. It was common knowledge among the followers of Jesus that Peter had always been impulsive. Jesus had once scolded Peter, even called him Satan, because Peter had said something he should not have said. Peter was also the one who had jumped out of the boat in the midst of a storm that raged in the Sea of Galilee. Peter had cut the ear off of the high priest's servant when Jesus was arrested. Peter was also the first to say that he would not betray Jesus, and yet he was the first to deny that he knew Jesus.

With Peter, John, and Mary Magdalene gone, a quiet calm, like the calm of the eye of a storm, filled the room. It was as though no one wanted to speak. Salem motioned for Elizabeth to sit on the pillow that was next to his. After they both sat down, Salem turned his face toward the lovely Elizabeth. "This is hard for me to say . . . I still love you and I always will!"

Gently, Elizabeth touched his face with the back of her hand and started to gently caress it. He reached up and took her hand tenderly in his. As he touched her hand, it became apparent to Salem why she caressed his face with the back of her hand rather than her soft palm. The soft hands that he had once cherished so much were now calloused. He realized that after he had departed Nazareth in shame, the life of his dear Elizabeth had drastically changed. The many laborious tasks that she did not have to do in Nazareth, she now had to do. The death of his mother and her separation from Jeru only increased the burden on these hands.

Salem turned the palm of her hand toward his face and moved it up and down his face. Without a word between them, he had told her that he loved her the way she was. The sudden remembrance that she had remarried, caused him to pull away and then turn away from her.

"Do not worry! I have been freed from my debt to Timothy," she said as she came near him. "Timothy gave me an ultimatum. He said that I could stay or I could go. But if I chose to leave, I could never return. As I gathered my things to leave, he said that since you were alive, and not dead, you were my legal husband. He knew that you still loved me!" There was a moment of silence. "He could also tell that I still loved you."

"Where is our son?" Salem asked.

"He is with a friend. Would you like to go and see him?" Elizabeth asked. She expected Salem to be excited about seeing Matthew for the first time, but all she saw was agony. "What is wrong?" she asked.

"The desire to look upon, to hold, to kiss my son has consumed me from the very moment that I learned I had a son. Yet, I have committed myself to a dear friend, and if I keep my word, I will not see my son." He then told her of the trip that he and Cleopas were to make to Emmaus this very day.

"I will relieve you of the responsibility of what choice you must make. You keep the promise that you have made. I will go and prepare Matthew and make him presentable for his father," Elizabeth stated. They both knew that it would not matter to Salem exactly how Matthew would look the first time he saw him. To the father, the child would be beautiful.

Salem accepted her suggestion and then they both reclined together and held each other tightly. Of all the uncertainties that Salem had encountered, of this one thing he was certain: he loved the woman that was in his arms. They had not planned on going to sleep, but they both fell asleep even though the world around them seemed to be in total disarray.

†

The soldiers that had fled from the tomb of Jesus slowed down from their run when they reached the East Gate of the wall of the city. Breathlessly, one of the soldiers asked, "What were those beings?"

"I am not well versed with this Jewish religion. I once heard them called angels," the captain of the guard offered as an explanation.

"What is an angel?" the man asked.

"From what I have learned from their stories, angels are spiritual beings that do the will of the Hebrew God, Jehovah," the captain answered.

"This Jehovah must be a powerful God!" one man stated.

"These Jews believe that he is the one and only true God!" the captain replied.

"What are we to do now?" another man asked.

"We will go see the chief priests in the Jewish Temple and tell them of what we have seen and heard. We will let them make a decision on this matter," the captain answered. Normally he would have gone to Pilate, but he was afraid that he would be put to death.

They made their way to the Temple and explained all that they had witnessed. The chief priests were not pleased with what the soldiers told them. They assembled the elders and took council.

Jeru was not a true religious leader, but because of his service to the religious order in Israel, he was called in for the council. Many other men, like Jeru, were allowed to witness these proceedings, but were not allowed to vote.

Because the meeting of the Jewish religious hierarchy had taken so long, the soldiers had become frightened that they would lose their lives. They were totally unprepared for what happened next, but they accepted it willingly.

"Here is your . . ." one of the chief priests stated, then paused as though he had to think of the next word, " . . . reward!" Everyone in the room knew that the priest meant "Bribe." The man with the captain reached for the bag of money that he knew was quite generous. The priest pulled the bag back toward his body and said, "This is what you will say to whoever will listen or question you about what you know about the body of Jesus not being in the tomb. You will tell them that his disciples came in the night while you slept and took the body."

The chief priest noticed the concern on the soldier's face. It was a common fact any soldier in the Roman army that was asleep at his post would be executed. "And should these words fall upon the governor's ears, we will persuade him otherwise, and protect you from him!" the chief priest said as he handed the soldier the money.

The money offered was received. All parties in this deception were pleased. The chief priests were happy because they did not want people to continue to follow after Jesus. The soldiers were happy because the version of what the chief priests had told them to tell would be easier for others to believe than the truth.

Jeru was not happy that the body of the Jesus was missing, yet at least a very plausible replacement story would be used. "Who could ever believe the story, a man was raised from the dead?" Jeru said to himself. "If they continue to spread the word that Jesus is alive, I will spend every pence that I have to track down every believer of Jesus and put them to death."

†

"I hate to wake them," Bedar said as he looked at the man and woman that slept together on the floor.

"It is time to go," Joseph stated.

Before Bedar could shake Salem, Salem woke up. The still sleepy man could see the smiles on his friends' faces. Salem knew that these two men would be happy that he had his wife again, but they would still have the same concerns that he himself had earlier. Salem explained all the details that Elizabeth had told to him. Both men accepted and were pleased at the results of what great fortunes had come Salem's way. Then he remembered something important and said, "How could I have forgotten?" as he rose to his feet.

Both men looked at Salem with a puzzled expression on their faces and both asked simultaneously, "Forgotten what?"

"Have you heard that they could not find Jesus' body?"

Joseph and Bedar both nodded their heads. "You tell him," Joseph said to Bedar.

"No! You tell him," Bedar said.

"More has happened," Joseph said. Salem listened anxiously as Joseph continued. "Peter, John and Mary returned to the tomb." Salem nodded his head to signify that he remembered. "John ran on ahead of Peter, but Peter was the first to enter the tomb. The grave clothes were there, just like Mary said, but his body was gone. John and Peter departed the tomb but Mary did not leave. She stood outside the sepulcher and wept. As she wept, she looked into the sepulcher, and saw two angels in white apparel sitting, one at the head, and the other at the feet, where the body of Jesus had lain. They said to her, 'Woman, why weepest thou?'"

Elizabeth was awake and now stood by Salem's side as Joseph told them what Mary had said, "Mary said to them, 'Because they have taken away my Lord, and I know not where they have laid him.' And after she had said that, she turned to leave. Then Mary saw a man standing there that she thought was the gardener. The man said to her, 'Woman, why do you weep?' Mary said to him, 'Sir, if you have taken him away, tell me where you have laid him, and I will take him away.' He said to her, 'Mary.' She turned and said to him, 'Rabboni,' which means 'Master.' She said that when he called her by name, she knew that it was Jesus. She wanted to take hold of him, but he forbade it because he had not ascended unto the father yet. Jesus told her to go tell the disciples, 'I ascend unto my Father, and your Father; and to my God, and your God.' Mary Magdalene did as she had been instructed. She went and told the disciples that she had seen the Lord, and that Jesus had spoken these things to her," Joseph concluded.

The words had no more been uttered when Cleopas walked up and asked, "Salem, are you ready to go?" For a short time, they talked more about the strange occurrences, and then Salem introduced his wife to Cleopas. Cleopas had seen her several times since the first day that Jeru and his family arrived from Nazareth, but he had never met her.

All the preparations had already been completed for their trip, and they were ready to go. Both Salem and Elizabeth hated to part the other's company, even for just a few days. "I have been separated from you for too long. When I return, I will never leave your side." Salem had previously never been the type of person to show his affections openly in public, and it was not common among many of the people of this land, but Salem savored the moistness of her sweet kiss.

"Wine could only wish to taste as sweet!" Bedar waxed poetically.

After Salem and Elizabeth finally broke away from each other,

Salem said to Elizabeth, "I love you. These next three days will be an eternity."

"In three days we will be together again!" she replied.

"Will you still be here, my friend?" Salem asked Bedar.

"I should have departed early this morning, but with this latest development, I just do not know what I will do next," Bedar commented.

"My desire is that you would remain, but if not," Salem said as he embraced his friend, "May the God of Israel bless you, and your family!"

Finally, Salem and Cleopas walked away to begin their trip to Emmaus. It had not been easy for anyone. The news that Jesus was alive diminished the purpose of this trip, but he had already promised Joseph that he would go.

Salem and Cleopas had only just started to get to know each other, and already they had found out that they had many things in common. They both knew Joseph, some of the disciples, Bedar, Jeru, and Jesus. Both believed that Jesus was the Messiah, and both were horrified at the death that the Son of God suffered. Neither man could fully understand what they had heard just before they left Jerusalem.

Each one took their turn to explain how they knew Jesus. Cleopas listened intently as Salem told the story of his life as they walked. Cleopas had seen many miracles that Jesus, had done but he had never heard a story quite like the one Salem told him.

Cleopas apologized to Salem that he had misled him when he first came to Jerusalem. Salem accepted the man's apology and understood that Cleopas had only obeyed his orders. Cleopas sighed heavily just before he began to tell the story of his life. "I was born in a foreign land, because my parents, who were Hebrew, had been sold into slavery. My father owed a debt that they could not pay." Cleopas explained to Salem how his parents had ended up as slaves even though he had not been asked. "They taught me how to speak the language of their native tongue, and of the Romans, and of the nation that I grew up in." Salem did not want to interrupt the man who had patiently listened to him, so he did not ask what nation he had been a slave in.

"At a very young age I could speak three different languages fluently," Cleopas boasted. "Forgive me if I sound prideful, but it was the foresight of my parents that deserves any praise. They knew that one day, with the ability and knowledge of many tongues, I could rise above the state of slavery. My father did not want what happened to him, to happen to me." Salem nodded his head to show that he understood.

"When I was only twelve years old, I was sold to a very wealthy nobleman who traveled in a large caravan that was on its way to Israel. They needed an interpreter. Along the way, I learned the reason of this journey," Cleopas said, then paused. Salem knew that this man had not forgotten what happened next, but that he only reflected on how the next events had changed his life. "We came to a small town, and a small band of sheep herders, fishermen, and carpenters came to the camp and wanted to speak to the leaders of the caravan. It was not until I interpreted for these men that I learned that I, we, were in Israel."

It was not Salem's intent to interrupt Cleopas' story, but he could not contain his excitement. "Mashic, the man that I spoke of earlier when I told you of my life, he was one of those visitors! He must have told me that story several hundred times."

Cleopas remembered the first Hebrew man other than his father that he had ever spoken with and how persistent he was, yet cordial. He remembered how Mashic reacted when he found out the reason why the caravan passed by Nazareth. Cleopas told Salem that Mashic seemed nervous when he first entered the tent that night so many years ago. "A divine peace settled over Mashic when I interpreted for him what the king told me, 'We followed that star that lead us to the King of the Jews.'" Cleopas continued on with his story of how he learned about of the birth of the King of the Jews. He told of the caravan's journey to Jerusalem, then to Bethlehem. Salem had heard this part of the story before, as told by Mashic from the shepherd John's point of view, but he did not hinder Cleopas. "After the wise men had visited with the child king, the man who had bought me gave me my freedom. I had no sooner been set free than the caravan left the country in a different direction than they entered. I had heard that an angel had visited them and told them to leave immediately and leave from a different route than they had entered."

Cleopas' voice cracked several times, so Salem said, "Mashic has told me about the massacre that took place in Bethlehem. I will understand if you do not wish to talk about it." Silence fell over the duo after

Salem mentioned the slaughter. Salem prompted Cleopas to continue his story. "If the man set you free, then how did you get that scar on your ear?"

The mood of Cleopas changed and he answered Salem's question, "The wise men were in such a hurry to leave, my master had forgotten to remove the ring from my ear. I was young and did not know how to remove it myself. With no other choice, I pulled it out. I thought I was going to die, but the blood did not flow long." He rubbed his ear gently as he thought of the past.

"It did not take me long to get a job in the Roman court," Cleopas said, "and I moved up quickly. It was a mundane operation, until just about three and a half years ago. The news that a leader had arisen amongst the Jewish nation excited me. The first time I saw Jesus, I knew he was that same child I had seen in Bethlehem. I had to be very careful in how I dealt with this most delicate matter, and with what I said. There are many believers, like myself, in positions that could not allow them to openly support Jesus."

"Were you afraid?" Salem asked.

"I stayed in my position in hopes that I could assist in the bringing forth of his kingdom in this world, but I have learned a great deal more of the true purpose of Jesus. With what Jesus, the apostles, Joseph, you, and other people have testified, I now know that Jesus did not come to set up an earthly kingdom, but to begin the Kingdom of God on earth," Cleopas answered.

The more they talked, the faster they walked. Their emotions scaled from the highest elation of the wonderful things that they had witnessed and heard of Jesus, to the somber realization of the remembrance of the evil that had been done. Both men were saddened at that remembrance, and of the possibility that Jesus was alive. They were visibly shocked when a man asked, "Why are you saddened so?"

Cleopas answered the man, "Are you a stranger here? Have you not heard what has happened in Jerusalem?"

And the man asked them, "What things?"

As they walked to Emmaus, they explained to the man the things that concerned Jesus of Nazareth who was a prophet, mighty in deed and word before God and all the people. They told him how the chief priests and rulers had delivered him to be condemned to death, and had crucified him. "But we trusted that it had been he which should have redeemed Israel: and today is the third day since these things were done. Yes and certain women also of our company astonished us. They went early to the sepulcher. When they did not find his body, they came, and said that they had also seen a vision of angels, who said that Jesus was alive. And some of them that were with us, went to the sepulcher, and found it as the women had said, but they did not see him."

Then the stranger said to them, "O fools, and slow of heart to believe all that the prophets have spoken: "Ought not Christ to have suffered these things, and to enter into his glory?" The stranger began with Moses, then went through all of the prophets as he expounded to them all the scriptures that concerned Jesus.

As they drew near the village where they headed, the stranger talked as though he would go no further. The travelers constrained him and said, "Abide with us: for it is toward evening, and the day is nigh over."

Cleopas led the way to where they should go. The stranger went in the village with them. Both Salem and Cleopas sat with the stranger to eat. As the stranger sat to eat meat with them, he took some bread, blessed it, broke it, and gave it to them. Immediately their eyes were opened, and they knew who the stranger was, but he vanished out of their sight.

Salem said and Cleopas agreed, "My heart did burn within me, while he talked with us on the way. The way he spoke opened the scriptures to me in a way that I have never understood. We must find and tell the eleven that are gathered together, that we were with Jesus!" Then Salem said, "I hope Joseph is not upset that we did not complete this task for him." Cleopas assured Salem that Joseph was a very understanding man, and that the news that they had seen Jesus outweighed the less significant task that they were sent there to do. Immediately they rose up and returned to Jerusalem.

Cleopas and Salem found the eleven apostles gathered together, and the other people that were with them. After they entered the house, the door was secured behind them. Salem looked around and noticed that Elizabeth, Bedar and one of the disciples, known as Thomas, were not present. Cleopas said, "The Lord is risen indeed." They told the group the things that were done on the way to Emmaus and how Jesus had made himself known to them when he broke the bread.

"I have known Jesus all my life and yet I did not know him. It was as though scales had been placed over my eyes, until he broke the bread. Immediately we knew that it was Jesus," Salem said as he looked over at Cleopas to agree with his statement.

As they spake, Jesus himself stood in the midst of them, and said to them, "Peace be unto you." They were terrified and very frightened, because they thought they had seen a spirit. Jesus said to them, "Why are you troubled? And why do thoughts arise in your hearts? Behold my hands and my feet, that it is I myself. Touch me, and see; for a spirit does not have flesh and bones, as ye see me have." And when he had spoken those words he showed them his hands and his feet. The scars from the nail were clearly present.

Jesus asked of them, "Do you have any meat here?" They gave him a piece of broiled fish, and a piece of a honeycomb. He took it, and did eat before their eyes. Then he said to them, "These are the words which I spoke to you, while I was yet with you, 'That all things must be fulfilled, which were written in the law of Moses, and in the prophets, and in the psalms, concerning me.'" Then Jesus opened their understanding, that they might understand the scriptures, and said to them, "Thus it is written, and thus it behooved Christ to suffer, and to rise from the dead the third day: And that repentance and remission of sins should be preached in his name among all nations, beginning at Jerusalem. You are witnesses of these things. And, behold, I send the promise of my Father upon you: but tarry you in the city of Jerusalem, until you be endued with power from on high." As he had entered, Jesus departed from them.

Salem went to Joseph and apologized that he and Cleopas had not completed the mission that had been assigned to them. "It is I who should apologize!" Joseph admitted. "Bedar and I were very concerned for your mental state, so we came up with this plan to get you out of the city for a couple of days. Bedar believed that you would not refuse anything that I would ask of you. After your wife had been returned to you, and with the resurrection of Jesus, we had our doubts that we had done the proper thing. I almost confessed to you my scheme, but it was too late to withdraw from the project."

"Do not blame yourself for what has happened. The Lord has guided you to do this thing. If I had not been on the road to Emmaus, I would have not had the great honor to see Jesus and talk with him at great length," Salem reassured his old friend. "Where are Elizabeth and Bedar?" Salem asked.

"Bedar has returned to his home," Joseph told him.

"Elizabeth?"

"She did not expect you back until later!"

"Can you tell me where she is?"

Before Joseph could answer Salem's question, Thomas returned to where the remainder of the disciples were. The disciples tried to tell Thomas that Jesus had been there, but he refused to believe it. "Until I shall see the print of the nails in his hands, and put my finger into the print of the nails, and thrust my hand into his side, I will not believe," Thomas said doubtfully.

With the excitement of Thomas' return now quenched, Salem again went to Joseph to inquire about his wife. As he came near to Joseph, Joseph lifted up his hand to stop Salem. Salem stopped. "Upon your arrival, I sent a messenger to inform your wife of your return," Joseph told him.

Salem opened his mouth to speak, but Joseph put one finger up as if to tell Salem to be silent. The elderly man pointed his finger toward the ground and made a circular motion. At first, Salem did not understand what his host tried to tell him. "Turn around!" exclaimed Joseph.

Salem began to move his head, and then his body followed. What he saw when he had completed the simple maneuver caught him by surprise. He expected to see the same woman that he had seen when he departed for Emmaus. Elizabeth was adorned with the apparel of a virgin bride. This would be their wedding night. The child that slept in her arms did not awaken as he embraced them both. Once again the couple wept, but this time it was with tears of joy. Matthew awoke as Salem began to cover him with his kisses.

†

Eight days later, again Jesus' disciples were together. Thomas was with them this time. Like the last time, the doors had been shut and secured. Then Jesus appeared and stood in the midst of them, and he said, "Peace be unto you." Then Jesus said to Thomas, "Reach here with your finger. Behold my hands; and reach here with your hand, and thrust it into my side. Be not faithless, but believe."

And Thomas answered and said to Jesus, "My Lord and my God."

Jesus said to him, "Thomas, because you have seen me, you have believed. Blessed are they that have not seen, and yet have believed."

For forty days Jesus showed himself alive after his passion by many infallible proofs that were seen by the apostles, and spoke of the things that pertained to the kingdom of God. And being assembled together with them, Jesus commanded them that they should not depart from Jerusalem, but wait for the promise of the Father.

Jesus said, "You have heard of me. For John truly baptized with water; but you shall be baptized with the Holy Ghost not many days hence."

When they were together, they asked of Jesus, "Lord, will you at this time restore again the kingdom to Israel?"

And Jesus said to them, "It is not for you to know the times or the seasons, which the Father hath put in his own power. But you shall receive power, after the Holy Ghost has come upon you. You shall be witnesses for me both in Jerusalem, and in all Judea, and in Samaria, and unto the uttermost parts of the earth."

When Jesus had spoken these things, while they beheld him, Jesus was taken up in a cloud which took him out of their sight. As Jesus was lifted up and while they looked steadfastly toward heaven, two men in white apparel appeared by the people who watched Jesus ascend up into the clouds.

They said, "You men of Galilee, why do you stand and gaze up into heaven? This same Jesus, who is taken up from you into heaven, shall so come in like manner as ye have seen him go into heaven."

"Of all the things that I have heard and all the things that I have witnessed, all the scriptures that were opened to me, all the truths revealed, the scars that I saw on his hands and feet and side, these things reveal the power of God that rests in Jesus. It all still amazes me," Salem said.

Then the disciple whom Jesus loved testified, "We know that his testimony is true. And there are also many other things which Jesus did, that if everything would be written, I suppose that even the world itself could not contain all the books that should be written."

   Amen.

John 15:3

Now ye are clean through the word which
I have spoken unto you.

Epilogue

I have always liked to hear how a singer got a special inspiration for a certain song, or why a director made a movie a certain way. I sometimes enjoy the special features on a DVD more than the movie. That is why I wrote this special chapter for "Unclean." With the details of why there is a book called "Unclean," it makes it more special for you, the reader.

It is a miracle that Unclean was ever written. I am not a professional writer, nor am I a Bible scholar. Those two things should have told me not to write a story about the most important man of all time, Jesus. However, the still small voice of the Holy Spirit would not let me rest. God used an unprofessional writer and sometime Bible teacher to bring this story to you.

One day in church while listening to a sermon (sadly I must admit I forgot what about), I got the inspiration to write, "Unclean." The idea was to tell the life of Jesus from his neighbor's point of view. I also wanted to make Salem the leper who went back and thanked Jesus for healing him and the other nine. Here was this man who was just a couple of years younger than Jesus, came from the town that rejected him, and now he must ask for his help. That was my original thought until I sat down to begin the typing of the book. I remember this event as though it just happened moments ago. I sat down at my computer, and I heard the Lord speak to my spirit, "Don't you think you should at least read the story about the ten lepers first."

Many of us have heard the Bible stories several times over. When someone else mentions them, you can recall the gist of the story, and usually forget some of the details. This was what happened to me. I opened my Bible to the story of the ten lepers and began to read the Living Word of God. It was then that I realized that my "plan" would not work. The one leper that went back and thanked Jesus was a Samaritan; if that man was a Samaritan, then he could not have grown up with Jesus.

I immediately said, "What am I going to do now?" That still quiet voice returned to me and said, "Make him one of the nine." Man can teach man, but man can never give man understanding. Either you are going to get it or you're not. A teacher can pound it in to you, but that does not mean you are going to understand it. With the Lord Jesus Christ, it is possible. With those six words, I knew the rest of my story. God did not tell me what the rest of the story was going to be; he revealed it with understanding. "Make him one of the nine." I knew that the man who grew up with Jesus, became a leper, and was cleansed (but was not thankful), would spend the rest of the story trying to find Jesus. He would not be able to thank him, until he saw him on the cross.

Unclean was originally written as a three-act play, "The Carpenters Shop," "In Exile," and "In Jerusalem." When I typed the last word to the play, I said, "I'm done!" The Holy Spirit said, "No you're not." So began the three year journey to bring to life the story "Unclean."

I could lead you to believe that I spent three grueling years typing and doing research for "Unclean." Like I stated earlier, I am not a professional writer; I had to work for a living. I would run to the computer as often as I could to work on it, and as the Holy Spirit lead me. That constant running to the computer and repeating beating of the keyboard keys lead my precious wife to utter the infamous phrase, "When are you going to be done with that?"

When writing a play, you have to consider many factors, i.e. "Where is it going to be produced, like a church or regular stage." Many items, like past events, have to be mentioned rather than presented. Case in point: in the opening scene to the play, Mashic entered Jeru's shop and they began to talk about the Roman occupation of Israel. Mashic mentioned to Jeru, "Don't you remember several months back when that caravan pasted through on its way to Jerusalem?" When I began the novel of "Unclean," I started it exactly at that same point. When I typed their conversation, I got the thought, "I don't have to mention it, I can take them there." The first section of the story about Uriah, the grasshopper, the sheep and all the way to where the Mashic had proclaimed that the Messiah had been born was added to the story.

As I began anew with this inspiration, I received the idea of a small shepherd boy watching his father's sheep. I know that little boys get distracted very easily, thus the idea of the grasshopper and the plan to eat it. I wanted to show how customs were important to this region and to the story. My favorite part was where Uriah reached up and took his father's hand.

Somewhere in every story, the title, or the reason for the story appears. I did not want to use UNCLEAN until the first leper said it, so I had to cleverly use other words throughout the story if the subject of unclean items came up. In the opening story about the grasshopper, I used "on the list of items that were lawful to eat."

When I originally wrote it as a play, I wrote the opening of one scene very specifically. Mashic walked into the shop and mistook Salem for Jeru. That scene showed the audience that some time had passed. This scene was so entrenched in my story that I wanted to include it in the book the same way. During the transition from play to novel, God kept telling me to make Mashic the father of Salem. I flat out refused. Mashic was a righteous man, a good man, and I did not want to change that fact. I refused to make that critical aspect of the story, but God was loving and patient with me. The story developed nicely, until I got a bad case of writer's block.

Unclean was my first attempt at writing a novel, so I cannot call it "writer's" block. I had a case of "Holy Spirit" block. Anytime I would stray from the Bible scriptures, I would not get any inspiration at all, "NONE." "None" that is, until I would research that particular event again. When I would see where I strayed from the scripture, my story inspiration would return.

Changing Mashic from a righteous man to an adulterer was not a Bible story, so I was not going astray there, but I was still missing God on this one. I had still been able to write about half the book with the full intention of not changing my mind. I was so frustrated when I hit that "block," that I decided to go drive around. As I was thinking about what I wanted to do with "Unclean," the Lord impressed upon me again to make that drastic change to Mashic. Finally I said, "Yes Lord, I will do it." Immediately the rest of story came to me in full revelation. Not every detail was given to me; I got the inspiration for the rest of the story.

By saying yes to God, the Holy Spirit released the hindrance that I had built up. Everything that I had written up to that point finally made sense. Even though I had declined God's plan of making Mashic an adulterer, all of the details in the story in the first chapter had already been written. When I said yes, all of those things that were already typed now made sense. God had already been guiding me to that end. I fought this change even up to the part where Mashic revealed the truth to Salem.

Jeru's attitude changed over the years. I wanted to show how a person who denied his religion, his heritage, and eventually his God, could turn evil. Jeru was dedicated to his work first and foremost. He was only religious when he had to be. Jeru used his Jewish faith only when he wanted to condemn someone else. When he was confronted with the truth, "Jesus," he rejected him. When he found out that his wife and best friend had disgraced and lied to him, he turned to murder.

Here are just some more tidbits of information about "Unclean." I have always loved to play with names. Other than the common names, I created all the other names. I would use the Text to Speech option on my computer to hear what I just wrote. When it would read Mashic, it would say Messiah. I created Salem's and Jeru's names from a very special source. I did not want to reveal the source of the name until Jesus was on the cross, so I had to strategically place their names in specific order until I wanted it revealed. I got their names by splitting the name "JERUSALEM." Except for the times that I used the actual name Jerusalem, I never allowed Jeru and Salem to appear together. I would use things like, "Jeru, Martha, and Salem," or "Salem and Jeru." I wanted to show that Jeru Salem stood before the cross on which the Messiah had been crucified.

I wanted my story to align with the Bible, not change the Bible to match my story. I used a chronological list of events concerning the life of Jesus to help me mold my story. Using that list, I would read the next event and figure out how I could adapt my story to flow from the previous event to the next. If an event occurred that my characters could not have been at, then that event would not be included at that time. Sometimes I would have a person tell one of the characters at a later time about an event that had happened earlier, Example: Salem would not have been at the well in Samaria when Jesus asked the woman for some water, so Bedar told him about it after they met. I generally knew how the story was to take place, but I was relying on the Holy Spirit to guide me along the details. I would not research the next event until I was finished adding the last event to my story. I did not want to get my facts mixed up, so I took it one story at a time.

The Lord gave me the name of Cleoiphous for the Roman worker early in the writing of the story. I knew in the beginning that Cleoiphous would be a believer and that the information he learned inside of the Roman Government would be useful. I wanted to use him and Salem to make the journey from Jerusalem to Emmaus. When I started setting the story up for these two men to make this trip, I decided that I'd better do some research first

Like I said earlier, I knew the stories, but sometimes I forget the details. In the play version I had used Salem to challenge Peter after Jesus had been arrested. In one Gospel I could use Salem to make that challenge. As I was doing research for Unclean by combining all Gospel versions of the same story, I realized that I could not use Salem. Even though Peter had been challenged three times, somewhere in all four Gospels, it is revealed who those three people were (except for the woman, and Salem could not have been her).

I did not want to make that mistake with Salem and Cleoiphous and their trip. If the people were named, then I would be in trouble. I opened my Bible to the story of the two people on the way to Emmaus. I shouted for joy when I read that only one man was named and his name was Cleopas. The name that God had given me at the start of the book was so close to the actual name in the Bible. I knew and still know that it was a miracle, and divine inspiration.

"When I first started working on "Unclean," I had an approximate amount of pages that I wanted my story to be. I was at about half the pages that I wanted it to be when I got to the part where Salem and the other nine lepers were healed. It was during my research of the crucifixion of Jesus that I realized how much of the Gospels dealt with that one week. By the time I was finished with that short period of time, I was very close or over the number of pages that I wanted this book to be.

From the time that I finished writing Unclean to the time that I sent it to a publisher was almost six years. At first I was scared to send it off. I viewed my writing skills as very amateurish and my language skills as horrible. Most of the people that read it encouraged me to get it published, but I waited.

When the circumstances occurred that I was able to send Unclean to be reviewed by a publisher, I knew the time was right. At first it was my fears that held me back, but I think God used my personal fears to make me wait, wait for the right time. God's timing is perfect.

We can all look back on our lives and see how God has moved us from one place to another for a particular purpose. When I was in the US Air Force, being a Texan, I made the comment, "I will never live in Louisiana." One month after I got out of the military, God moved me to Louisiana. It was in La. that I met the woman who later became my wife, and the mother of my son. I worked at a petrochemical plant until they laid me and fifteen hundred other people off in one day. When I worked as a cook at Holiday Inn, a fellow worker's husband hired me to work as a government contractor. I worked there for eight years, until they decided to close that site down.

I transferred to a Texas site as a supervisor and worked there for eleven years. During this time, I wrote "Unclean." God placed several people (the two most helpful are mentioned in the introduction of the book) in my life that helped me write the novel. They didn't actually help me write it or decide how the story would go; they mostly told me where I messed up. At the very beginning, I messed up a lot. With their patience and sticking with me to the end, I was able to complete the task. There was a lady at that facility that displayed her son, Marcus' artwork in her office. Everyone admired his work and talent. A little over a year before I left that job, her son got a job in the same department as mine, and we became very good friends.

When the opportunity to move to another government facility in northern Texas came up, I accepted. It was here that some very small and unexplained events happened in one night so that I was able to send Unclean to this publisher.

"Unclean"

written by:
Jeff E. Frazier

When I knew that Unclean was to be published, I presented Marcus with the opportunity and challenge to design the cover. I sent him a black and white drawing (pictured above) that I originally made for the cover of Unclean the play. He accepted and his work is wonderfully displayed on the cover.

The publisher really didn't want to get an outside source for the cover (they had their own people to do that), but when they saw the original chalk drawing, they were pleased. I pray that our Lord and Savior Jesus Christ will bless Marcus Taylor for his wonderful and inspired work.

Contact Jeff Frazier
unclean_novel@hotmail.com

or order more copies of this book at

TATE PUBLISHING, LLC

127 East Trade Center Terrace
Mustang, OK 73064

888.361.9473

Tate Publishing, LLC

www.tatepublishing.com